THINNING THE HERD

THINNING THE HERD

All My Best!

KEVIN J. RYAN

To order additional copies of this book, contact:
Xlibris
1-888-795-4274
www.Xlibris.com
Orders@Xlibris.com
663883

PROLOGUE

IT HAD AWAKENED. There had been no alarm. In fact, there was no clock where it slept. There was no need for a clock. Predators needed no clock. Predators knew when it was time to awaken. Only humans needed clocks and alarms, fancy beds, and curtains. It did not need these things; it was a predator.

The predator stretched out and yawned. It was a long, luxurious stretch. It licked under its arm and liked the taste. There was no need to hurry. The sun had just begun to peek over the horizon. The predator sensed a lack of humidity and knew it would be a pleasant day. The predator felt no hunger, and therefore would not hunt. It would be hunting soon though, as it had not hunted in a while. There was time, there was always time. Nature knew how to cull out the weak. Nature knew how to cull out predators that were not fit. A fit predator knew how to be patient. A fit predator would survive.

It was going to be a busy day. Soon humans would die. It needed to be prepared. The deaths would be satisfying and appropriate. But the humans were too stupid to see the glory, the wonder of the predator's plans. The predator knew this, but this thought did not detract from the wonder of the plan, or the beauty of the predator. They would think the predator evil, but there was no evil in its lithe body; only intelligence, hunger, and need. It only did what came naturally. It only did what it had been taught to do.

It stretched again. It purred majestically and licked its knee. The knee tasted good. Today was going to be a good day, and soon the days would be glorious.

These new people were different. At first they would suspect nothing, but after a time they would know something was amiss. It was a question of how long it would take to put the pieces together. They would sense the danger and mount a search. Smarter and more effective law enforcement would be at play this time. It, the predator, would know when it was time to stop hunting.

It opened its eyes. Darkness flooded the room; the sun a full half hour from daybreak. It was a good time to rise; a good time to stretch, breath, think and plan.

The predator stood and walked across the room. The predator lingered before the picture window, naked. There were no curtains and the blinds were always open. The predator did not care if someone saw it naked. It was beautiful, like a cat. It wondered if the cornered mouse beheld the beauty of the cat. When the chase was over, and the mouse was unable to run away, despite its fear and loathing, did it find the cat so beautiful that in its last moments of terror, it could not take its eyes off the beauty?

The predator believed this. The predator believed that snakes did not hypnotize their prey, but that in the final moments of their lives, the prey recognized the power and the beauty of the predator, and gave itself up willingly to that beauty.

They were like sheep, and thinning the herd was as natural as breathing. The human herd needed constant thinning. The predator breathed in the delicious morning air and dreamed delicious thoughts.

CHAPTER 1

EDDIE WALKED DOWN the street with a nice little bounce in his step. He wore a thin, gray Michigan sweatshirt, a Philadelphia Eagles ball cap, and a pair of jeans. His Nike's were lightweight cross trainers. He had an mp3 player attached to his ears, but there was no music. If someone asked him a question, he could shrug and point to the earplugs. His dog was a medium-sized mutt that had been appropriately sedated so that he would neither bark nor wander. Eddie and his dog fit into the neighborhood just like they lived there, just like they belonged. That was the idea.

Eddie had scouted the neighborhood several times, careful to use a different car each time, and casually observed its residents in daylight and at night. He'd counted the number of houses, the number of cars, the ages of the kids, and the number of animals running about. He had a real feel for the neighborhood, and he was confident that he could stroll unnoticed by the casual observer. However, the Nike was made for running, and he could run like a deer if the situation changed. The dog was on its own.

You couldn't tell by looking at Eddie in the slightly oversized outfit, but he was in great physical shape. He ran, he worked out in his living room, he swam, and he climbed. He knew that the best way to get around was to walk; the slower, the better. Only guilty people ran. Eddie walked, slowly, unobtrusively. He spent a great deal of time practicing walking. Eddie was a professional.

It was a warm night. It was September 6. The neighborhood had no streetlights, and it was slightly overcast. No one noticed

Eddie when he strolled up the driveway at 161 Maetten, and the dog
led him to the back of the residence. There were lights on inside,
apparently a hall light and an entrance light, but he wasn't worried;
he was confident that no one was home. Underneath his sweatshirt,
he carried an array of tools, everything a good burglar needed and
more. Eddie was quite good at his work.

Once Eddie had walked around to the back of the house, he
loosely tied the dog to a bush and commanded it to lie down. The
dog did what it was told and appeared to go right to sleep. Eddie
then donned surgical-style gloves. They were thin and dexterous.
Even at close range no one could see that he was wearing gloves.
The gloves had a slight skin-toned tint so that at night, unless you
were right on top of him, you probably wouldn't even notice he was
wearing gloves. That was the idea.

He very gently tried the handle on the doors to the back
bedroom. They were locked. He glanced about and checked the
frames for inserts, wires, or connectors, and finding none, popped
the lock with a small device he had personally designed for such
purposes. He carefully put his ear to the glass for a full ten seconds,
waiting for any kind of noise that might indicate that the small
snapping sound he made while popping the lock had been heard
inside.

Convinced that there were no noises coming from inside, he
slowly and carefully opened the door and peered inside. Then
Eddie did something that had served him well over the years, and
that no other self-respecting thief would think to do in a million
years: Eddie softly, but clearly, called out, "Excuse me, anybody
home? I need some help. Anybody here?"

CHAPTER 2

EDDIE HAD BEEN twenty-three years old and out on his forty-third burglary since he began his professional career at the age of seventeen. That first time as a junior in high school, he had gained entrance to the back of a seemingly empty row house with a simple lock pick. Once inside, and knowing he could not be seen from the street, Eddie had turned on the kitchen light. Within seconds, a woman had appeared in the kitchen, too startled at seeing him to scream. Seemingly born for the trade and without thought or hesitation, Eddie said, "Lady, are you all right? I thought I heard someone screaming in here. Couldn't see in. Came around back, found the door open, and thought something terrible might be happening. God, are you all right? Are you OK? Should I call the cops?"

The middle-aged woman, who'd been awakened from a booze-induced slumber, was so relieved that she wasn''t about to be killed that she made both of them coffee and assured him that she was all right and that there was no need to call the police. By the time it was over, he thought, he could have been in her pants. Bad thought. He remembered a line from a song, "Breath was hard as kerosene." His intended victim's breath had, in fact, been that bad. His intended victim had been something else.

She had commented on how nice a young man he was. By the time he left her home the woman had determined that she'd actually been talking in her sleep and that her talking had attracted him. Eddie had been an average student in school, but in the world of professional burglary, he was magna cum laude. He learned fast and he never forgot a lesson. He was still able to steal a number of items from her home because she left him alone while she went to the bathroom on two occasions. He had simply taken something valuable on each occasion and put them just outside her front door for him to retrieve when he left.

Fortunately, there was no answer to his question at 161 Maatten. Eddie closed the door without so much as a click and turned on his penlight. His heart was steady, his breathing slow. Unlike most burglars, he got his thrill on the plan, not on being inside. This fact more than anything else had kept him out of jail; in fact, it had kept him out of the courtroom. With one minor exception, he'd compiled a clean record. The police had no clue that Eddie was on the other side of the legal fence. That was the whole idea.

Without difficulty he had found the nightstand-type dresser, right where he was told it would be. On the top in the back corner, the jewelry box lay open. Eddie pulled out its drawers, one by one, and emptied them into ziplock baggies which were strapped to his leg. Most of the jewelry consisted of earrings that shimmered under the tight beam of light. When he'd emptied the contents of all the drawers, he deftly turned the box over and began manipulating the panels until one of them slid neatly away, revealing a small inner compartment. The inner compartment also contained earrings, but they were significantly larger and the stones sparkled in his penlight. He then uncovered a small pouch which contained five large, loose stones, which varied in color and size. The information he had received had been accurate.

He carefully put the box down and crushed it with his foot. He turned it over and crushed it again until the box was broken into various pieces. He stopped and listened. He knew that it was time to leave, but he had the nagging feeling that he'd heard a noise. He was also quite convinced that he'd smelled something out of place, and although he recognized the smell, he couldn't place it.

Eddie had a great nose; he could smell trouble before it happened. His nose told him it was time to go. He tossed the pieces of the box gently around and reached for the handle of the door, but as he did he heard the noise again, and the smell was even stronger.

CHAPTER 3

EDDIE MOVED DOWN the street the same way he'd come, with his dog at his side. He was moving slowly. To the casual observer, he appeared to be singing to himself as his dog wandered down the sidewalk. Just a man walking his dog, but Eddie was nervous, no Eddie was downright scared. He could barely contain himself. He could feel himself sweating underneath his clothes and his knees were weak. His nose had been right; he'd smelled trouble, bad trouble.

Once you smell blood, you don't forget it, he thought. Eddie smelled blood and that was not part of his bargain.

Just take it a step at a time, he thought. Only three blocks and you're home free.

Two children on bikes moved lazily down the other side of the street, one saying something to him and the other waving. Eddie casually waved back and kept moving. He didn't look back; he never did. Eddie turned the last corner, placed his dog in the back seat, entered his car, and slowly, casually drove away. The smell of death lingered in his nostrils.

CHAPTER 4

"THERE'S BEEN A shooting. I heard the shots." The automatic recording system of the 911 control center for Chester County had turned on a microsecond before the operator answered the call. The digitized tracking system had already determined the area code and the prefix numbers before the operator even spoke. The operator also knew immediately that the call was being made on a cell phone.

"Please give me the address of the incident." The operator was well trained and sounded calm, but she knew the prefix; she recognized it as Glenmoore, where her family lived, and was trying to blank out any thought that it might be someone she knew.

"It is 161 Maatten Court. I'm going to see what happened." The phone went dead before the operator could speak. She immediately pressed redial to try and regain contact. At the same time, she had dispatched a message to the local ambulance corp via modem, as the same message was being transmitted to Upper Uwchlan Township and the Pennsylvania State Police.

There were two simulated rings on the call back, and then a canned voice: "I'm sorry but the mobile phone operator is not available, please try your call again later. Thank for using LCI mobile systems." Click.

The operator had done all she could do to electronically alert the proper authorities. Now she could only follow up telephonically and wait. She went about her business, competently and methodically.

The person holding the cell phone pulled out the memory chip, dropped the phone down the sewer, hopped back into the car, and casually drove away.

CHAPTER 5

J ASON FEKETY GREW up thinking he'd like to be a policeman, perhaps even an undercover agent. At the age of sixteen, he'd been convinced by an older friend to go on ambulance runs for an evening. During that single evening, he helped deliver a baby, watched the crew administer to a young girl trapped in an automobile wreck, assisted a fire crew in treating three people (including the chief of a local fire company) for smoke inhalation, pumped the stomach of an attempted suicide patient, and completely lost interest in being a policeman. He completed high school with excellent grades, but with no interest in going on to college. He had trained for and become a paramedic. It was his life.

Jason was surprised when the call came in. The address was in Glenmoore and the report was for a shooting. Glenmoore was not the kind of place where people got shot. He considered the possibility of a crank call or even a hunting accident. Glenmoore was the type of place where one might call because of an accidental child poisoning from the garden supplies or a backyard swimming pool accident. But shootings just didn't occur in Glenmore. At least, not until now.

En route to the scene, the ambulance received a report on the radio from local police that a police officer had arrived at the destination, the scene was secure, and two persons had been critically wounded. The crew agreed that Jason would attend to the more seriously injured of the two, while his understudy, Irene, would attend to the other. They had already linked up their computer and radio to the trauma center located in Courther, and two surgeons were standing by to give them instructions on the scene until the injured could be removed to the hospital. The ambulance crew was informed that a helicopter had been dispatched, but due to the hilly nature of the neighborhood and the lack of a township road, it would be difficult to land near the site.

Traffic was unusually light driving north on Route 100 and the trip around the Marsh Creek State Park was uneventful. Most of the traffic pulled over to the side of the road before the ambulance was within a hundred yards of them, so the trip took less than nine minutes. The ambulance crew knew that time was everything when it came to emergency care; every minute of delay might mean the difference between life and death, the difference between complete recovery and brain damage. The driver of the ambulance, an electrician by trade, was serious, focused, and skilled at his job.

As the ambulance came up the driveway, the sliding doors flew open before the vehicle even came to a stop. Jason, Irene, and two ambulance crew members jumped out. Eighteen minutes and four seconds had elapsed since the 911 dispatcher had received the call. Two more policemen had arrived, one only partially in uniform. The partially uniformed officer wore his hat and jacket, but underneath the jacket he sported a Harley Davidson T-shirt tucked into a pair of jeans. He escorted the paramedics through the front door.

"The lady in the bedroom is dead. Jesus. What a mess. Guy in the hallway is bleeding pretty badly. Jesus." The officer was pale and one of the EMT's turned him back around, took him outside, and sat him on the lawn, where he promptly vomited.

A second officer stood over a figure on the floor in the entrance foyer. The house was huge. Jason guessed the entrance foyer to be thirty feet long and ten feet wide with expensive art adorning the walls and furnishings in every corner of the room. The ceiling, with skylights and an enormous chandelier, towered twenty-six feet above them. The exquisite beauty of the room stood in stark contrast to the horrific scene below. Linda rushed to Jason's side, startling him and bringing him back to the events at hand. Glancing a few feet in front of him, he found the second officer standing in a puddle of coagulating blood, shaking his head.

"This guy is still breathing. I didn't know what to do for him. He's bleeding awfully badly. Woman's in the bedroom. She's worse . . . think she's dead." The officer visibly sagged as if he had awaited this moment and now had been relieved of any responsibility.

"You did just fine, officer." Jason's voice was a study in control. Jason had a calming effect on everyone. The second officer headed for the front door, no longer viewing his presence as necessary and damn happy for it. Jason's assistant, Irene quickly went to work on the man before her, ripping open his partially torn shirt and examining the wound.

CHAPTER 6

JASON'S ASSISTANT QUICKLY donned her gloves and began examining the victim for the source of blood. She had determined almost immediately that there was a single wound in the abdomen, but she found it strange given the quantity of blood. One thing that Jason had taught her about bullet wounds was that no two were alike. Sometimes a victim would have a huge hole from a wound and be sitting there cursing his bad luck at being shot. Other times a small stream of blood came from a seemingly innocuous wound on the body of a person who had expired from that wound.

Exit wounds never made any sense. The victim could have been shot in the arm and the bullet could have exited through the back or even the shoulder. Exit wounds could be small or huge gaping holes depending upon the type of bullet and the angle of entry. This wound didn't look too bad to Jason's assistant, but this victim had lost a great deal of blood and was obviously in shock.

"I have a white male about forty-five years old in the prone position; face up with what appears to be a gunshot wound in the abdominal area. He has lost an inordinate amount of blood. He is pale and unconscious." Linda was now in her trance mode, thinking aloud, and by instinct transmitting everything she saw and thought to the surgeons twenty-three miles away.

"Linda, can you read me?" The speaker crackled to life. Linda moved the speaker to direct it at Jason so that he'd have a clearer field for hearing.

"Yes, but please speak up. It seems there's some interference."

Jason knelt in blood and by the time he'd cut away a portion of the injured person's shirt, blood covered his gloves, pants, shoes, and coat. If he was concerned, he didn't show it.

When Linda had peeled away the lower portion of the shirt and swabbed away the blood, she got her first good look at the wound.

"It's definitely a bullet wound just below the abdomen. It's ragged around the right edge. There are no internal organs protruding from the wound and it continues to bleed. There is some minor coagulation and the bleeding at this time seems to be light. This guy has lost a lot of blood."

The microphone crackled to life. "Is there any indication of an exit wound?"

"Patient is flat on his back, but the underside of his shirt appears to be damp from sweat, not blood."

"Give us your assessment. We'll interrupt as needed and when we deem appropriate."

"OK. His blood pressure is sixty over thirty. Pulse is eighty. He's definitely in shock. Pupils are dilated, and he is breathing really fast. The floor shows a significant loss of blood and his color is bad. He's breathing without difficulty and there appears to be no blood in his sputum. The IVs were started without incident. Skin is cold and clammy to the touch. We've placed the MAST trousers on his legs and elevated his head slightly. The bullet path does not appear to be near the spine and, unless it traveled a strange path internally, it didn't hit any bony masses."

"OK. Try to keep his blood pressure up and transport him ASAP. Medivac has been dispatched and should arrive within five minutes. They don't seem confident they can land very close to the premises. Dr. Evans will be here in a moment and will take over from our end."

"OK." The speaker went dead. Jason gave it a crack with his elbow and it came back to life. " . . . and load him on the ambulance for transport to the medivac. They're landing about three blocks away in a cul-de-sac called Thielane Court." The driver, who had been lurking nearby awaiting further instructions, was already out the door and getting a fix on the location of Thielane Court before Jason could issue the orders to do so.

"I'm sorry, your transmission broke up. Please repeat."

"Repeat. Please prepare the patient for the raft and get him to the ambulance as quickly as possible. Get two large bore IV's started. If he starts to lose blood pressure again, give him another one hundred cc of the butinezerene. If the blood pressure drops, you've got the green light to administer Rastin, but no more than five hundred CCs. The medevac unit will be landing three blocks away on Theilane Court. Did you get that?"

"Roger. Got it."

It took four of them to load the patient on the raft while keeping him as still as possible. He was lifted vertically and whisked to the back of the ambulance without incident. Five minutes later he was in the helicopter, being attended to by a hospital-based tech. Jason and Linda headed back to the house.

Although they had no doubt that the police knew a dead person when they saw one, the two paramedics went to check the status of the female victim. They approached the bedroom door, which was flanked by two state police officers.

"She's on the floor behind the bed." The older of the two men said and pointed to the corner of the room, as if they might have trouble finding her.

Jason checked her pulse. There was none. He held his stethoscope to her chest and listened; there were no sounds. Her eyes stared lifelessly at the ceiling. He cuffed her arm with the mechanized sphygmomanometer but there was no pressure. She felt cold and it appeared rigor mortis might be setting in.

Elaine Pierce Kauffman was dead.

CHAPTER 7

D R. CAROL EVANS was on her way to work at the trauma center where she was a staff emergency room physician, board certified in surgery, when the call came in from Brandywine Hospital on her beeper. Her car phone had the number in its memory and upon her voice command, "two," she activated the call. She had reserved number one for her father's number when she had the phone installed in the car.

"Dr. Evans, we have a shooting in the Glenmoore area. We have paramedics on the scene. We're gearing up here and I thought you might want to be involved from the beginning," the voice said. The voice speaking was the critical care nurse Sharon Webster who worked almost exclusively with Dr. Evans. Webster was cool under fire, never gave in to the dolts in hospital administration, and could stand steady on her feet for sixteen hours without food, water, or complaint.

"Thanks, Sharon. I do want to be involved. When the call arrives, can you forward it to my car? I'm about ten minutes from the hospital. I can pull the phone and stay in link when I get out of the car. You can pipe the call into the OR as soon as I arrive and get scrubbed."

"The audio tech guy says it's no problem to have it linked to the OR and your car at the same time, so we can hear what's going on from the beginning as well. Please chime in if for some reason you get disconnected or get pulled over for running the stop sign at the bottom of the hill again."

Evans chuckled to herself. "I'll be sure to come to a full stop this time."

CHAPTER 8

"OK, LET'S DO it." Carol was confident of herself and in the abilities of her staff. She loved her work. The adrenaline was already pumping through her body, and she made a conscious decision to put the car on cruise control so she wouldn't rap herself around a tree while on her way to save someone who had enough problems without losing their doctor.

It was certainly less difficult than it seemed to someone who was unfamiliar with medical procedures. As a practical matter, there were only so many things that could happen to the human body. The number of different ways they happened was absolutely limitless. For instance, she thought, a person could be brought to the trauma unit with a clogged air passage. The way that problem was approached depended largely on the age and condition of the patient and not on how the passage had been blocked.

Carol had been involved in one hundred and sixteen air passage blockages, and only thirteen of them had been from what she considered conventional means. There had been the college student with the ping pong ball, the baby with the JuJi fruits, and the football player with the mouthpiece. When her adrenalin was pumping, she often thought of these types of things. It did not affect her ability to concentrate; on the contrary, it helped her to focus.

Carol knew the techs were usually pretty good, but as a surgeon her ego rarely allowed her to give them any credit for their performances. Her mentor had once referred to the paramedics as puppets, "The less they can think, and the better they follow your instructions, the better the result." It was a good thing that the medical techs didn't know what most surgeons really thought of them, or they might have just stayed home at night.

Her phone was mounted on her dashboard to provide hands-on driving and hands-free phoning. She had an extra speaker added in the back to provide for more clarity in transmission. Both speakers crackled back to life.

"OK, can anyone copy me?" Carol waited her turn.

"Brandywine Trauma. We have you loud and clear. Dr. Evans?"

"Loud and clear. From now on everybody follows my lead. To whom am I speaking?"

"This is Jason. I'll give you the details." He didn't wait for her permission even though that was clearly the way she wanted it to go down. "We have a middle-aged male, about forty, found on the floor in his home. He is bleeding moderately from a wound to his abdominal area. Looks like a gunshot wound. There appears to be no blood underneath him so there is probably no exit wound. Subject is unconscious. Blood pressure is 60 over 30. Helicopter is en route, repeat en route. Over."

"Pupils?" Carol asked.

"Pupils are dilated, eyes are unresponsive, light in here is quite bright and it's noisy as hell. Subject is not responding to verbal commands and doesn't respond to pain. He is in MAST trousers and is bleeding slightly."

"Respiration?"

"Difficult to tell in here, but it appears clear and rapid. His pulse is hovering around seventy, but it appears erratic."

"You said that his bleeding is moderate. What have we got for an IV?"

"We immediately started two large bore IV's, and he has now taken three liters of fluids. Saline solution drip and a plasma drip as well. The amount of blood on the clothes and floor do not appear to be life-threatening from the standpoint of how much plasma he's taking in, I . . . "

"Thank you, Jason, but I don't need to hear what you think, just the data," Carol interrupted.

Jason bit his lip, but didn't say anything. He knew he was talking to one of the "gods," and no matter what he said or did, she would take the glory and lay blame elsewhere. It didn't bother him as much anymore; he had gotten used to it.

"Skin color?"

"He's pale, but not ashen."

"Temperature?"

"Pretty stable at one hundred."

"Any head trauma?"

"No trauma that we can see anywhere on the body except the wound. Bleeding is slowing. We've been applying a pack and gauze and it seems to be clotting."

"OK." Carol was pulling into her parking space at the rear of the hospital where the emergency room and trauma units were located. "I assume the helicopter is somewhere nearby now." No one spoke. "Hello, is anybody home? Where is the helicopter?"

Another voice came on the line. "We're having some difficulty getting the chopper landed because of the terrain in the neighborhood, wooded lots, and narrow streets."

"Shit," was all she said and headed into the unit on a good clip, but careful not to run. They weren't going to get here anytime soon, she thought. Let's hope he doesn't flat line on us before I can get my hands on that bullet. She gave no thought to the fact that she had accepted the tech's analysis that it was a bullet; she knew it was a bullet.

CHAPTER 9

FOUNDED BY A government grant and aided by corporate donations, the Brandywine Hospital's Trauma Center (BHTC) had been built in 1989 and was the only one of its kind outside of center city Philadelphia which could treat severe trauma patients from all over eastern Pennsylvania. The ability to save the lives of severely traumatized persons was in direct proportion to two factors: how soon the paramedics arrived after the trauma occurred and how quickly a trained trauma unit was able to treat the patient.

The helicopters provided fast and efficient transportation from the scene of an accident or, in this case, a shooting. The helipad sat right next to the BHTC with appropriate ramping, cover, doors, and access to provide a smooth transition from the helicopter to the operating theater of the unit. A ramp allowed the gurney to come out of the helicopter without dropping the gurney's wheels. The ramp led straight into the unit via two plastic door covers, which eliminated the need to open any real door and at the same time kept the unit sterile.

The trauma unit was extremely expensive to maintain. In order to be ready to treat a victim, the unit had to be staffed and ready to proceed at all times. In the event of multiple trauma victims, a second team remained on standby and a second operating theater stood fully equipped and ready for use. Trauma surgeons were a rare breed. Several cuts above any emergency room doctor and the average surgeon, they had to remain calm under pressure and maintain significant physical and mental endurance. Twelve hours of trauma surgeries after a major multiple automobile accident was not unusual. The team itself had to treat persons of all ages and with various previously existing conditions, such as diabetes, heart conditions, and even AIDS.

Tonight at the BHTC, eight people were assembled and awaiting the helicopter. The only two males in the group were orderlies, whose jobs it would be to move Richard Kauffman to the unit and to move anything else that needed moving, then to disappear. The other six were women all highly trained and skilled in their areas of expertise. Dr. Kristen was an anesthesiologist who had trained at Johns Hopkins School of Medicine and interned at Sloan Kettering. She had acquired a reputation as one of the finest young anesthesiologists in the nation and had been invited on two occasions by the Chinese government to visit China so that the Chinese Emergency Room physicians could watch her work. She had a sixth sense when it came to patient allergic reactions, something that had saved more than a few people's lives.

Sharon Webster and Teresa Domenic were both registered nurses with a combined twenty-nine years of experience. They had both been certified by the American Institute of Trauma Research as CTAs (certified trauma assistants), and both had more actual training than the average surgeon, despite not being MDs. They were good friends and made a great team. Sharon and Teresa were both tireless; both trained by running ten kilometer road races, swimming in the winter months, and lifting weights. Ann was married with three children, while Teresa, at age thirty-seven, had remained single by choice.

Karen Warren was also an RN. At twenty-six years old, she was the junior in the group by seven full years. Karen had graduated fourth in her class from Princeton University and, despite Papa Warren's desire for her to become his "daughter the doctor," she was determined to be the world's best trauma nurse. Her stop at BHTC was a temporary one and everybody knew it. Papa Warren's baby girl was not going to stay in the "sticks" very long, no matter how much experience it put on her résumé. Karen was not only a skilled medical technician, but she was absolutely marvelous with personnel and filled out administrative paperwork in her sleep. Everyone at BHTC knew she was destined for a desk job at a prestigious northeastern hospital (probably in Boston) at a very early age. Since Papa Warren was also Jonathan Besper Warren, MD, chief of staff at St. Christopher's in Nassau County, Long Island, no one had any doubt about Karen's future.

Dr. Beth Francis was the assistant surgeon on the team. At the age of forty, she was the oldest member of the team. She was a bundle of energy inside and outside the operating theater. She pitched for a local over-thirty softball team, coached her youngest daughter in recreation league soccer, and bowled every Tuesday night (trauma calls permitting) with her husband in a mixed league. Dr. Francis, an avid reader (and fan of anything remotely associated with H. P. Lovecraft), had no desire to be the head surgeon. She was tremendously comfortable with her role as assistant, ready to take over whenever necessary, and otherwise to assist in a calm and professional fashion under the most grueling of circumstances. She knew her strengths and weaknesses and dwelled on neither.

Dr. Carol Evans was the chief trauma surgeon for Team Gold. Her credentials were impeccable. At age thirty–three, her resume read like an encyclopedia. She had graduated college at the age of nineteen and had gone on to graduate third in her class at Cal Berkley Medical School in just three and a half years. Dr. Evans's family was well known in the medical community. Her great-great-great-grandfather had emigrated from Ireland at the close of the fourth potato famine and set up practice in an Irish ghetto in Union City, New Jersey. The family now sported no less than fourteen physicians around the country, with three more in various stages of medical school, and Evans's father was chief of staff at the most prestigious hospital in Newark New Jersey. Beyond that, no one knew a thing about her.

Carmen Nuestro Rodrigues was a homebody. She enjoyed cooking for her family. She loved to bake and had little or no interest in sports—unless her children were involved. As for her credentials, Carmen was simply the best nurse in the hospital.

As a team they were nothing short of spectacular.

CHAPTER 10

DANTE "SPAGS" SPAGNOLA had been a detective for eleven years. He'd been a police officer for five years before that. He'd received the call about ten minutes after the ambulance had been dispatched to the Kauffman home. He jumped into his car and called the officers at the scene. Unfortunately, he understood that no one was in charge because both the "staties" and the "locals" had somehow shown up at the Kauffman house. What he didn't know until he arrived was that two different local departments and the staties had all showed up together with an off duty cop and a retired security guard.

When Spags got out of his car in front of the house, he knew he was in for a bad evening. There were cars everywhere. The ambulance crew had come and gone (driving across the lawn leaving relatively deep gouges along the way), and the house was teeming with people. He had called the county lab on the way to the scene and requested the forensics unit to dispatch a team on the off chance that there would be something valuable to be found at the scene. He knew firsthand from experience that murders were usually committed by people who knew the victim and, in most instances, the murderer confessed shortly after the act. He had been informed of the woman's death en route.

Just looking around the outside of the house, Spags had a bad feeling that the forensics team was going to be useless. He walked up to the front door where three officers, all in different uniforms, stood talking quietly. He flashed his badge and announced that he was going to take charge of the crime scene until the forensics boys arrived. No one objected.

"What happened?" was all he asked.

A young, slender black statie was the first to speak up. "We found a white female in the master bedroom on the floor behind the bed. A neighbor, who's inside, a former security guard for Weston, identified her as Mrs. Elaine Kauffman, the owner." He was reading from his pad now and sounding quite professional, Spagnola thought to himself.

"She appears to have been shot twice, once in the hand and once in the chest. She was dead when the paramedics arrived. The second victim was Mr. William Kauffman, also identified by the neighbor. He was found in the entrance hall. He was shot one or more times in the abdomen and was medevaced to the hospital fifteen minutes ago. The ambulance crew said they believed him to be in critical condition based upon the wounds. I didn't get that directly from them, but this was relayed to me by a fellow officer, Sergeant Cottman of the West Darrinville Police."

"Thank you, trooper," said Spagnola. "Please show me around."

Spagnola followed the trooper through the front door, took one pace and stopped dead.

"Will you look at this fuckin' mess? This place looks like a MASH unit just got a load of marines off a beach. Shit," Spagnola said to no one in particular.

Pools of blood covered the hardwood floor and spattered the walls. Dozens of bloody footprints crisscrossed the foyer. The blood, which had now coagulated, could be seen in trails leading to and from the kitchen and the master bedroom. Pieces of gauze and cloth, together with wrappers and a syringe covers, littered the area.

Spagnola tried to be careful as he walked about the house, but his efforts seemed futile. After a brief walk through the downstairs rooms, including the kitchen, he followed the trooper into the bedroom. Although no one except Elaine Kauffman was in the room, the mess of footprints on the carpet made it apparent that many people had been there earlier in the night. He noted that everything in the house appeared normal except in the entrance hall, the bedroom, and the connecting hallway, all of which conjured up images of *Saving Private Ryan.*

Elaine Kauffman lay next to the bed. It appeared that she had been shot in the chest, through the quilt which partially covered her body. She may have been sleeping at the time she was shot, Spagnola thought, but sometimes these things were staged. He put on a pair of gloves and slowly lifted the cover, careful not to change its crease, and looked beneath it. The bullet had indeed gone through the blanket and sheet and into her chest, leaving a fairly small wound. Then the detective caught sight of her left hand, which had been partially hidden by the bed skirt. Mrs. Kauffman was missing two fingers.

Spagnola slowly glanced around the room. He noted mentally that the room was cozy and warm in its decorations. There was no indication of a man's touch in the room; everything was either neutral or feminine. The curtains and blinds made it next to impossible for someone to see into the room from outside, unless the lights of the bedroom were lit and the person was standing inside the shrubs that surrounded the house.

The only other thing of note in the room was that a small jewelry box lay on the floor opposite of Mrs. Kauffman's body. It had been broken into several pieces and was empty from the look of it. He did not touch it, hoping that no one else had touched it either and that maybe, just maybe, there would be some evidence for the forensic guys.

CHAPTER 11

As Detective Spagnola had guessed, the night of September 6 had been a bad one. The morning of September 7 was not much better. Spagnola had not slept since the previous evening, and at 6:30 AM, he was six Wawa coffees into the day, and he felt like hell. He knew he wasn't going to be able to sleep just yet, and was sitting at his desk staring out the window at the two-hundred-and-ten-year-old township building, hoping for inspiration. The view gave him nothing.

The crime scene had been a zoo. As Spagnola had figured, the forensic team took one look around and told him they might as well go home. There was nothing they could do; everything had been trampled. He'd convinced them to stay and photograph the scene as best they could and check out the door to the outside from the bedroom and, of course, the jewelry box. Reluctantly they had done so, so at least he would have pictures, for what they would be worth. An examination of the box did not reveal any forensic evidence. The first mystery had already been solved. Mrs. Kauffman's fingers had been ripped off of her hand by the impact of a bullet that had later been found lodged in the bedroom wall. The forensics team chief, a young Korean man with a sharp mind, determined from the sight of her hand and the gunpowder residue that she had put her hand out to fend off the attack and had her fingers shot off for her trouble. Defense wound, mystery solved.

Spagnola didn't have much information, but he did have a handle on a few of the details. Mrs. Kauffman had seen her killer, or at least the gun, and knew she was going to be shot. The intruder had been able to get very close to her without her moving, so she either knew the intruder or had been asleep and had not heard the intruder. It was also possible that the intruder had entered the bedroom, pointed the gun at her so she couldn't or wouldn't move, and then killed her.

Spagnola also knew that the circumstances of the 911 call were suspicious. The systems operator had said that the call had come from a blocked cell phone, so they had no source. More importantly, it appeared that the call came in as much as half an hour after Mrs. Kauffman had been shot, according to the medical examiner, who said she would know more later on after testing the temperature of the victim's liver.

Why would someone call 911 on a cell phone and not leave their name? Spagnola picked up his pocket tape recorder, checked to see that it contained a fresh tape and began dictating:

"Tuesday morning, September 7, six o'clock. Observations regarding homicide of Elaine Kauffman."

CHAPTER 12

C ARMEN HAD NEVER wanted to be anything but a nurse. She was the daughter of a light-skinned black mother and a Puerto Rican father, who, while smaller than his mom, was as macho as they came. Carmen had her mom's size and skin tone, with all of her dad's attitude. She never wanted to be a doctor. Doctors were assholes. Nurses helped people.

Carmen was very good at what she did in the emergency room and as a trauma RN. She held degrees in both, she was good at her job, and she let you know she was good.

She held the emergency room doctors in full contempt, but she made small allowances for the trauma surgeons. She knew they were assholes, but they were talented assholes.

Carmen trusted Dr. Evans. She didn't necessarily like her, but she trusted her. Carmen didn't believe the doctor was truly an asshole like so many others in the hospital. Most importantly, Carmen knew that Dr. Evans was very competent.

When the call came in, Carmen was having a cup of coffee, reading an advanced trauma journal. She not only stayed on top of the latest techniques, she prided herself in knowing them before the docs. She heard the call and raced to scrub in, and on her way she tossed her half cup of coffee in the trash, not spilling a drop on the floor.

"Carmen drains a three!" yelled one of her co-workers while trying to finish his breakfast. "Don't take any guff from the gowns."

"Never have, never will," Carmen muttered, but her mind was already gearing to her work.

The scrub room was abuzz, since one of the surgeons and the anesthesiologist had just arrived and had walked straight in as the call came from the paramedics.

"Gunshot to the gut, Carmen," said the youngest of the assembled. "Nasty business. Evans will be in her element on this one. Make a mistake and its peritonitis city."

"They don't pay us to make mistakes," said Carmen, her game face on and her voice carrying a little edge. "Just make sure that security knows that we're the good guys, not the badges, and keep them out of our hair until we've got a live one. They always expect us to pop the bullet out on the police time table, and then they expect us to keep the patient alive and well as an afterthought."

Carmen had grown up in a lower middle class neighborhood that was a melting pot of Hispanics, blacks, and white manual laborers, where the police were definitely not your friends. She recognized that the police served a purpose in society, but she didn't take any guff from them either.

The patient was being transported to the helicopter and would arrive in ten to fifteen minutes. Dr. Evans was en route and would arrive shortly. The rest of the team was already on the premises. "This should be a good one," Carmen mused. They usually were with Dr. Evans. She didn't take any guff from anybody either.

CHAPTER 13

D R. EVANS WAS more than smooth. She conducted the trauma theater with the grace of a prima ballerina and the passion of a head coach of a hometown football team at halftime. She preached, cajoled, pleaded, barked orders, and implored, all while singing or humming most of the time, getting the best out of her team and setting the tone for success. She talked to the patient when she wasn't otherwise occupied. She willed the patient to good health and recovery by the sheer strength of her own will, her sublime confidence, and, in the end, her almost limitless knowledge of the human body.

"The techs did a good job," she said. "Carmen, make a note to send them a thank you note and some candy. We must keep the linemen happy if we're ever going to complete a long pass."

Everyone knew she was kidding and would no sooner compliment a paramedic than she would shine her own shoes.

"You don't send me candy, anymore," the doctor sang. "Hey, Mr. Kauffman, you're doing great, and we are the best, the absolute best thing that ever happened to you. You hang in there, we'll have you up and singing in no time." She swirled around the table, barking orders and checking clamps, bleeding, sponges, lividity of skin, and subtle changes in breathing that the machines could not record. She was in her element; she was also considered to be slightly nuts by everyone who worked with her.

Then suddenly, Dr. Evans became quiet. She asked for and received a scalpel and without so much as a moment's hesitation, she was slicing into the patient's skin just below what appeared to be a fairly neat hole on the right side of the patient's abdomen. Within two minutes she had discarded the scalpel for long thin tweezers and, after cocking her head to one side and then the other, as if she were listening to her patient, she retracted the tweezers. At the end was a single, slightly mashed bullet, ensconced in blood and tissue, but apparently whole.

"Voila," she whispered. The bullet was deposited in a sterling steel bowl. "For the gendarmes," she said. She looked around at those assembled. They all knew what was coming next but there was nothing to be done.

"Where the hell are the x-rays? How the hell am I supposed to work when those doctor wannabees in radiology can't develop a roll of film from a brownie instamatic?"

She then started humming and moved in close to the patient's ear. Those assembled looked at the vital signs and could see the tangible upswing in the vitals as she hummed some soft ballad from a long forgotten Joni Mitchell album.

Dr. Evans was the best, and she knew it.

CHAPTER 14

WHEN THE X-RAYS arrived, Dr. Evans said nothing. Dr. Fong hung them on the permanent x-ray light stand and flipped on the illumination.

Dr. Evans did not so much as turn her head, but kept humming her song. Dr. Fong knew not to speak until she was done. He had assisted her many times and had learned her idiosyncrasies, some through funny exchanges, others in more hazardous ways. It helped to know her quirks before assisting her in surgery. She was a tough, but fair, taskmaster and nothing short of a genius in her work. Dr. Fong was quite pleased to be able to add her name to his résumé, and a recommendation from her held weight throughout the nation.

Finally, she stopped humming and cocked her head to one side, away from the x-rays. "OK, big Ed," she said. Dr. Fong stood five foot three inches tall in his shoes. "Tell me the truth. There's no more bullets in our healthy, handsome man. Tell me I'm right. Let it happen, Cap'n."

Dr. Fong cleared his throat. He shook his head as he scanned the x-rays back and forth. "There's no indication of any foreign objects in the patient. There appears to be no broken bones. X-rays are rather unremarkable. We should take another set of pictures as soon as he is stable to be sure nothing was dislodged when the bullet was retracted." He smiled a thin, ingenuous smile and held his head in her direction, waiting for the storm.

It didn't come. Instead, the good doctor slowly turned around, stared at the patient, and gently patted him on the head.

"You're going to be just fine, Mr. Kauffman. Sleep long and sound and remember to send us all cards on Christmas." Then to Fong she said, "You won't find any." She pulled off her gloves, dropped them on the floor, and left the theater. If it were permitted, the team would have applauded on her way out. She had been, as usual, magnificent.

"Excuse me, Dr. Evans, should I bag and tag the bullet?" asked Carmen, one of the few who would engage the good doctor after her denouement.

"No, Carmen, that's not necessary, and besides, they'll claim we tampered with the evidence," she drawled as if she were suddenly possessed by a southern belle. "Just make sure it's safe."

CHAPTER 15

*B*ILL KAUFFMAN COULD *hear voices and music but couldn't focus. He had no idea where he was, nor who was around him. Initially the music sounded like rock 'n roll but it eventually slowed down and sounded more like a familiar folk song he couldn't identify. He felt odd, not in pain, but odd, and he did not like the smell around him.*

He sensed a conversation was occurring around him, but he couldn't distinguish the voices from the other sounds in his head. He was confused, but strangely he didn't seem to care. He was cold on the outside, but felt warm within. He was not in pain but kept searching himself, semi-aware that there should be pain somewhere.

In certain ways he felt like he was dreaming; in other ways he felt like he had had too much to drink. He was trying to place the smell around him, but that seemed to be too much work, and in his mind he simply faded away.

CHAPTER 16

DETECTIVE SPAGNOLA HAD worked for Uwchlan Township for sixteen months. He was one of two detectives hired by the township to assist the police force with the investigation of "serious crimes." Uwchlan Township did not have a significant number of serious crimes, a fact which greatly influenced Spagnola's interest in the job. As part of a cooperative effort with other local law enforcement agencies, Detective Spagnola was occasionally on loan to the Upper Uwchlan or West Pikeland townships. The two other townships requested a detective when they did not want to involve the state police or the county detectives' office. This made Spags a busy man.

Dante Angelo Spagnola was thirty-three years old. He'd been a detective for eight years, six and a half of them in Philadelphia, of which four were spent in homicide. Dan, as the police called him, was good at his job and knew it. He prided himself on his closure rate and didn't tolerate incompetence. He was trim, fit, and had a casual way about him that led witnesses and perpetrators alike to trust him. He could be tough as nails when he needed to, but found that he got a lot more information with the proverbial "honey."

Spags knew just about everything there was to know about homicide. He had studied at the academy in Quantico, the University of Pennsylvania forensic graduate school, and, finally, had investigated homicides first hand in Philly. He had seen far too many of them, first as a squad car cop and then for fifty-one months as a full-fledged homicide detective.

In the beginning, he was the rookie and was assigned cases that were virtually impossible to solve: bodies found in sewers, bodies floating to the surface of the Schuylkill River, bodies uncovered in landfills, bodies that turned up mummified and inside walls of buildings being demolished. Most of the homicides to which he was assigned early in his detective career involved bodies of people who had not been reported missing, had no identification, and had been dead for a long, long period of time. *Dead ends*, Spags liked to jokingly call them. Whoever perpetrated these murders was usually long gone. The detective received little time, no money, and no manpower to assist him in solving these crimes, so he had to rely on his own instincts and skill if he wanted to bring the perpetrators to justice.

Spags knew that the types of murders he investigated early on in his career represented a very small percentage of the overall number of murders that occurred in the United States. Statistically, the majority of American homicides shared several common denominators.

First, the victim typically knew the killer. Dan found it amusing that despite this fact, the average person believed that strangers on deserted streets committed homicides late at night in bad neighborhoods.

The second truth about most homicides was that the victim and the killer were usually related by blood or marriage. *So much for public perceptions,* Spags thought to himself as he continued the list of common denominators.

The killer or the victim or both were often high on alcohol or drugs when the death occurred. Family gatherings, such as weddings, birthdays, holidays, and family reunions, could be deadly.

None of these factors applied to gang-related homicides, however, which shared a separate list of commonalities. In these murders, the killer was a teenage male, high on drugs, intoxicated from alcohol, or both. The weapon of choice was a gun, and the victim was virtually never the intended target of the killer.

The killer, Spags mused, was usually an idiot. The killers were not nearly as tough as they portrayed themselves or as they were portrayed by the media and perceived by their peers.

Dan had seen it time and time again. The gang members spent hours getting high and talking about how tough and vicious they all were. They sometimes spent days jacking themselves up to commit the shooting. Then they would run or drive up to the victim and open fire with a semi-automatic weapon, while trying to escape at the same time.

The result? They misidentified their target, were too high and scared to take the time to aim, and usually killed an innocent bystander.

There was plenty of time, money, and manpower to investigate the homicide of a seven-year-old bystander accidentally killed by a gang member. It made good headlines, depicting a sympathetic police department and highlighting gang violence as a serious problem. The TV crews who wouldn't walk through these same neighborhoods in broad daylight would suddenly be sent filming there at eight o'clock at night, feeling safe with a significant police presence around them. Pure political bullshit, Spags thought to himself.

The third, and much smaller, category of homicides consisted of felonies such as robberies, rapes, burglaries, and drug deals gone bad. Because the public saw these murders every week on the national news or on popular cop shows, they usually believed that these types of homicides happened on a regular basis. In reality, a burglar wants property, not confrontation; the robber usually wants cash, not resistance; and the rapist usually wants to hurt the woman, not kill her.

Then there was the fourth category: the outcasts. Bums, homeless persons, prostitutes, runaways. Detective Spagnola left Philadelphia because there was no time, no money, no manpower, and no media coverage for those poor souls. The department assigned rookies to those homicides without providing much help or instruction. All the rookies got was a knowing smile from their supervisors. The politicians wanted these cases closed quickly, and didn't particularly care about pursuing the perpetrators and bringing them to justices.

Unfortunately, in the haste to close cases of victims for whom no one cares, some homicides were not investigated at all. Spags knew that there were real predators out in the world: people who didn't fit the mold; monsters that kill prostitutes, bums, the homeless, the mentally ill, and the runaways; monsters that killed for sport or pleasure. Spags knew because he'd seen their work. Spags knew because he had a sense for patterns in unrelated homicides that belied his years. Spags knew because he had met two of these monsters and looked into their soulless eyes.

The first time Detective Spagnola met a monster, he had been a patrol officer. The police had received a call from an elderly lady who complained of a series of loud noises and awful smells emanating from the apartment next door to her. It turned out that her neighbor had killed his roommate and the body had begun to decompose before the killer attended to the body's disposal.

A search of the apartment following the neighbor's s arrest had led to the conclusion that the killing wasn't his first. In all, he had killed somewhere between six and ten roommates over the course of four years. He had readily admitted the killings to Spags once he'd been caught. Most of the victims had been itinerant workers looking to share the cost of an inexpensive apartment so that they could make ends meet; they often sent some money back home to Puerto Rico or Mexico. He told the police that he had killed them for sport, because he was bored.

The second monster had been Ted Smythe.

CHAPTER 17

TED SMYTHE WAS in every nightmare that Spags had dreamt since January 23, 2012. Ted Smythe was the reason Spags had left the Philadelphia homicide division, a policeman's dream, for the quiet of suburbia.

Ted Smythe graduated from the prestigious Erwin Academy in Gladwyne and obtained a degree in economics at the University of Pennsylvania. He formed his own search company one year out of college and earned over two hundred thousand dollars that year. He was athletic, handsome, well off, and earned his living finding people to fill jobs in the medical industry. He did searches for doctors, nurses, paramedics, physician's assistants, and attendants. Smythe developed a software package that allowed a person who was longing for a position in medicine to enter his or her qualifications and salary requirements into a personal computer, and for a fee, he matched the candidate with an employer. Smythe was competent at his job, charging both the employer and the employee a fee for his successful employment matches. The system worked well, needed very little care, and provided Smythe with a handsome income and lots of free time.

Ted used his free time to accumulate data on runaway boys and girls. He liked them to be between twelve and sixteen years of age. If there were a chance that the runaway had come to Philadelphia, he would track them down. He found that tracking teenage runaways was much tougher than matching employees with employers, but he also found it far more rewarding.

Late in 2011, Homicide Detective Spagnola noticed a pattern in some seemingly unrelated homicides. The pattern involved the deaths of a number of runaway girls shortly after they had contacted a parent or loved one. The contact had come out of the blue, according to each parent interviewed, and had come a long time after the previous contact, if any. There were no other connections between the homicides; not family, not friends, not location, not past schools, nothing. They were all simply runaways in Philadelphia appearing to reach out to their families just before they died.

The common denominator was that they all ended up dead. One body was found in the river, one found in a dumpster, one found in the woods at Fairmont Park; one died of strangulation, one by a blunt instrument, one by stabbing. All were twelve to sixteen years of age, and all were murdered.

Spags brought his theory to his immediate boss, a senior detective with fifteen years on the force.

"Dan, you need a vacation. You're seeing multiple murderers in your sleep," his boss said.

Spags knew from experience that the last thing anybody on the force wanted to hear was that a serial murderer was in town. The cops in suits tried to believe they didn't exist. Serials were hard to detect, harder to catch, the hardest to convict, and, above all, publicity nightmares.

Once a newsman got a whiff of a connection between two serious criminal acts, whether they be robberies, rapes, or murders, the press went crazy. It made for great reading, great newspaper sales, and great late night news. Suddenly, everyone wanted to hear quotes from former FBI agents who specialized in profiling and jailhouse interviews with convicted serials and their families. News channels capitalized on all the hype by airing TV specials on serials killers of the past, serial killers of the eighties, Jack the Ripper, the first known serial killer Vlad the Impaler, and any other tantalizing story they could get their hands on.

Spags remained undaunted. He spent his spare time worrying about the case. His marriage had hit the rocks three months after he began working as a homicide detective. He, like Smythe, had lots of spare time.

With a great deal of hard detective work and not an insignificant amount of good luck, Spags found a runaway who claimed to have known the last victim, a young woman whose real name was Cheryl Anderson. The runaway, Lori, told an intriguing story to him. Lori told Spags that she and Cheryl had lived together for a short period of time in an empty office space above a restaurant on Eighth Street.

After a couple of square meals, Lori began to feel comfortable with Spags and realized that he wanted nothing from her but information. She trusted him in an odd fashion and eventually told him Cheryl's story.

Apparently, like many runaways, Cheryl had run out of money and had no place to live. She did some tricking in the theater district and waited tables at a small café that didn't even ask for her social security number, no less proof that she wasn't an illegal alien. A man had approached Cheryl as she waited tables and said that he was a runaway tracker but had not been hired by her mother or stepfather. Cheryl's real father, Lori told Spags, was dead.

The man claimed that he worked for a nonprofit organization that specialized in helping runaways establish a life free of the sex trade, while trying to establish some form of family contact. No strings attached, no fees, you could quit the deal anytime you liked. No cops, no telling the family where you were. It sounded like a good deal to Cheryl, and she took the man up on his seemingly generous offer.

The man also told Cheryl one thing that Lori had found a little strange. He told her he could only help her if she kept his identity and the identity of his nonprofit organization a secret from everyone, no exceptions, not even other runaways. Cheryl promptly told Lori this, in case Lori wanted to get involved too. Lori declined.

The man was described by Cheryl as young, hot, and sophisticated. He gave her cash to go shopping for clothing but insisted that nothing be trashy or suggestive. He refused to have sex with her when she offered. He told her his organization had strict rules and stricter principles. He eventually convinced her to call her mother, using his cell phone and assuring her that the call couldn't be traced if she held the conversation to under ninety seconds.

Spags remembered asking the question, "Did she make the call?"

Lori said, "I don't know, I never saw her again."

The thought of the conversation still sent chills down Dan's spine; it always would. At that point he knew his hunch was correct.

CHAPTER 18

S MYTHE WAS CLEVER and productive. A fourth dead girl was found six weeks after the third. She'd been stabbed eight times. The first wound had killed her, according to the medical examiner. After talking to her parents in Canton, Ohio, Dan learned that ten days prior to the discovery of her body, she had called home for the first time in over six months. The call had been made somewhere between twenty-four and forty-eight hours prior to her death, according to the medical examiner.

It took Dan two full months after that to find the 'tracker,' Smythe. It took three days of intensive surveillance to garner Smythe's routine. It took four hours to determine he had a young lady in his apartment on Thirty-Third Street.

Smythe, it was learned, maintained an apartment near Rittenhouse Square under his own name. The apartment on Thirty-third was in the name of a Grace Carenutos, a supposedly safe place for runaways to stay.

Smythe did not know anything about forensics. He had worked one summer at the county courthouse as an intern and had been fingerprinted by the county sheriff's department. He had left a thumb print on a plastic trash bag he used to dispose of the fourth victim. He'd also left hair, a small amount of blood, and even some semen. They all came back matching his blood type and the thumb print was identified as his. A Philadelphia common pleas judge barely read the affidavit before signing a warrant for his arrest and a search of all of his known premises.

The judge had asked just two questions: "Are you guys sure?" and "Can you get there fast?"

The Philadelphia Police Department was large, compartmentalized, and tough. When things got tough, they got tougher. Cooperation was hard to come by except in an emergency; then everybody pitched in. Smythe and his current runaway had become an emergency.

The command decision was made not to treat this as a hostage situation. Smythe did not have permits for firearms and nothing in his past or in the girls' murders indicated that he was armed with a gun. According to his record, there was no other history of violence for Smythe, nothing.

The apartment was one of four in the building, about half a flight up the stairs. Each residence had a small landing with a door that led into the apartment. In the back was a common fire escape. Surveillance had pegged Smythe entering the building at two-thirty, prior to which no one had known whether he was in the apartment or at large. At 3:30 PM, the detectives obtained the warrant.

The command plan was simple. It also mirrored the plan on the scene. A couple of two-man SWAT teams were positioned in the back of the building to cover the windows, fire escape, and roof. At the front door, an entrance team consisted of four uniforms: one with a hammer to knock the inside door off its hinges, two detectives, and a lieutenant. The lieutenant would, of course, remain outside on the landing.

Because one of the rear windows to the apartment had been partially open despite the frigid temperatures, it was impossible to enact a simultaneous dual entry since clamoring up the fire escape would produce too much noise.

It was January 23, 2012, and the sun was about to set. The entrance into the hallway was easy and quiet. Tiptoeing up the stairs was noisy, but soon loud, heavy metal-type music could be heard from the apartment on the full second floor above Smythe's apartment. The music deadened the sounds of the policemen's movements. The landing in front of apartment 1-B was small, so that only the hammer officer and one of the uniformed officers were able to be on it when they hit the apartment door. The door cracked like a gunshot, not only coming off the hinges, but cracking down the middle and exploding into the apartment entrance. The sides of the door took two large chunks of the molding with them and nails clanked and sprung all over.

The lead uniformed policeman moved into the apartment, ducked into the kitchen on the left, and yelled:

"Police! Ted Smythe, you are under arrest! Please step out where we can see you!"

"Police! Mr. Smythe, we have a warrant for your arrest! Please step out where we can see you!"

The second uniformed officer sprinted down the hall past the kitchen as soon as he heard the call, "Clear!"

The third uniformed officer continued down the hall to where the second officer was crouching and entered the living room area off the first bedroom with Detective Spagnola right behind him.

Someone turned the music down in the apartment upstairs and yelled, "What the fuck is going on down there?"

Suddenly, an eerie silence pervaded the apartment.

CHAPTER 19

SMYTHE STOOD WITH his back to the wall, in between two back windows. He was dressed stylishly, his hair groomed. He was absolutely calm. In front of him, Smythe held the fourteen-year-old girl, Kate Sugers in a form of a headlock with his left arm. In his right hand he held a .22 caliber purse pistol, the barrel stuck to Kate's young temple. She was trembling and did not say a word. She looked from cop to cop in a silent plea for help, not understanding what was happening before her.

"Welcome, gentlemen. To what do we owe this honor?" Smythe had a smooth voice and his question showed no hint of fear or apprehension.

"We have a warrant for your arrest. This doesn't need to be hard, Ted. Let go of the girl, put the gun down, and nobody gets hurt." Spags wanted to sound in control and wasn't sure if he succeeded, but knew that he didn't feel in control.

"Hey, pal . . .," started one of the uniformed policemen, a veteran of many armed encounters and arrests.

"'Pal' is it? Quite informal of you," mocked Ted. "Didn't know we'd been introduced. I have a splendid idea: you guys put your weapons down, back out of here slowly, and then we can talk, like pals, like you have some right to call me Ted. I'll give you my phone number, and we can talk."

Nobody flinched, nobody moved.

"Mr. Smythe, you must know that we can't surrender our weapons. Rule number one for us cops: we can't give up the weapon."

51

"Can't give them up." It was Dan again. He hoped to distract Smythe by forcing him to look back and forth between them, spread out as they were.

Smythe wasn't buying it.

The lead uniform took a slow step to his left.

Smythe grinned but kept his eyes on the first uniformed officer. "Going to outflank me, pal? Do that again and I'll begin to think you're not here in good faith." His voice was deliberate, like ice, but not showing any strain.

A crackle erupted from one of the officer's radios as it sputtered to life. "Give us your status entrance team. Where are you? We can't see shit through these windows because of the glare. Over."

"Ah, so we are not alone, eh?" Smythe began to giggle, seemingly uncharacteristic of him. It was a nervous giggle. Two of the three uniformed policemen began to think the same thing; Smythe was actually enjoying the dilemma.

"Do we agree that I can't possibly shoot all five of you policemen with this innocuous looking piece of metal?"

"What's your point, Mr. Smythe?" It was Detective Regan.

"I'm willing to put the gun down, but in the process I don't wish to be shot." Smythe was calm and sounded like ice again. "I have a feeling you, gentlemen, do not have my best interests in mind here."

"No one is going to shoot anyone. Just lay the gun down." The first uniformed officer appeared calm, and his voice was easy and reassuring.

Smythe let his eyes move slowly around the room. "I think not. With the gun still in my hand on the way down to the floor, one of you shoots me, case closed. No messy trials." His voice had gone up a few decibels.

"Look, here's how we'll play it," Smythe continued. "I will, in a single motion mind you, throw the safety on this toy, throw it forward, and slowly let go of the young lady. But you must point your guns up at the ceiling while I do that, so we don't have any mistakes. You admit that I couldn't possibly shoot my way out, so where's the harm?"

"Not a chance," said one of the uniformed officers.

"Then I shoot her."

"We will train our weapons three feet above your head. No more, no less. We do this on the count of three, by four you better have put the safety on, thrown the weapon to the floor, and released the girl, or your brains are gonna be on the wall."

"Sounds fair," he said. Detective Spagnola recalled how at ease Smythe seemed to be in such extreme circumstances. It was eerie, like a movie.

They all counted to three like a children's game. The police fully expected him to shoot at them on the count of two and were ready to duck and fire, even if it meant hitting the girl; there wouldn't be any choice at that point. They also knew that he could shoot her at any moment so this appeared to be a way out for everybody; nobody got hurt. They couldn't chance shooting him and having him reflexively shoot her, and there was no guarantee even a head shot would kill him right away. This wasn't the movies.

"One." Nothing.

"Two." Nothing.

"Three." All three of the uniformed policemen raised their guns as did the two detectives.

"Four." Smythe's gun was falling through the air and headed for the floor.

"Five." Ted Smythe stared straight into Detective Spagnola's eyes as he cut Kate's throat with a razor he had hidden in the palm of his hand. As she fell to the ground, blood spurting from her throat, mortally wounded, Detective Spagnola fired three shots, two into Smythe's chest and one in his jaw, and then two more into his torso on his way to the ground.

Smythe's smile never faded as he died on the floor.

CHAPTER 20

T HE CANVASSING OF the Kauffmans' neighborhood by the uniformed police officers had shed no light on the shootings. An inspection of the Kauffmans' backyard by the police revealed nothing the first time around. The second time, the yard was inspected by Spagnola. He noted three things, all missing from the uniforms' and state policemen's reports, all unrelated, and all of which he carefully jotted down on his notepad. He would transfer his notes onto his computer later.

The first thing that he noticed was that the lock on the back door had been tampered with. The marks were not very large, but they were very new. This was not the work of some junkie, or an amateur. The marks were slight, the hand that made them was steady, assured, and practiced. The lock was a good quality dead bolt and not easily opened without a key.

The second thing that Spagnola noticed was the dog print. It wasn't very clear, but it was definitely a dog print, and as far as he knew, the Kauffmans had no pets.

The third thing that he noticed was the flower garden. It was at the back of the yard; it was large, meticulously maintained, and blooming. It also had a small, well-worn path leading to it from the yard of the house behind the Kauffman's. That path did not lead back to the Kauffmans' house, but rather seemed to head off and stop under a tree. An examination of the area under the tree revealed multiple foot impressions; some were made by sneakers, some by other shoes, and all seemed to be the same size.

Spagnola didn't know what this meant. He didn't know that it meant anything, but knew he would need to find out. *Peeping Tom?* he wondered silently. *Stalker? A neighbor friend of Mrs. Kauffman's?*

Spagnola examined the yard and the back of the house one more time. He found nothing else that caught his eye and headed back to his car to look again at the reports of the uniforms who had canvassed the neighborhood.

CHAPTER 21

SPAGNOLA STOPPED HIS car in front of 16 Dever Drive and turned off the engine. The front yard was absolutely immaculate. The bushes appeared to be trimmed and there wasn't a weed to be seen. Mums bloomed everywhere.

He got out of the car, looked around the street, noted that it was as quiet as could be with no cars, no kids, no dogs, and no workers. He walked up the stone walkway. The front door was a dark wood with beveled glass, and there were a variety of flowers in concrete planters all around the porch area. Vines hung from an artificial trellis and wind chimes hung at both ends of the house.

He rang the doorbell and cringed as the opening line of "Some Enchanted Evening" rang throughout the house. He listened carefully and heard some movement from within, but no one answered the door.

Spagnola pulled out his cell phone and his day timer, found the Yeldon number, and dialed. On the third ring a man answered.

"Hello . . ."

"Hello, Mr. Yeldon, this is Detective Dante Spagnola of the Uwchlan Township Police Department."

"Uh . . . what can I do for you, sir?"

"Not to be impolite, but you can open the door. I'm standing outside and I need to speak with you." There was no response, but the turning of a dead bolt lock and the opening of the door.

"May I come in?" asked Spagnola.

Yeldon was six foot one, a bit gawky, and slightly overweight with a very young looking face that belied his age.

"Yes, of course . . . I guess I've been expecting someone."

Mr. Yeldon returned with two cups of coffee and a small tray containing milk, sugar, and Sweet'N Low. He did not look up when he put the tray down.

"Help yourself, Detective," Yeldon said, and Spagnola noticed that the man appeared to have shrunken down.

Detective Spagnola just stared at him, but Mr. Yeldon would not look up. He just stared into his coffee.

Finally he looked up, looking a little relieved, and spoke. "It's all my fault, detective. You probably already know that. If it weren't for me, Elaine would still be alive."

Spagnola had expected that this visit would be revealing, but a confession was not what he was expecting.

"Mr. Yeldon, please, hold on just a second. There's something we have to do before you say anything more. You have the right to remain silent. You have the right to counsel of your choice. If you cannot afford counsel they will be appointed for you without cost to you. Mr. Yeldon, do you understand those rights?"

Now it was Mr. Yeldon's turn to look surprised. "You're reading me my rights? My rights? Do you think I actually did something physical to hurt Elaine? Are you mad? I loved that woman. Loved her. Do you understand that?" His voice was rising and Spagnola thought that he might turn violent, so he put his coffee down and backed his chair away from the table.

"Elaine was the only good thing to happen to me in the past seven years. She's dead because I didn't get her to leave that worthless husband of hers. Because I didn't have the guts to do the right thing and convince her to divorce him. I didn't hurt her for God's sake. I just failed to save her. Do you understand that?"

Spagnola didn't know quite what to make of Mr. Yeldon, but he didn't doubt his sincerity. Whether or not he was somehow involved in the murder was still a question, but that he loved Mrs. Kauffman, there could be no doubt. Over the years, Spagnola had learned that men were very poor at pretending to be passionate about anything, especially women.

"Mr. Yeldon, I'd like you to accompany me to the Uwchlan Township building to answer some questions. Take a minute or two if you'd like."

"Andrew," Yeldon responded.

"Excuse me?" asked Spags.

"My name is Andrew. No need for the Mr. Yeldon thing."

It took Spagnola a moment to catch on. "Yes, of course, Andrew. I just didn't want to seem, you know . . . "

"Am I . . . under arrest or something?"

"No, sir. At this point I am not going to charge you with a crime, but I think it would be beneficial if I could get an official statement from you. I think we would both prefer that you come with me voluntarily, you know, for Elaine's sake." Spagnola knew that throwing Elaine Kauffman's name into the conversation was risky, but he was banking on Mr. Yeldon wanting to avoid a scandal, even after her death. He was right.

"Sure, that's OK. Let me put the cups in the sink and put the milk away. Will this take long? I'd like to water the backyard flowers before sunset."

"I promise to have you back here well before the sun sets."

"Thank you, that's kind of you." Mr. Yeldon had shrunken again and his voice was barely audible. He didn't speak again until they entered the police station.

CHAPTER 22

THE UWCHLAN TOWNSHIP Police Station was a hodgepodge of buildings, strung together without a true master plan, with original walls in one portion dating back one hundred and fifty years, and additions dating anywhere from two years to ninety years old. Some of the architecture was mid-nineteenth century, some early twentieth century, some midcentury, and some twenty-first century. Most of it was sided with modern aluminum siding and the entire building was secure. The police chief was a stickler for detail, and when it came to his station being secure, nothing stood in his way.

The holding cell had been moved when he took command so that in the unlikely event that a detainee escaped the cell, he or she would enter a secure area, devoid of weapons, phones, or any hope of taking a hostage. The interrogation room was a short distance from the holding cell and its door locked inside and out with a distinctive click. It could be opened with a combination or a master key, but could not be opened from inside or out without one or the other. It emptied into the same secure hall of the holding cell. The interrogation room did not have a phone, the furniture was bolted to the ground, and the glass was shatter resistant and bulletproof.

Spagnola had locked Mr. Yeldon in the interrogation room. He had not handcuffed him or taken away his shoes. He sat in the observation room and watched Yeldon on closed circuit TV while he and Sergeant Foster had a cup of police coffee and chatted.

"Doesn't look much like a killer," the sergeant commented, "but then I guess most people don't." He cocked his head toward

Spagnola who seemed to be more absorbed in his coffee than in Yeldon.

"Seems more likely that he would have killed Mr. Kauffman than Mrs.," the sergeant added, trying to get some response from the detective.

"You ever notice, Sarge, that every once in a while, you put the damn creamer in the coffee and it looks like its gone bad? It's not real cream, can't really go bad, doesn't smell or taste bad, but it looks like hell. Ever notice that?"

"Sure, it's one of those mysteries of life kind of a thing. Keeps me awake at night sometimes . . .," the sergeant laughed.

"Well, killing someone is very personal. Sometimes the guy who does the killing looks OK, sounds OK, usually acts OK, but when you put him in the mix, he looks like hell. Our Mr. Yeldon smells and sounds OK, but he currently looks like hell. I can't figure why he'd kill the missus either, but we don't have her side of the story."

Yeldon stood up and looked around. He seemed lost, completely lost. He wandered around the room looking at the walls and then at the ceiling. He mouthed words but because he made no audible sounds nothing was recorded.

Spagnola looked at the sergeant, gave him a wink, and said, "It's time, you watch. Make sure the tape recorders are working. It's time."

Sergeant said, "Yeah, of course, it's time and I got your back."

Spagnola counted to ten then pressed the code into the door, heard the click, turned the knob, and walked in on Mr. Yeldon's private, silent conversation with himself.

CHAPTER 23

"OK, YOU PIECE of crap, you know damn well you weren't the only guy that Mrs. Kauffman was dancing in the dark with, and there was a good chance she wouldn't ever leave her meal ticket, Mr. Kauffman, so you went over there, walked down your secret little path, and tried to kill them both. But you didn't succeed, you big shit. No. You came close but you didn't get the job done. Mr. Kauffman is alive and awake, and he fingered you as the mother fucker who crept into his home and tried to kill himself and his wife."

Yeldon was visibly shaking. He moved his lips and hyperventilated. He couldn't speak, could barely breathe, his knees buckled, and he sat on the carpeted floor.

"Don't even try to deny it. You have gunpowder residue all over your hands because you didn't think to wear gloves or even wash your hands when you were done, because . . . because . . . you petty little shit, you never even considered that your killing of two people might draw the attention of the police. Don't even bother to deny it. We have you dead to rights. You have the right to remain silent. You have the right to an attorney . . . "

At first there was no movement or sound from Yeldon. The room was perfectly still but ever so slowly Yeldon began to take deeper and deeper breaths. Sweat trickled down his right temple.

"Noooooooo!" Yeldon's voice was a piercing scream when he finally got enough air in his lungs to say anything at all.

Spagnola sat back and glared. He had no intention of saying anymore. Yeldon still did not look up.

Yeldon put his head in his hands, seemed like he was about to retch, then straightened up with a menacing look in his eye, and stared, without blinking directly at Spagnola. Spagnola tensed, ready for an attack. In the other room, the sergeant pulled his mace out with his left hand, his baton out with his right hand, and moved to the door, expecting serious trouble. He and Spagnola both knew the look that Yeldon had on his face. It was the look you saw on someone's face just before he became seriously violent.

CHAPTER 24

T HE TENSION LINGERED in the air. It was as if time had stopped. Then Yeldon, sweating and breathing heavily, slumped his shoulders, let out a sigh, and laughed softly, as if only he knew the joke. Spagnola didn't let his guard down and the sergeant still maintained his vigil by the door, fully expecting Yeldon to explode across the table at any moment.

Then Yeldon ran his hands through his hair, rubbed his temples, and laughed again.

"You guys got any aspirin? My head's killing me. I know you don't believe me but what more can I say? I don't have it in me to kill anybody. Hell, I have trouble killing spiders on my porch. Bill Kauffman was a 'dyed in the wool' son of a bitch, lying, cheating bastard. Elaine deserved better. Tell you what, though, I couldn't have killed him if my life depended on it. Just not my nature. Lock me up if you need to, but I can't give you anything more; there isn't anything more. I loved Elaine, no question . . . best thing that ever happened to me was meeting her. I can't believe she's gone. She wouldn't hurt a fly, she had no enemies . . . .I loved her."

Spagnola sat as still as he could. *Rule number one*, he thought, *once the suspect was talking, let him go until he ran out of steam.*

Yeldon started again. "So what do you want, Detective, a confession? I can't help you there. Information on the murder? Can't help you there either. So what do you want?"

Spagnola just stared. Then he slowly, purposely rose from his seat. He turned sideways to Yeldon, dropped his pen on the desk, and spoke.

"You have just made some statements about Mr. Kauffman which I frankly don't understand. You are the one who was in a cheating relationship with this man's wife. You were the one in his home, with his wife! How do you call him names? Where does that come from?"

Yeldon rubbed his head again. "I can back up everything I just said. The Kauffmans hadn't been in a real marriage in years—everyone knew that. But right now my head is killing me, and I want a lawyer."

Spagnola sat at the table quietly. Other than an occasional blink, he didn't move a muscle. He was tense and ready to react if Andrew Yeldon came across the table or became violent in any way.

Spagnola analyzed Yeldon's physical appearance in an attempt to determine if he looked like a murderer. Yeldon looked to be in his mid-fifties, overweight, out of shape, and did not carry himself like an athlete. This guy might have been the type to use a gun in a crime of passion, thought Spagnola, but probably not the weapon involved in this crime: a hammer, a knife, or an ax.

Yeldon had begun to sob softly. His lips were moving, but he wasn't saying anything. Spags fully expected that a confession of sorts would be coming forthwith. He'd seen it a hundred times before. Psychologically, once an accused was in police custody, he often felt the need to tell the truth—to get it off his chest. Even though Spags was the tormentor, it was often the tormentor that the criminal looked to unload his secrets.

A minute went by, then five, then ten. Yeldon still sat there quietly sobbing and moving his lips. He slowly raised his head and stared with bleary, tear-soaked eyes at Spagnola.

"I told you back at my house that Elaine was the best thing that ever happened to me. I would never hurt her. We met innocently enough in the backyard where our gardens were only a few feet apart. The little trail you found was mine. I walked that little trail almost every day for the past two and a half years. It all started innocently. Chats about flowers, fertilizer, ground hogs, woodchucks . . ." Yeldon stared off into space for a few moments. "I know it all sounds ridiculous: a grown man having a garden relationship with the woman who lived behind him. Believe it or not, for over two years it was strictly on the up and up. We'd chat, occasionally have a cup of coffee or a donut together. She would sit in my kitchen or I would sit in hers. It never went any further than that."

Yeldon put his hands on his head and leaned forward with his elbows on the table. He almost looked like he was finished speaking. Spags knew it was a good time to speak up.

"OK, Andrew. I hear you and let's say for the moment that I believe you. What changed? What happened? When did it become something else?"

"A couple of months ago I was out in the garden several days in a row and didn't see Elaine. I became concerned and went over and knocked on her back door. She didn't come to the door, but she called me into the kitchen. She was sitting there over a cup of coffee, crying.

"I'm no good when it comes to a crying woman. I think that's how I lost my first wife. She'd cry. I wouldn't know what to do. I'd go outside and garden and eventually she took my inability to handle her situation as apathy.

"I guess it was easier talking to Elaine than talking to my ex-wife. I asked her what the matter was. I poured her some more coffee. At first she told me she couldn't talk about it. Eventually, she just shrugged her shoulders and said, 'Why not? You're my best friend.'

"She told me she suspected her husband was having an affair. At first I could barely hear what she was saying. The thought that I was her best friend really struck me as odd. I don't think in my entire life I had ever been anybody's best friend. It had bothered me when I was a teenager, but once I got to college and found the world was full of nerds like me, it had stopped bothering me. In any event, when I began to catch on to what she was saying, there were clear signs that her husband was coming home later than usual. He was finding excuses to be out on Saturday afternoons when previously, he had always been plopped in front of the television watching sports. He began wearing better clothes and started having his hair cut at a salon instead of a barber.

"I told her that it might be a midlife crisis. I told her that I was sure her husband loved her. How could anybody not? I told her she was a great person and a lovely woman. After a while, I realized

I was professing my love for her, not just comforting her. At that realization, I felt quite awkward and reverted back to being my quiet, nerdy self.

"She said to me, 'Thanks for your kind words. But when I found a box of condoms in his gym bag, I knew there was someone else. I started snooping around and found some credit card receipts which showed that he had rented rooms in a couple of locations, always a fair distance from here. Since he was never gone overnight, I assumed he was having sex with someone and then coming home to me.'

"That's what she told me.

"I walked around the kitchen table, patted her on the shoulder, and kissed her on the cheek. Literally, the next thing I knew we were in her bedroom. I'll be honest with you, Detective. I hadn't had sex in several years. Not real sex anyway. I'm not above going to a hooker once in a while, usually when I'm traveling. You know, Las Vegas, Miami, whatever. But this was different. This was soft, this was tender. This was amazing."

Yeldon suddenly bolted upright as if he had been hit with a charge of electricity and glared at Spagnola. "Why the hell am I telling you that?"

Spagnola waited a count of 1-2-3-4-5, and then answered, "Well, you're either trying to convince me that you wouldn't harm Elaine, or giving me a perfect reason to throw your ass in jail for murder and attempted murder."

Yeldon shook his head slowly, side to side and then looked up at the ceiling. He let out a low whistling noise and again stared at Spagnola.

"Well, Detective, if it's the latter, I'd like to call a lawyer now."

Spagnola got up from the table and walked to the door. "I heard your request and I'll honor it. Just give me a few minutes and I'll be back to you."

Spagnola stepped out the door and looked the Sergeant in the eyes. "What do you think, Sarge?"

The sergeant shook his head from side to side and chuckled. "Sorry, Detective, but I don't think that milk toast could kill anybody. What are you going to do?"

"I'm going to bring him a phone and if he wants to call a lawyer, all well and good. I'm going to tell him, however, I have no intention of charging him. I would like to know anything else that Elaine had to say. This could be related to the husband's affair. Let's face it. If he was having an affair, maybe he was having an affair with a married woman. Maybe his girlfriend's husband did this, or her boyfriend. Who knows?

"I have to agree with you though. As mad as Yeldon got in there he didn't so much as raise a finger, and I don't think he ever would have thought of the idea of staging a burglary to cover the murder. In the heat of passion, people don't think that way. More than likely, he would have thrown the gun on Elaine's bed and walked out, gone home, had a cup of coffee, and waited for the police to arrest him. Can't rule him out completely, but he's got to be pretty low on my list."

Spagnola returned inside the interrogation room with a phone and hooked it up to the cord in the wall.

"Here's the phone. If you'd like me to leave the room, I will. If you need a telephone directory for your attorney's number, I'll provide that. If you want to avoid that, I'll give you what's known as reverse Miranda warning. Then we can finish this conversation and you can go home. What I'm holding in my right hand is a Philip's Executive Style Pocket Memo 491. It's got good working batteries in it and we can record my reverse Miranda warnings. When we're done, you can acknowledge it and I can acknowledge it on the tape. I'll hand you the tape, we can continue our conversation, and when we're done, you can go home. Your call. No pun intended."

Yeldon scratched his head.

"I don't want to sound dense, but what's Miranda? How does any of this help me and why are you going to let me go?"

"Ever watch a cop show? When they are arresting the bad guy, the cop always says you have the right to remain silent. You have a right to an attorney. It goes on from there. Those are called Miranda warnings. They come from a case a long time ago called *Miranda v. United States*. By law, you're now entitled to those warnings if you are going to be interrogated and if you're a suspect in a criminal matter. If I give you a reverse Miranda warning, and you have a record of it, nothing that you may say can be used against you in a court of law because I'm telling you that one, you're not a suspect and two, you don't need a lawyer. If I do those two things, I can't use anything you tell me.

"I'm not trying to trick you in any way here. If you still feel a lawyer is necessary, that's fine. I don't think you committed this crime. I can't be sure, but I don't think so. I would like to know, however, any other conversations you had or anything that might help me to find out who really killed Elaine. I know you want to do that, but I respect your decision to call for a lawyer if that's what you want to do."

Yeldon thought about this for a moment and then said, "I really do want to catch Elaine's killer. I wasn't lying when I told you she was the best thing that ever happened to me. I know I'm never going to find another Elaine. Let's see if we can find her murderer. Let's get on with the reverse Meronda."

"That's M-i-r-a-n-d-a. Not that it matters a whole lot." Spagnola switched on the Pocket Memo 491.

"Mr. Yeldon, this is Detective Spagnola, the date is September 17 and I'm informing you that during the course of this conversation nothing you say to me can or will be used against you in a court of law. You have a right to an attorney . . ."

Two hours later, Detective Spagnola delivered Andrew Yeldon to his driveway. They shook hands and Spagnola left.

CHAPTER 25

*I*N THE DISTANCE *somewhere, there seemed to be a dull ache. If Bill concentrated on it, the ache appeared to be in the lower right side of his stomach. Bill Kauffman couldn't really feel any pain, but he knew somewhere in the fog, the pain was there. He knew it should be there, but he also knew he couldn't feel it.*

Someone hovered over him. They were close enough to smell. The smell was neither sweet nor pungent, just the smell of a person. Then the feeling of pressure against his stomach.

His shirt was torn, or it was tearing. He knew he should feel the pain, but he couldn't. He tried to reach his hand up to feel the wound, but his arm was stuck. He tried to move because it felt as if his arm was stuck beneath him, but moving didn't help. His arm was still stuck.

There were no colors in this dream, no taste, only smell and sound. He was not alarmed by the dream but confused by it.

He could feel the scalpel against his skin, not a pain, just pressure, still no pain. He tried to open his eyes, to cry out, but he drifted back into the fog, and the dream was gone.

CHAPTER 26

IT LAY ON the grass in the outfield of the park baseball field. It smelled the grass and listened to the animals move about. The night had become chilly and there were no insect sounds. The time was 9:45 PM and no one was in the park. The police would come by in fifteen minutes or so and look about, but they would not notice It: dressed in black spandex from head to foot, dyed black cross trainers, and a small, black skull cap. Even if they put a spotlight on It, there is no way the police could see It; the camouflage was too good and the human eye too poor.

Ah, the human eye . . . great for picking up motion. Without that motion detector, man would have perished long ago, the predator thought. Too bad that the humans can't see at night, see distance, or see accurately. Ah . . . but the predator could. Lasik surgery had produced not just twenty-twenty eyesight but ten-ten vision. Special training on the science and art of enhanced hearing, and even better yet the art of listening, put the predator at a distinct advantage over those around it.

Now was a good time to think, to plan, to outsmart them in advance. The humans were predictable. The humans would try to discern a pattern in the chaos. They would come up with theories; they would come up with suspects and motives. If they were lucky, they might even link some of the deaths to a single source or sources. Then, just as they thought they had a pattern, the pattern would change, the death would be different; they would not see the relationship. They couldn't. What they would be seeing and dealing with did not exist within their philosophy.

The deaths to come would not fit within their beliefs about their own patterns of behavior. The deaths to come would not fit within their theories, their educations, or their practical experiences, because they couldn't let those deaths fit in. Their brains couldn't conceptualize the reasons behind these deaths.

The predator needed to take swift action. There would need to be confusion, doubt, subterfuge. The predator had limited human weaknesses. It had no need to act out fantasies, obtain sexual gratification from the commission of a crime, or deal with some psychological damage inflicted in its youth. The predator hunted from a directive to hunt and thin the herd; all of its other needs were satisfied through other means.

The police car arrived several minutes early. The officers turned on the spotlight and ran the light quickly around the park, more to scare off teenagers than to actually search for anything. The beam of light never approached the place where It lay in the shadows. Within minutes the police car had exited the parking lot and the predator was left to plan and scheme, until late into the night.

The jogger, a thirty-one-year-old real estate salesman, was completing his day just as he had four days a week, every week for the past eight months. He had shed thirty-five pounds of fat and tightened himself up from working out in the gym and playing the occasional game of hoops. He felt good. His job required that he be available until roughly 8:30 every evening. As a result, he had gotten into the habit of jogging first thing in the morning or last thing at night. His five-mile course took him through the park and down into the Marchwood development, before going across the highway and up into the Rhonda neighborhood.

The jogger was about two miles into his course when he crossed Route 100 near Lionville Middle School. He entered the park just behind Evangelista Little League Field, about six hundred yards from the outfield in which the predator lay.

The predator was distracted from its scheming. A soft, barely audible sound had invaded the park. It was rhythmic in its composition and familiar in its tone. It was the soft touch of jogging sneakers on macadam. The predator slowly rolled over onto its side and directed all of its senses toward the sounds. It took several seconds to locate the jogger. The jogger was a male, perhaps six feet tall, wearing a Gore-Tex suit with silver reflection strips that caught the street lamps and passing car headlights and made him highly visible, even at night.

The predator calculated a good point at which to intercept the jogger. This would be a rare and spontaneous kill, hand to hand, predator against human athlete. Even It needed to practice Its skills. The jogger actually presented an even more baffling murder because he confused and misdirected Its actual intentions. The predator carefully watched the jogger's stride. Unless the jogger was very skilled in self-defense, this would not be a long contest, It thought.

The predator began to jog and then sprint toward the point of intersection somewhere just shy of the pavilion above the soccer field. It remained well behind the jogger and to his left. In the darkness of the outfield and with the aid of a small slope, Its presence was well shielded from the jogger.

He did not see the predator spring into action in the outfield. He did sense something, and he looked around straining to see after having come in from the lights along Route 113. His pupils had not yet adjusted. He began to feel a tingling on the back of his neck, like someone was watching him, and his body switched to a higher state of alertness, but he still neither heard nor saw anything as the predator closed the distance between them, running on an intersect line now about fifty yards from making contact. Something had given the jogger the willies; some primeval instinct that kept mankind alive in the prehistoric days when nature, the elements, and the odds said mankind should perish. The jogger's suspicion led him to believe that someone—a mugger, or worse— might be waiting at the darkened pavilion, a mere hundred yards ahead.

The predator did not anticipate the runner's abrupt change in direction. It had run three full sprinting strides toward the original intercept point before It was forced to alter Its course in pursuit of the jogger. The predator changed direction with the agility of a cat. It accelerated toward the jogger, but It had lost over twenty yards due to the jogger's change of direction.

Part out of hunch and part out of panic, the jogger suddenly darted across Hoffecker field running at a ninety-degree angle from his original path. He started to sprint for no discernable reason and had decided his sprint wouldn't end until he rounded the corner onto Devon Drive where he would be in the safety of the lighted high school grounds. He thought he detected the sound of running behind him but decided not to take the split second to turn his head and peer back into the dark.

It made up the twenty yard differential quickly, and although the jogger continued to sprint, It began to close the gap between Itself and Its prey. The predator was much faster than the jogger, but It quickly realized that it could not catch up with the jogger before he exited the park, so It changed direction and slowly jogged back to the baseball field.

The jogger continued across the field and ran through the gap in the fence, leaving the park and heading back out onto the well-lit Devon Drive.

Without knowing it, the jogger had lived to jog another day.

CHAPTER 27

I T WAS ALMOST two days following Elaine Kauffman's death before the unofficial preliminary coroner's report landed on Detective Spagnola's desk. The report had been hand delivered by an aide who worked in the coroner's office. Much to his annoyance, the aide had made the detective carefully fill out the appropriate paperwork for receiving the report before leaving the detective's office.

The cover sheet contained only the essential items: name, address, DOB, DOD, EIN number, and the case number. The inside cover consisted of a crude index by page number and the opposite page contained the beginning of the report.

Spagnola leafed to the end containing the conclusions. They were succinct.

"Cause of Death: Gunshot wound from a .45 caliber pistol fired at a range of no more than six or less than four feet. No surprise there," he said to no one. He popped the top of a Skinny Water, put his feet up on his desk, pulled out his handheld dictation device, and began to read from the beginning.

The coroner's office was thorough to a fault. With the exception of their on-loan homicide expert Saw Bones (called SB by everyone), the employees of the coroner's office did not often see a homicide. As a result, they took extreme pride in the handling of the victim's remains and in the handling of the entire investigation into the victim's death. They took blood, urine, hair, nail, and skin samples. They tested for the presence of alcohol; ran numerous tests for prescription, over-the-counter, and illicit drugs; performed skin scrapings, tongue swabs, rectal, and vaginal examinations; and checked the ears, nose, throat, eyes, and teeth of the victim for clues about the cause of death and for any marks left behind by the perpetrator.

The coroner's office never jumped to conclusions. They recorded their comments during each autopsy with microphones that automatically picked up their voices. Detective Spagnola had not requested the tapes, but if he uncovered anything puzzling, he always had the option of listening to the autopsy live and hearing the physicians' comments as they occurred.

The coroners had removed, weighed, and examined each organ, and had performed tests upon those that required further investigation. The contents of Elaine Kauffman's stomach had revealed some light hor d'oeuvres and a quantity of merlot wine. Her blood alcohol level suggested that she had consumed more than one glass of wine, most likely less than three, but certainly not enough to cause her injury or, given her body weight, to create an intoxicated state.

There were numerous observations and conclusions about the destroyed finger on her left hand. The bullet had literally exploded the finger and only a small amount of it was actually recovered. The bullet had been fired at very close range suggesting that she had awakened, had seen her assailant, had extended her hand in a futile gesture of defense or a plea for mercy, and had had her finger shot off for her troubles. The second bullet had killed her. After the second shot, she had continued to bleed, suggesting that she had lived for a short period of time afterward, until her heart eventually ceased to pump blood through her system.

There were no other defensive wounds, no telltale signs of abuse, and no signs of sexual assault. It was determined that she had had intercourse within twenty-four hours and the semen retrieved was being tested for DNA. Without wanting to jump to conclusions, Spags was fairly sure that it was Yeldon's semen, and Yeldon had already given them a voluntary DNA sample for comparison.

Tons of information, tons of test results, tons of data. But nothing was of any help to the detective. The phone rang and it was not good news. The hospital was reporting that they had misplaced the bullet which had been removed from William Kauffman during emergency surgery. Spagnola was suddenly more pissed off than he was perplexed.

CHAPTER 28

DETECTIVE SPAGNOLA KNEW that something wasn't right about the lost bullet. He couldn't fathom why anyone associated with the surgery would purposely mishandle the bullet. Checking the online profiles of the doctors and nurses in the trauma unit produced a picture of intelligence, dedication, and competence. By state law, they could not work in the operating theater of a federally funded trauma unit if they had convictions for any felony offenses or had any addiction problems.

Although he trusted that none of the trauma unit staff had any direct connection to the crime, Spagnola knew from experience that sometimes hospital employees collected evidence for another reason: a souvenir. He knew this was unlikely, but it would not be the first time that a criminal investigation had been hindered by someone looking to grab a piece of memorabilia or save a victim or his family from embarrassment.

Detective Spagnola had been a rookie in Philadelphia when he and a senior homicide detective had been summoned to the scene of a suspicious death. They had arrived at the brownstone of an elderly couple to find the front door wide open, a grieving widow, and a perplexed set of paramedics. The paramedics swore they had been dispatched in order to assist a gunshot victim who apparently had been attacked inside his home after returning from a movie.

The detectives were quite beside themselves when they found the victim inside the living room in a brand new suit, with no signs of holes or blood, seated across from the grieving widow who was drinking tea and expounding on their long and happy marriage.

As it turned out, the wife, a devout Catholic, had panicked upon finding her husband shot and called 911. When she regained her composure, she had undressed her husband, disposed of the suicide note and the gun, dressed him, and concocted the story of the robbery gone wrong.

Spagnola had heard of other similar incidents. There had been the neighbor who had kept the murder weapon, which he had found in the street, fouling up the entire murder investigation for months. There had also been a homicide case in which the paramedic had stolen the murder weapon, an ornamental knife, because it contained over ten thousand dollars' worth of inlaid jewels. The list went on and on.

This didn't have that same smell. This had the smell of something else, something more professional, but Spagnola just couldn't fathom what that might be. The only thing left to do was to conduct background searches on all eight persons who had the opportunity to steal or lose the slug. He would turn that over to the county detectives who had far greater resources, not to mention the ears of some county judges should the need for search warrants or court orders arise. In the meantime, Spagnola would head to the trauma unit and begin interviewing the hospital staff himself.

CHAPTER 29

DETECTIVE SPAGNOLA WAS not a happy person. He rarely was happy on Mondays, but now he was genuinely on the warpath. The fact that the bullet that had been removed from Mrs. Kauffman was missing was going to screw up the investigation and possibly the prosecution of the case.

"Listen, you people. I'm here to tell you that there's a section of the crimes code here in Pennsylvania that fits you guys to a T. You are responsible for the proper removal, care, and storage of any projectile removed from a person under suspicious circumstance until the projectile is turned over to the proper authority. And that's me, goddamn it. What the hell were you people thinking?"

The anesthesiologist looked pale. The nurses sat and stared at the ground. The only person with her head up was Dr. Evans. She just glared at the detective, not saying a word.

"Let's go over this again, shall we?" He said, dripping with sarcasm and sounding like a wounded Sunday school teacher.

"We take the bullet out of poor Mr. Kauffman. Then we . . ."

"Detective, we didn't take a bullet out. I personally extracted the bullet with great care and skill causing no further damage to Mr. Kauffman and no discernable damage to the projectile either. The bullet was carefully dropped onto a tray which was carried to the table by the attending physician's assistant who is not in the hospital at the moment. The bullet was then tagged and removed from this room. After it leaves this room, it is hardly our responsibility."

It was now the detective's turn to glare. He rolled his eyes in an exaggerated fashion and then began to speak very slowly and precisely like one would speak to a recalcitrant child.

"Oh, we have a law degree on top of our license to steal, do we? Well, let's just think about this for a moment. You tell me, that *you* removed the bullet."

"Extracted the bullet, Detective," she responded, tempted to spell it for the detective but thinking better of it. "And I have a number of licenses and even more degrees, and I don't intend to suffer you much longer if you continue to rant and rave."

"Extracted, madam doctor, with great care, as you said. Now, when was the last time any of you saw the extracted bullet. Hmm?"

Nurse Ellenby was the first one to speak up. "I saw the bullet on the tray and Phil carried the tray over to the table to bag it and tag it."

"Phil would be the missing Phil Thompson, physician's assistant?"

"That's him," she said, seeming a little braver now that Doc Evans had shown her mettle.

"Great, now maybe we'll make some progress so we can all get home for dinner." The detective made an exaggerated show of looking at his watch, which read 11:22 AM.

"What happened to it from there?" He exaggerated every word trying to be as annoying as possible, and for the most part succeeding if the looks on the assembled faces were any indication.

No one spoke. No one looked around. The room was quiet. Even the detective did not look from side to side, but simply stared in the direction that Phil Thompson had taken the ill-fated bullet. He waited, what seemed an interminable amount of time, but no one spoke, no one moved.

"This is bullshit!" he shouted at last, causing everyone in the room except Dr. Evans to jump.

"Yes, it is," Dr. Evans said, evenly and quietly with a hint of annoyance in her voice, but loud enough for everyone to hear. Then she turned and walked out.

G. Lowry Fisher was a pompous, monied hospital administrator who knew little about medicine and less about running a hospital, but bore the title of president because he could fundraise with the best of them. He didn't like to work, didn't like to sweat, and didn't like to see the apple cart that was his hospital upset by anyone.

G. Lowry Fisher was very unhappy. It was 12:05. He had a lunch appointment at the trendy La Cage restaurant and a reservation at the window that he favored when sipping martinis, while trying to convince the local gentry to part with their money in the name of "health and medical treatment advances," as he called it.

Detective Spagnola was equally unhappy. Perhaps the detective was even unhappier than Fisher. The veins sticking out on his neck indicated that he was the most miserable of the two. Only the doctor seemed nonplussed by being summoned to the president's office at midday.

"I should charge you with obstruction of justice, lady, and hindering apprehension as well." Detective Spagnola was uncharacteristically beside himself.

"Now, now, I'm sure this is all just a misunderstanding. We can certainly sort this out, officer . . . "

"It's detective . . .," Spagnola injected angrily.

"Yes, yes, of course, Detective, but we must not lose our heads here. We simply need time to sort all of this out. I can assure you this has never happened before, and I'm sure we'll find that bullet in short order. Isn't that correct, Doctor?"

"I extract bullets, I don't move them, bag them, tag them, transport them, or store them. I have no more idea where the bullet is than I know where the detective learned his grammar, but I suspect both locations are near a dump. If you're going to charge me with something, let's get on with it, and I'll call my lawyer. Otherwise, I've got work to do." Her voice was calm, matter of fact, and carried no hint of fear or apprehension. Dr. Evans came from a wealthy family, from generations of physicians in fact, which employed numerous lawyers. From the time she was a little girl she had been instructed never to call, talk to, or assist the police or any authority without first calling the family lawyers.

"OK . . . that's it for now," the detective growled. Then staring at Dr. Evans he said, "We'll be talking again, Doctor." Turning to G. Lowry, Spagnola declared, "You and I will talk, right now."

G. Lowry groaned internally, knowing his appointment for lunch would surely be a casualty of this encounter.

CHAPTER 30

WHEN SPAGNOLA ARRIVED at his office, the official coroner's report on the death of Elaine Kauffman sat on his desk. It had been hand-delivered by SB himself. Spagnola had been out conducting interviews, so he had not been able to speak with the coroner in person. Like Spagnola, SB had come from the big city. He had worked for eleven years as head medical examiner for the city of Atlanta. While Atlanta was not a very large city, its homicide rate per capita was one of the highest in the United States for eight of those eleven years.

Atlanta attracted hundreds of thousands of tourists, as well as countless conventions, and was home to Ted Turner's TNT, the Atlanta Hawks, the Atlanta Flames, the Atlanta Falcons, and the Atlanta Braves.

Atlanta was also home to a host of violent predators, including rapists, child predators of every variety, and at least three documented serial murderers. SB, in a move similar to Spagnola's, had accepted the job as Chester County's medical examiner when the grim day in, day out task of documenting the cause of death for countless groups of murders grew to be too much to handle. SB was sharp, seasoned, methodical, and well-respected by prosecutors and defense counsellors alike. He didn't pull any punches. He didn't care if the evidence didn't fit the alleged crime. He was legendary for always sticking to the facts—no ifs, no ands, no buts.

The report on Elaine Kauffman, dated that morning, was no different. The first page bore the "Official" stamp and the subsequent pages would include all of SB's findings. The detective knew the report was subject to a variety of chemical blood and fluid tests, still to be coordinated and collated.

Spagnola placed his coffee on the desk in front of him, sat down in his all-too familiar office chair, opened the report, and spread the papers out. He did this as a matter of habit so that he could glance back and forth at the pages without having to fumble through the entire document.

His coffee had long since gone cold when he finally finished the document. He had read it three different times and marked some of the pages with a highlighter. Although it was still not complete, the report clearly indicated that there was no doubt as to the cause of Elaine Kauffman's death. She had died of a single gunshot wound.

The distance between the gun and Elaine's body had been no less than twenty-eight inches and no more than fifty-seven inches. She had died of exsanguination, a massive loss of blood, and the tearing of internal organs. The report also detailed the defensive gunshot wound to Kauffman's left index finger which had been blown off just below the first joint. The pieces of the digit had been discovered on the floor next to her bed where her body had been found.

The report stated that the homicide had occurred in the bedroom, on the bed, in fact, and that the body did not appear to have been moved after the shooting.

The contents of her stomach had been sent off for analysis but initial indications showed nothing significant. Her initial blood toxicology screen showed that she was coherent and that the small amount of alcohol in her blood had in no way exacerbated her death. In short, wine or no wine, the bullet wound would have caused the onset of sudden unconsciousness, and in the absence of immediate emergency medical treatment, she would have died.

There were four relevant footnotes to the report. The first two did not concern Spagnola. The third, however, grabbed his attention. In an attempt to focus himself and examine every detail, the detective began reading the report aloud. "Preliminary toxicology reports indicate a high level of melatonin. This leads us to conclude, subject to any further toxicology reports, that the victim was asleep just prior to the attack. This would be consistent with the placement of her body and the defensive wound, indicating that she waited until the last moment to raise her hand before she was shot at close range. It cannot be established at this time whether the melatonin was produced naturally or was a product of ingested melatonin."

Spagnola knew that people who had trouble sleeping often took the dietary supplement melatonin to help them fall asleep at night. He made a note to inquire of the medical examiner whether or not a high level at that time of day was unusual or was a product of someone regularly taking naps then. If the killer knew she took naps at that time of day, then maybe this random burglary homicide was not what it appeared to be. Spagnola knew it would not be the first time in the history of crime someone tried to cover a homicide with a burglary, robbery, or an arson.

Footnote four also contained some details Spagnola found interesting.

"The projectile recovered from the victim is virtually intact. Projectile recovered from the floor of the victim's bedroom is badly damaged. However, under plain microscopic examination, it is the preliminary determination of this office that the striation marks on both bullets are consistent with being fired from the same weapon. The striation marks are slightly unusual and will be forward to CODIS to determine if the national database contains files on bullets with similar striation marks."

Spags reviewed the numerous notes he had made on the preliminary report and in his notebook.

Elaine Kauffman was known to wear jewelry at all times. Apparently she had been stripped of her jewelry and was either wearing none when she was murdered, or her murderer stripped the jewelry after she was dead. Immediately, alarms began going off in Spagnola's head.

Although the average citizen believed that a burglary and a robbery were the same crime, the detective knew they were nowhere near the same crime, were not committed by the same type of criminal, were not punished by the same statutes, nor did they involve the imposition of the same prison terms.

Burglaries involved the criminal entering a private place, be it a business or personal residence, with the intention of committing a crime. The crime intending to be committed was usually theft.

Therefore, someone who broke into a home with the intentions of stealing a stereo was a burglar. Burglars were hard to catch. Burglars stole items that were easily sold: jewelry, stereo equipment, and worst of all, guns. Most illegal guns on the streets of America had been stolen from homeowners or businesses that legally possessed them as defensive weapons. In many instances, burglary victims failed to include the theft of a weapon, particularly a gun, in their burglary reports for a variety of reasons. Oftentimes the gun or guns were not registered, sometimes a wife did not know her husband had a gun in the house and sometimes a relative living in the house had a gun but never told the owners. Sometimes the owners had prior criminal records and were not legally permitted to own a gun. Consequently, police departments could only guess at the number of guns that were out on the streets in the possession of criminals all across America.

Amateur burglars tended to be children and teenagers. Occasionally, a junky got into the act as well. Professional burglars were usually interested in stealing and selling to buy illegal narcotics; a precious few committed the act to earn a living. The ones who made a living were the hardest to catch. They left the least amount of clues, usually led fairly innocent lives outside of their burglaries, and often held legitimate jobs as well.

The vast majority of burglars did not carry weapons. Burglars planned carefully so as not to come upon citizens in their homes or places of business. They wanted to enter and exit alone, and disappear. Confrontation was bad for the burglary business.

People who committed robberies were a different breed altogether. Some psychologists believed that robbers enjoyed violence, very much the same as rapists did. Robbers were not interested in the theft itself. Robbers armed themselves with weapons: a screwdriver, a knife, a club, a gun, or just their fists. A robber's intention was usually to physically confront someone, to take whatever he wanted (a watch, wallet, jewelry, or cash), and in many instances to beat, stab, or shoot the victim, anyway. Robbers were much easier to catch. They often didn't wear ski masks or any other disguise because these interfered with their terrorizing of the victim. Robbers often stayed at the scene far too long, deriving pleasure out of beating, shooting or stabbing someone, instead of fleeing with their loot.

A robber rarely could make a living on street robberies because few people carried cash and panicked people had difficulty removing their own jewelry. It was not unusual to read in the newspaper that a robber had beaten an elderly person and stripped the victim of a wallet or pocketbook, only to get away with some petty cash. Robbers were extremely dangerous to society and were often given long prison sentences once they were caught and prosecuted. A robber was often the kind of perpetrators that good, honest, decent policemen found themselves beating silly because of the violent way in which the criminal had attacked the victim only to make off with a l couple of dollars.

To the experienced detective, the shooting of Elaine Kauffman seemed to be incongruous. It could have been a home robbery, a serious almost lethal crime, or it could have been a burglary gone bad. The problem with the second theory was that most didn't carry weapons. The last thing they wanted was an extra five years added on to a light burglary sentence and a rash of unwanted attention from carrying a gun they never intended to use.

Spagnola was worried about this one. He knew that forensic evidence would be essential to convicting the perp. However, the crime scene had been terribly compromised by the initial police and medical personnel on the scene. When it came time to prosecute this guy, Spags knew he might be in deep trouble in a court of law.

CHAPTER 31

IT WAS TUESDAY morning at 10:25 and already Spagnola's head was aching and his stomach was growling. Good work on the part of the desk sergeant and a patrol officer who had tracked down a life insurance policy on Elaine Kauffman that was less than a year old. Grey's Funeral Home had provided the lead to a financial planner located in Exton who had been eager to provide the details of his sale to the police. He had assured everyone that everything was on the up and up, and that Elaine Kauffman had been quite healthy when the policy was written.

The beneficiaries were not her brother and husband as Mrs. Kauffman's brother had suggested. Only one beneficiary was listed—Mr. Kauffman. No contingent beneficiary appeared on the policy. In the ordinary course, a husband buying a five-hundred-thousand-dollar life insurance policy on his wife eleven months before she was murdered without a motive would make Mr. Kauffman a prime (if not the only) suspect. There was one little rub: Mr. Kauffman himself had been critically injured and lay in semicoma in the Brandywine Hospital intensive care ward. The injury had not been self inflicted.

Spagnola punched a Philadelphia number on his cell phone. After three rings his call was answered.

"If you're a bill collector, the check's in the mail, if not leave a message . . ."

"Hey, Detective Mike, this is Spagnola. If you're home please pick up the phone so I can give you a headache."

There was a long pause followed by the indication that the phone message had stopped recording. Just as Spagnola was ready to hang up, a gruff, gravely voice came on the line.

"Spagnola, you were never a good enough cop to give me a headache, but your ex-wife always gave me a hard on."

Spagnola chuckled. "Faint praise by the sage from the East."

"Screw you. Why are you waking me up? I have important things to do. You have no idea how busy you can be when you're retired. I may clean my socks today. I may play Russian roulette with my old service revolver. But listen, while I got you on the phone, what kind of problem can I solve for you and how much of your paycheck are you willing to pay me?"

"Two beers and Kielbasa at Corky's, and not a nickel less."

"Promises, promises," the retired detective said.

"OK. Here's the deal. Wife is found shot to death in the bedroom of her home. Husband is on the floor in the entranceway of the house with a bullet in his gut, same gun, same caliber, no ballistics match . . . and don't fucking ask me why. Kicker is no gun in the house, not a suicide-murder because there's no powder burns on the husband, but, and this is a large but . . . husband took out a life insurance policy on the wife less than a year ago for five hundred large. If he did it, how did he do it? By the way he's in a semicoma from the bullet wound which was damn near fatal."

"I thought you were gonna give me something tough. It's easy. He had an accomplice. Accomplice decides not to split the five hundred and shoots to kill; only your husband didn't die. The perp doesn't know that and takes a hike. Your husband can't tell you nothing because he's in a coma. Only question is, how was the accomplice gonna get the insurance money? Wake the bastard up and lean on him a little?" After a brief pause to consider this possibility, the retired detective asked, "Have you physically ruled the husband out yet?"

"No," said Spagnola, feeling just a little foolish and naïve. "Fact is, he's in a coma."

"So physically rule him out. Get yourself a paraffin test on him and rule him out. Earn your pay, son, earn your pay."

Although Spagnola had the utmost respect for Detective Goodall's instinct, he couldn't see this crime happening that way.

"Thanks. I owe you two and one at Corky's . . . "

"Yeah, yeah, promises, promises." Detective Goodall hung up.

CHAPTER 32

BILL WAS STANDING on a rock, looking out over a field of grain, flowing in the summer breeze, the sun hanging low on the horizon. The scene was spectacular and the colors were dazzling. He heard a voice speaking somewhere in the distance, as if it were coming through a speaker. The voice was summoning a person to the nurses' station. This struck Bill as odd.

When he blinked, the grain had turned into waters of a stream, long, wide, and shallow. He looked down and could see his feet on the bottom, where the rock had been. He could not identify the smell surrounding him, but he knew they were not flowers or water or anything else that smelled good.

When he looked up he saw a person standing on the shore, no more than fifty feet away. The shore had been as far as the horizon the last time Bill had looked, but it didn't matter. Bill tried to raise his hand to wave but could not lift his arm. He tried the other arm with the same result. He tried to say hello but it came out nothing more than a mumbled mess. He turned to face away from the figure standing on the shore.

Bill knew that if he were able to speak or wave this whole thing would end and he could go on his way. He felt rather than heard the person come across the water to where he was standing. Bill was suddenly afraid. The water became rough and deep and loud. Bill could no longer see his feet, and the water had turned a deep shade of gray with whitish foam at its tips.

He turned around and suddenly the person was looming over him. Bill noticed that the person was holding a pistol and was aiming it right at him. Bill tried to move but he couldn't.

Bill struggled mightily and sweat began to pour out of him and then his dream was gone.

CHAPTER 33

D ETECTIVE SPAGNOLA DECIDED to take his mentor's advice. Until he eliminated Bill Kauffman as a suspect, he had overlooked a prime candidate for the crime. Statistically, people didn't murder people they didn't know. Statistically murders were committed by husbands, wives, boyfriends, girlfriends, brothers-in-law, sisters-in-law, etc. He knew the drill and he knew he had made a mistake. He intended to rectify it immediately.

He arrived at the hospital with a county detective and a young technician. The young technician had brought with her a forensics kit, including a standard paraffin test, a more current and less reliable pore test, and a blue light that was used to try and obtain indications of cordite or gun powder from human hair.

The young tech was excited about her work and eager to have an opportunity to use her expertise. She had babbled all the way over in the back of the detectives' vehicle, but a lot of what she said was quite informative. She told the two detectives that the average person who fired a gun had watched at least some television crime shows and knew of the paraffin test. They would therefore wash their hands with soap and hot water after discharging the weapon. This was usually a mistake because the hot water opened the pores and actually allowed the gun powder residue to enter the skin in a place where it was much more difficult to remove. If they had used mild soap and cold water, washed and rewashed, there was a better chance the gun powder would evade detection.

She had also told them that very few of the people she had tested or who had been part of testing realized that their wrists needed to be cleaned as well. Many times the blue light detected the residue of cordite or gun powder on wrist hair, even though the hands had been thoroughly cleaned. Some of the perpetrators even went the extra step of dipping their hands in Clorox. She had never met anyone who had a good explanation for why they dipped their hands in Clorox if they hadn't fired a weapon and been seeking to avoid detection.

She did explain, however, that there was a problem with this particular case. Bill Kauffman had obviously been shot. It was very possible that his hair (at least on his head) would show traces of gun powder and cordite from having been shot at what appeared to be close range. The shirt that had been taken off of his body certainly showed gun powder and cordite, but in an odd pattern as if he had been turning at the time he was shot or had perhaps been shot at multiple times. The detectives listened and pondered the young tech's insights.

A second-year intern met them at the nurses' station. He was very full of himself and wanted everyone to know that he was in charge. Both detectives and the technician quickly surmised that the intern was nervous and attempting to cover it up by trying to play the big shot.

The second year intern explained the rules as he saw and interpreted them and let them know in no uncertain terms that the patient's well-being came first. They all nodded and politely gave him what he was looking for, an acknowledgment that he was in fact in control. Satisfied that they had listened to him, he walked them down to Mr. Kauffman's room. He rapped quietly on the door and stepped inside asking, "Mr. Kauffman, are you awake?"

There was no movement from Bill Kauffman. No one really expected that there would be., He was suffering from shock and significant blood loss and therefore was heavily sedated.

Despite this, the young doctor explained to the unconscious Mr. Kauffman each procedure, including what the detectives and technician would be doing and how it would feel. The intern instructed Mr. Kauffman to relax during the examination. Were it not such a grim situation, the county detective thought, the entire scene would be humorous.

When all the tests had been administered, Detective Spagnola thanked the doctor, who said he had important things to attend to and to please not touch the patient or the charts without him present. They assured him this would not happen and he left.

"What an asshole," said the tech.

The county detective looked down at Bill Kauffman and said, "Not in front of the patient, please," in his best imitation of the intern.

On the car ride back to the offices, the tech gave her preliminary analysis of the tests.

"I'll check under the microscope, of course, but I don't think the paraffin pulled anything out of his hands or wrists. As you know, he was wearing a short sleeve shirt when he was shot. There could be residue on his arms and arm hairs from his own gunshot wound. I didn't see anything under the blue light that would indicate any cordite or gun powder in his hair. But it is very possible that his hair has been washed since he got here. They would use a type of shampoo that was antibacterial, which would interfere with the blue light big time. If I had to testify right now, I'd have to say that in my opinion there was no evidence that he fired a weapon. It has been two days though, so who knows?"

In a way her report made things more difficult for Detective Spagnola, but in a way he felt good because his first instincts had been correct. Despite whatever else he might have been, Spagnola thought, Bill Kauffman was probably not a murderer.

CHAPTER 34

B Y THE TIME he returned to his desk, Spagnola had, to his own satisfaction, eliminated Bill Kauffman as a suspect. Although not quite ready to do so, he was fairly confident that the neighbor was not involved either. *There might be some connection though*, he thought. These days, it was a little hard to fool around without eventually being caught, even if it was with your next-door neighbor. The detective made a mental note to keep Mr. Yeldon in the back of his mind.

Spags still hadn't sorted out the burglary portion of the crime, the position of the bodies, and the timing of everything. It was a fact that the call to 911 had occurred at 6:24 PM; this had been documented in several different fashions. It was also clear that the call had been made by a cell phone, but there had been no luck in retrieving the number or the owner. In fact, the cell phone had been blocked, leaving no trace of the caller.

It was also a fact that Jason Fekety had entered the house some nine minutes later as this had been logged through the 911 system as well. Those facts created problems.

The first problem was that the coroner's office had established the time of death for Elaine Kauffman as somewhere between 5:15 PM and 6:15 PM. When pressed, SB had indicated on the telephone that the fifteen minutes at either side of that were remote possibilities. That left Spagnola with a time of death between 5:30 PM and 6:00 PM. If the shot had been heard by the anonymous caller a minute or two before the call to 911 at 6:24 PM, what shot had that person heard? Right now, Spags had three shots to consider:

two fired at Elaine Kauffman and one at Bill Kauffman. The two bullets that had struck Elaine Kauffman had been recovered and matched to the same gun. The bullet that had been extracted from Bill Kauffman was still missing.

What did the killer or killers do in the time between shooting Mrs. Kauffman and shooting Mr. Kauffman? Why did they hang around the house so long? Why is it that only the bedroom appeared to have been subject to the burglary and not the entire house?

Spags tried to run through scenarios that made sense. He couldn't do it. He examined a diagram of the Kauffman house and marked it up with a pencil in an attempt to assist his analysis. The next steps, he thought, would be to try to eliminate some of the irrelevant facts he had gathered and to see if the other facts fit into some logical explanation.

The first fact he eliminated due to irrelevancy was the burglary. Perhaps the burglary had occurred independently of the homicide and attempted murder. If that were the case, the shootings might make sense. Although Spagnola could not yet determine the motive, if the killer had been trying to kill both of them, the best way to do it would have been to identify the Kauffmans' routine. That would have allowed the killer to know how long it would be until Mr. Kauffman would arrive upon the scene, so he could isolate Mrs. Kauffman and kill her before killing her husband when he came home. This seemed to make sense and would account for the differential in time between the shooting of Elaine and the shooting of Bill.

Spagnola's mind drifted momentarily to his favorite television show of all time: *Star Trek*. He let no one know about this hobby of his. He thought it would be bad for his image and that he wouldn't be taken seriously if people found out. He watched the show (and all of its spin offs) religiously. He even owned some of the final seasons on DVD. One of his favorite lines came from the large-eared Ferrengies, "Where is the profit?" In Spagnola's line of work, profit equaled motive. Who stood to profit from the Kauffmans' deaths? Profit could be measured in money, revenge, power, sex, or opportunity.

This led back to the question regarding the burglary. If the burglary had been a cover up for the homicide, that would make sense too. If it was a phony burglary, it was a good one. Whoever had committed the burglary had taken the time to carefully pick the outside door lock and had come in through an easy-access entryway. No broken windows, no broken glass. Amateurs trying to show that a burglary had occurred often took a shoe, smacked a window from the inside out, and unlocked the door. Even amateur detectives knew that professional burglars rarely broke glass, and when they did, they did it from the outside in, not from the inside out.

The burglar at the Kauffman house, if there really had been one, was efficient in his or her work. The criminal hadn't wasted any time and appeared to have snagged the jewelry and left. The interviews conducted with the neighbors revealed that Elaine Kauffman's love for her jewelry was well known. She owned a significant amount of it and wore it on a regular basis. These things would lead a burglar to believe that she kept her jewelry on the premises and not in a safe deposit box. The burglar probably assumed that, like most women, she kept it in her bedroom, easily accessible to wear and just as easy to steal.

Despite all of the information that made sense to Spags, a few things still unsettled him. Although the dog prints were problematical, the biggest problem was the missing bullet. Without it, Spagnola would never know if the same gun was used twice or if two different guns had been used. Different guns could mean different motives. If only one gun had been used, then the crime was probably premeditated because Elaine Kauffman's killer who was in all likelihood a burglar would not have hung around after killing her. A burglar would not have waited for Bill to come home.

A murderer with intent to kill Bill . . . would have.

The chances that two different guns were used were a million to one, Spags thought, but if there had been more than one intruder, it was possible. In addition, there was the extremely remote possibility that the death of Elaine and the death of Bill were separate and distinct events, with separate yet equally deadly motives. Spags tried to put that scenario out of his thinking because if there were two shooters with two motives, the hopes of solving both cases were pretty slim.

A thorough search of the hospital produced nothing. There were no other bullets being stored there so a mix up was an impossibility. Unfortunately, it appeared that the bullet may have been thrown in a red bag and disposed of in the ordinary course of hospital procedure. If so, it was lost forever amidst hundreds of tons of medical waste from all of the areas of the hospital that was carefully picked up and taken to an incinerator on a daily basis.

Spagnola needed a break. The doctors at the hospital had told him there was a good possibility Bill Kauffman would not remember what happened to him because of the trauma of the incident and the length of time he had been unconscious. It was also very possible that whatever Bill's recollections might be, they would be tainted by his subsequent dreams, imagination, and details filled in by his subconscious. That would mean that, despite being the victim, he might well be an unreliable witness. Spags's headache increased.

CHAPTER 35

THERE WAS A dull ache in the lower left side of his stomach. Someone was kneeling astride him, but he felt no pain. The pain was somewhere off in the distance . . . it should have been right there in his gut, but it wasn't. Bill searched for the pain, but all he felt was the pressure.

His shirt was wet. Warm and wet. It was wet down his side too. Bill tried to reach up and feel the wound but his arm was stuck. At first he thought maybe the person above was kneeling on his arm, but it didn't feel that way; his arm was just stuck.

He could smell the person, actually smell his breath. The person was mightily exerting himself and was beginning to sweat. Bill somehow sensed that he was sweating too; he could smell himself. He went to move his left arm, but it was stuck also.

He didn't know where Elaine was. He wasn't sure where he was. It was so hot and foggy. Bill was afraid.

Bill could actually hear the scalpel as it tore into his skin. He had been shot, hadn't he? And someone was pulling the bullet out! Bill tried to move his arm again, but it was still stuck. Bill felt as though he was going to wake up but then he was aware of someone fiddling with the bag of liquid next to his bed. His eyes slowly followed the tube from the liquid bag, and he noticed the other end of the tube was in his arm. Then he felt a sudden warmth, and as he drifted away, so did the dream.

CHAPTER 36

THE FAX MACHINE in Spagnola's office kicked to life. It startled him out of his reflective mood. When he saw the top of the page, it reminded him of his inquiry to York County about his hate affair with Dr. Evans. Thinking about her really rubbed him the wrong way. She was arrogant, self-assured, and not afraid. *Kinda reminds me of myself,* thought Spagnola.

He blamed her for the missing bullet and she refused to accept that blame. Probably if she had done a few mea culpas, he would have let it go. She hadn't, and he wouldn't. Spags couldn't figure out how she fit into this unless she was a souvenir taker. Given her profession, that was a distinct possibility.

The report on Dr. Evans from York was three and a half pages long, single spaced, and full of detail. It provided York County statistical information on the period of time from three months before Dr. Evans accepted her job at York County Hospital, until sixty days after she left. The analysis showed the following:

1. There had been no evidentiary snafus at the hospital during her tenure.
2. There had been three homicides in York County during that period of time and eleven other attempted homicides. Dr. Evans had performed surgery on three of the subjects who were shot, all of whom had lived, with the recovery of all of the bullets in all three matters.
3. The three homicides were unrelated. Two had involved drug deals gone bad, and one involved a wife shooting her

husband for infidelity. Only one of the homicides had been
handled by York County Hospital on an emergency basis
and none of them involved Dr. Evans.

Statistically, the period of time when the doctor was at the
hospital was no different than the period before she arrived or the
period after she arrived from a police statistical standpoint. The
report, however, did show that she was apparently an excellent
surgeon. There had been no details of any serial murder activity
in the county during that period of time, or homicides that could
be linked together.

The hospital records regarding Dr. Evans showed exemplary
work and admiration from her colleagues. It also indicated her
respect for, but no deference to, her employers. Evans was the
last of the hospital employees he had investigated. None of the
employees had any prior criminal history, none of them had
any brushes with the law, none of them had been suspected of
tampering with evidence or taking souvenirs, and none of them
had any real connection to the Kauffmans. There was a footnote
from his pal in York. It said that the Doctor had been reported
as a possible witness to a homicide in Maryland but York had no
details...just the phone number of a State Trooper.

It was a thorough report, but it gave Spags nothing.

CHAPTER 37

SPAGS WAS HALFWAY through reading the coroner's report a second time when a line in the text struck him as odd. It read, "In the examiner's opinion, the lack of defensive wounds would indicate that the deceased either knew the assailant or was awakened by the assailant shortly before the weapon was fired at her. However, the fact that the deceased was fully clothed and apparently lying on the bedspread at an early hour does not lend credence to the latter scenario."

Spagnola thought it odd that a burglar had gained entrance to the residence and that she had not awakened until he was within feet of her bed. There was no good indication as to whether the burglary was complete at that point and no precise sign as to when Mr. Kauffman had entered the house. An interview of Mr. Kauffman would be key. Despite the interviews with the neighbors, the phone records, and the cell phone calls, Spags could not establish a specific time line; and to determine exactly what had happened, Spags was going to need Mr. Kauffman to talk.

In the meantime, the detective had policemen out interviewing everyone a second or even a third time and checking on neighbors who had been away during the incident, in order to add to the existing database of information. Nothing of interest had materialized as of yet, so he returned to the report.

He knew it was not unusual for people to take a late afternoon nap, or even to doze off after a few predinner cocktails of choice. Given that the marriage of the Kauffmans was in no great shape, it was possible that this was a routine that Mrs. Kauffman had fallen into since she really would not have been all that excited about the prospect of her uninterested husband returning home from work. However, her boyfriend was of no help in that regard claiming that Elaine never consumed too much liquor and never dozed off.

What was it that the Irish say? Spags thought. "Your ne'r drunk so long as you can hold onto a blade of grass and not fall off the face of the earth!" Spags knew that Yeldon's impressions of Elaine were seen through a starstruck lover's eyes and had to be tempered with reason. Still, he didn't like the "fall asleep" scenario one bit, and he wasn't exactly sure why.

Elaine was an active woman. She had an interest in gardening, she got up early in the morning, she was in reasonably good physical condition, and she was getting laid on a regular basis. Did this sound like a woman who would fall asleep after two small glasses of wine at five o'clock in the afternoon?

It didn't add up. At this point, nothing did.

Spagnola speed dialed the coroner's office. He knew SB was a workaholic who spent most of his time at his office. SB's one true passion other than his work was golf. Since it was a Sunday morning, SB might have opted to hit the little white ball rather than deal with his scalpel or peer through his electron microscope. The phone at the coroner's office picked up on the third ring.

"Assistant Medical Examiner Begozian here."

"Hey, AME," answered Spags. "Any chance SB is around?"

"Sure. If you're around the tenth or eleventh hole at the Coatesville Country Club, I'm sure you'll find him. How can I help you, Mr. Detective?"

Spags thought for a second, trying to focus on what was most important. He didn't want to waste the medical examiner's time, but at the same time, some nagging questions had hit him. "Melatonin. I've looked it up on the Internet. I'm familiar with it from health food store, but I'm not sure I understand. You take melatonin during the day and it builds up in your system. How in the hell does it help you sleep at night and what prevents you from falling asleep in the daytime?"

"That's easy," said the examiner. "You're thinking about it all wrong. Melatonin isn't a sleeping pill. It has no similarity to any drug that affects your ability to remain awake. Melatonin is naturally produced in your body. It is believed that low levels of melatonin in your body can create a situation in which it is more difficult to enter specific states of sleep. The most important rest for humans is REM sleep. In nonscientific terms, this is the type of sleep where you have deep dreams and where your body and mind actually get rested in the traditional sense of the term. Ever slept for eight hours and woke up tired? That's because your body and mind never got into REM sleep, therefore, you never got the real rest that you needed. Soldiers on the battlefields have been known to sleep for fifteen or twenty minutes, awake fully refreshed, and ready to fight. The proper levels of melatonin in the system assist the body and the mind in getting to the REM state."

"Well, what do you think of the high level of melatonin in Elaine Kauffman's body?"

"Professionally? Probably nothing. Gut instinct? Significant of something, but I'm not sure it has anything to do with our homicide. From her skin it would appear that at the time she died, it was relatively cool in her bedroom. Perhaps she had the air conditioning cranked up. But the reports don't indicate that the air conditioner was on when the police and ambulance arrived at the scene."

"It sounds like a punch line to a bad police joke." Spagnola mocked a laugh. "I've seen criminals do stupid things, but why would even a dumb criminal stop to take the time to turn off the air conditioner after he just killed two people?"

The assistant medical examiner laughed on the other end of the line. "You're the detective big guy, you tell me. Is there anything else I can do for you?"

"No, just don't spill any of your chicken soup into the evidence. Talk to you later. Thanks for your help."

CHAPTER 38

THEY CALLED HIM Injun Joe. He was not an Indian and his name was not Joe. He was born Stewart Heideman and was called Stew or Stewie until eighth grade, when a ninth grader from Bishop Shanahan thought he looked like an Indian at one of the youth dances and dubbed him "Injun Joe." The name stuck.

Joe was now twenty-seven years old, unemployed, an alcoholic, a bum, and known by everyone as Injun Joe. He had grown up in the West Chester area, but had found that the handouts and the places to sleep peacefully were more abundant in the Exton area, so he had migrated the six miles north and called Exton his home.

He walked or hitchhiked wherever he needed to go. He knew all of the bars that would serve him, when they would serve him, when they would cut him off, and how to get a ride. He also knew that when he was good and drunk, there was no point in hitching because no one would pick him up, except the police.

This particular evening he had received a dose of good fortune. While wandering around the Exton Mall (and evading the security officers who escorted him out on a regular basis), he had stopped to help a woman who had spilled all the recent spoils of her shopping on the ground. The woman had handed him a twenty dollar bill, thanked him, and told him to get a haircut. He told her he would.

His plan for the twenty dollars was simple. He had walked over to Burger King for a Whopper with cheese, fries, and a Coke—his absolute favorite meal when he could score it.

He then walked to the LCB liquor outlet in Marchwood Shopping Center and purchased a quart of Tango and a pint of brandy. He still had sixty-eight cents change.

He sauntered out of the liquor store and headed behind the shopping center. After a quick look around, he slipped into a small wooded area where he could drink unobserved. His plan was to drink the Tango right away and save the brandy for later. Get a buzz on, he thought, but not too much. He would use the bathroom at the Welcome Center to clean up a little, then hitchhike up to Pottstown to see if he could find some friends and drink with them. He would be willing to share his brandy if they would share their beer. He loved to have a plan. This plan seemed good to him, and he wasted no time finishing off the ice cold Tango.

The sun had gone down and he knew he wouldn't spend much time hitching on the corner of Marchwood Road and Route 100 before the police got him.

I'm not a dummy, he thought. He would walk up to Worthington Road where he imagined people might think he had just come out of church and needed a ride. He was a little fuzzy on that idea at this point, but it still seemed a good plan to him and he didn't mind the walk.

Stewart was caught by surprise when the first line of traffic produced a minivan that pulled over about fifty yards past the intersection. At first he hesitated, thinking maybe they had stopped for some other reason. Then he figured, what the hell, and ran up to the passenger door. He opened it and thought, *Something's wrong here!* Then the thought drifted into his Tango, and he hopped in the van.

"Hey, thanks, I don't usually hitchhike but my car's busted."

"Uh huh. Where are you headed?" the driver asked.

"Pottstown, see some friends."

"OK," the driver replied. "Just need to make a quick stop along the way. Only a few minutes off 100. You OK with that?"

The Tango now had its haze all over Stewart. "Yeah, sure." The only thought in his mind was whether to offer this Good Samaritan a swig of his brandy.

Stewart was not the least bit surprised when the car pulled into Placid Park.

CHAPTER 39

I T SAT IN the dark on the lawn and laughed. The grass was cool to the touch, but dry. It knew that they would not find the body until the morning. It had been an exceptional stroke of luck to find that miserable hitchhiker, intoxicated and just waiting to die as he thumbed his way down Route 100 for the last ride of his pathetic life.

The coroner would be very thorough in his autopsy. The coroner did not have many opportunities to examine such a body in a county like this. Not like a good large city, It thought, with all the horror and death that only a good large city could produce.

The coroner would find the clues that It had left. The homicide would befuddle him and disturb the police for some time. It laughed again.

It knew how predictable those guys were. They all went to the same schools and academies. They all studied under the watchful eye of the all-knowing FBI. They were all "pigeonhole people." They only knew protocol; they only knew statistics; they only knew patterns. They knew nothing of the nature of a true predator. They never suspected anyone of trimming the human herd. They knew nothing at all.

It had been through this before. It knew when it was time to hunt, and when it was time to move on. They always looked for a pattern, a connecting activity, a profile . . .

They would of course suspect a stranger, someone who came to town just to wreak havoc. They would believe the stranger was abused as a child, possessed fair intelligence, worked at a decent job, and was personable so as to seemingly fit into their society. They would call the FBI. They would engage a profiler and try to determine what the clues meant. They would believe that the killer was criminally insane, a psychotic. They would speculate that the killer's crimes would accelerate, become more daring and more reckless, giving them hope that they could catch him quickly. They would ask, "Who could do this?" and "Why did he do this?"

"Who could do this? Indeed," It said out loud to no one, "that is the part they will never understand, not 'who' but 'what?'"

It would be difficult to sleep tonight. Delicious thoughts . . . so much to remember, so much to think about. So many duties lay ahead. So much still to be done.

Difficult indeed.

CHAPTER 40

S PAGNOLA WAS ON his way to work when the cell phone rang. The desk sergeant alluded to a crime wave and said not to bother coming to the station, but to head up to Placid Park. They needed a detective, now, he said.

There had been a homicide. That much was clear. As Dan walked from his car to the scene, he shouldered his way through the dozens of people milling around. The crime scene itself was taped off and only three people stood inside the tape. The coroner's assistant was taking pictures, a uniformed officer from Upper Uwchlan stood facing the crowd, and an off-duty officer was talking on a police radio.

"Hey, Dan, nasty business," said the uniformed policeman. Spagnola didn't recognize him but since Spags was the only detective around, everyone knew him.

"Any idea what happened?"

"No. Guy jogging came by at six o'clock and at first didn't know what he was looking at. Thought maybe it was vandals and paint. Got closer, got sick, jogged back to his car, and called 911. At first they sent an ambulance because what the guy described sounded like some terrible accident, and he wasn't making much sense."

"Hey, SB," Spagnola called to the coroner.

Spagnola stood looking at the tarp that had been hung by the coroner to prevent unwanted news photos. He turned to the uniformed police officer.

"Let's clear the park . . . the crime scene. Nobody allowed in until I say so."

"Except the press?" the officer asked.

"Especially the press."

"They are gonna howl. Whoa."

"Let 'em howl. By the time they get their attorneys involved, I'll be done."

"It's your ass, Detective," the officer said with a smile and a wink.

"Hey," yelled Spagnola, pointing at his own butt, "this has been chewed off so many times there's nothing left to chew anyway."

SB got a good chuckle out of the detective's remark. He liked Spagnola. No nonsense, no bullshit, not looking for a promotion or to move onto politics; just doing the job, doing a good job at that, and trying to put bad guys away.

It took about fifteen minutes to clear the park. Satisfied that the press was not in a position to photograph, even with a telephoto lens, he signaled SB to remove the tarp.

The detective stood straight in front of the tarp as it was removed. When it was completely off, he cocked his head to one side then the other. Finally, he shook his head.

"I have to say this had the same effect on me. I wasn't sure what exactly I was looking at. I understand why the jogger didn't know. I've seen some bad stuff, but other than car accidents, I've never seen anything like this."

"Help me here, SB. What the hell happened to this guy?"

"As best as I can tell, without going through all of the detail . . . my best professional guess is that most of the damage occurred, mercifully, after he was dead. But not all of it. I have no idea what weapons were used, but this took some time. It would appear that the people who did this were either mighty pissed off or mighty high . . . most likely both."

"Anything to indicate ritual?"

"Too early to say for sure, but I don't think so. Nothing carved in the torso, nothing in writing, no special markings that I can see, but the body is so mutilated that the autopsy will tell us if there was any attempt to communicate a message before things really got crazy. He seems to have all of his fingers and toes, eyes are still there, little hard to find, but they are there. Ears were severed but they are on the ground right next to the body." SB's voice started to shake a little and he stopped. He was accustomed to gruesome death, but there was something different here, and it started to choke him up.

"I'm going to take a short walk, think a little, maybe puke a couple of times, and then I'll be back." Spagnola turned his back on the grisly scene and rubbed his head. He had trouble making out the human form beneath the torn flesh and blood. There was literally no face left and parts of the body appeared to have been peeled open with a dull instrument.

"Who the fuck could do this to another human being?" Spagnola said to no one. "Who?"

CHAPTER 41

THE CORONER'S OFFICES and Chester County Morgue were located, of all places, at the back of a business park in East Goshen Township. As the county grew, very little thought was given to where to house a state of the art morgue and proper facilities for a modern medical examiner's office. *It is bad enough,* SB thought to himself as he sat at his desk, *that they still called it the coroner's office when everybody else in the world was calling it the medical examiner's office. Hell,* he thought, *doesn't anybody watch CSI? They were calling it the medical examiner's office on Quincy re-runs for crying out loud.*

The more SB thought about it, the more he realized he didn't much care what they called his office as long as he could still get the funding that he needed to conduct topnotch autopsies and coroner inquest work. SB was called in on major cases throughout the Commonwealth of Pennsylvania. He hated to admit it to himself, but he was looking forward to this autopsy and had requested his top AME, Lester Stahl, to assist him to give him firsthand experience in a mutilated body case.

SB knew that the toughest thing to do in a mutilation case, or fire death, was to avoid jumping to any conclusion. As the famous FBI agent Frank Jules used to say, while imitating Peter Lorre, "He had a bullet in his head, a knife in his back, and a hatchet in his chest . . . The police were trying to determine who poisoned him."

SB was lucky to work in such a state-of-the art morgue, complete with a voice-activated recording system. SB was a creature of habit and kept a cassette running to ensure that he never missed a detail. He pushed record.

"This is Dr. Julius Constantine. Testing. Play back, please."

After several seconds he heard, "Playback. This is Dr. Julius Constantine. Testing. Please, play back."

"OK, this is September 18, . It is approximately 4:00 PM. I am at the coroner's office of Chester County, being assisted in the autopsy of an unidentified white male by Dr. Lester Stahl, assistant medical examiner for the county of Chester. This autopsy is being done as part of the official investigation of the death of the unidentified male whom we'll call John Doe.

"Visual examination reveals a male, age indeterminate, with slight build; clothing has been removed and tagged for further testing. Subject has brown hair. Subject has a tattoo on his right arm that appears to be a heart with an arrow through it. The tattoo contains no discernable lettering.

"Subject was measured and weighed at five foot eleven inches and one hundred forty-five pounds. Subject is Caucasian. He appears to have been intoxicated at the time of his death and his body smells strongly of sweet alcohol mixed with blood. We will begin the autopsy by thoroughly examining his wounds."

For almost an hour, the two doctors took turns examining specific parts of the body for scars, moles, bruises, cuts, and other wounds, detailing each one and photographing each portion of the body from several angles. The doctors were careful to be sure that no trick of lighting or angle would spoil the ability to recreate the wound in court, if it were needed to help make a case.

All in all, they took seven rolls of film (SB hated digital) containing three hundred and ninety-two photographs. They also videotaped the autopsy through remote cameras, but most times the footage was more fanciful than effective.

They saved his face for last. It was, in nonmedical terms, a mess. It appeared that someone had taken pruning shears, stuck them up the victim's nose, and began unceremoniously removing his face.

As they folded the skin back from the right side of his face toward his left ear, Dr. Stahl noticed something that seemed out of place.

"Hold on, there is something underneath the skin." He selected small tweezers from his operating tray and maneuvered the skin around the object. While he held the skin with the tweezers, SB used an even smaller set of tweezers to get a hold of the bloody object and slowly extract it from the victim's face.

At first he held it up to the light, and both doctors peered at the foreign object. Then SB carefully laid the object on a tray and photographed it.

"It appears to be a piece of folded paper. It could not have accidentally ended up in the position under the victim's facial skin. It appears that it may have been purposely positioned there."

There was a long pause as both doctors just looked at one another. The inference was there but unspoken: the murderer had left a message. This was the kind of occurrence that murder mystery novels were replete with, but in real life Stahl had never witnessed a body, even in forensics school, that actually had an intentional message left from a killer, in any form whatsoever. SB had only seen such a thing twice.

CHAPTER 42

"WE SHOULD TRY to carefully unfold it. It is drenched with blood but otherwise appears to be intact. Ready?"

Dr. Stahl nodded. They each held their tweezers as if they were doing a delicate operation on a living patient, not unfolding a reddish scrap of paper. The video cameras would later reveal just how macabre a scene the unfolding of the paper had been.

After nearly twenty minutes and some gentle, but firm, coaxing, both doctors lay the paper open, face down. SB turned it over gently. It was, in fact, a note from the killer:

HE DIES NOT FOR WHAT HE WAS
HE DIES NOT FOR WHAT HE COULD NOT BE
HE DIES NOT FOR HIMSELF
HE DIES THAT YOU WILL SEE MY GREATNESS

"Let's photograph it first, read it into the record, and then get some samples of what appears to be blood covering the paper, and save it for diagnostic," SB said.

"Uh huh." Dr. Stahl was lost in thought.

They took twenty-one photographs of the writing. They took shots from either side with different lighting, close up and far away, until they were satisfied they had not missed anything. Dr. Stahl then took the scrap of paper by the tweezers, inserted it into a tube, covered the top, and placed it in the vacuum machine.

The vacuum machine, as it was called by almost everyone involved in forensic science, was actually a pervismometer, which literally sucked the air out of a tube and replaced it with a mild and light phuric gas, the latter being injected to prevent the collapse of the tube. In doing this, it prevented the air from deteriorating the piece of paper while keeping it in a vacuum-like environment. The device was the invention of the long-forgotten scientist Arman Pervis. Originally, these machines actually created a virtual vacuum. However, it was found that certain objects completely disintegrate when there is no atmosphere around them, including certain varieties of paper when wet. With the paper safely in place, the doctors decided it was a good time for a break, neither knowing exactly what he should do next.

They were both very well trained, had significant experience in the area of autopsies, and had attended the latest and greatest schools on forensic science, but they had very little experience with what they both knew they were looking at: a note from a serial murderer.

CHAPTER 43

T HE DOCTORS HAD decided it was in everyone's best interest to complete the autopsy before they called Detective Spagnola. It was not good procedure to jump to any conclusions, even though they had both come to the same conclusion, both as to the cause of death and the type of murderer.

Off camera, they had quietly run through a variety of scenarios. They had discussed the possibility that someone had a motive for this killing and, in order to cover it up, had written the note to throw them off. They discussed sexual motivations, rage, homophobic behavior, and a variety of textbook similarities to classic killing scenarios. In the end, they knew they were wasting their time with these theories.

When they had completed the autopsy, the victim resembled a dissected frog more than a human being. They had cut open the body and sawed through the rib cage. They had removed each lung, the heart, the kidneys, the liver, the pancreas, the stomach, and the small and large intestines. They had carefully weighed, measured, and photographed each organ, noting with each one what years of smoking, alcohol abuse, and poor diet had done to the poor victim.

The cigarettes, alcohol, cheeseburgers, and fries had done nothing compared with what the killer had done. The victim had been severely beaten. He had been methodically hit with a variety of objects and had not died fast nor easily. Whoever had done this had not wanted him dead too quickly. There was internal bleeding all over the body and bruising that showed he had died after dozens of blows, inflicted over some period of time, as much as an hour.

They discovered no other telltale clues. They found virtually no fibers or foreign matter in his wounds. The killer had delivered most of the blows over the victim's outer clothing so that bits of his clothing were in his wounds, but nothing else. It appeared that several wooden objects had been used to inflict the damage: a blunt instrument like a hammer, at least two knives, and a screwdriver. None of the items had been recovered at the scene. Whoever had done this was strong and unrelenting.

Test results would tell whether the killer hade left any DNA behind, but it appeared that trace DNA was a long shot. There didn't appear to be any defensive wounds on the victim, so whatever fate he suffered, he did not have an opportunity or perhaps the strength to fight back. It appeared that all the damage was done to him at the scene so that his killer had not taken the chance of leaving Injun Joe's DNA in another location either.

The victim's clothing and shoes had been stripped off and each article lay in a separate plastic bag, tagged and photographed.

When the coroners were finished, SB called Detective Spagnola, reached his answering machine, and left him a message. They then stripped off their gowns, took searing hot showers, and opened a bottle of Johnny Walker Red that SB kept hidden in a gauze cabinet.

"I never thought I'd see the day—not here, not now."

"They can't classify it as a serial unless there are at least three killings with sufficient cool off time in between each one."

Dr. Stahl sighed. "Do you have any doubt that the person who did this has done it before?"

"No, I'm afraid not . . . and I'm afraid he'll do it again." SB closed his eyes and turned on the CD player, which intoned the Manheim Steamroller's "Toccata."

"And again."

CHAPTER 44

B ILL'S IMAGINATION HAD kicked in. He was lying in the foyer of his home. He was groggy and dazed and he could smell his own blood. His eyes were closed, so he couldn't see, but he could hear. He was puzzled. A streak of lightning went through his mind, but he knew it wasn't real.

He heard someone nearby, but couldn't tell if the person were actually in the house or just outside. Bill felt as if he were standing in a fog, and that everything lay just beyond his grasp. He sensed that he had been shot, but by whom? He could still hear the report of the bullet as the hammer struck the shell casing and the bullet zoomed out of the barrel toward him. At the same time, he thought that part was just make-believe; who would want to shoot Bill Kauffman?

It dawned on him that his wife didn't love him. Maybe she had shot him. That would make sense, he thought.

Another bolt of lightning without sound ran through his dream. He was standing beside a river and his wife was drowning; he pulled a beer from his backpack and began to sing. Even in his fog he knew that was silly. He couldn't sing, his wife wouldn't shoot him, and his wife, a good swimmer, would not be drowning just off the shore.

She didn't call for him to help. He heard the sirens and some voices just beyond his front door. He recognized some of them as his neighbors, but it was too much effort to keep this dream going, so Bill drifted away.

CHAPTER 45

THE INVESTIGATION OF the operating team, the orderlies, and even the people who cleaned the operating theater (numbering eleven in all) at Brandywine Hospital provided little interest to Spagnola. He was still annoyed with Dr. Evans, and he read over her materials again for what seemed like the fiftieth time.

The doctor had previously been on staff for eighteen months at York County, where her record was nothing short of remarkable. She was well respected (if not particularly well liked) by everyone from the custodian to the CEO. She had been effective, tireless, and successful in treating near-dead victims of everything from car crashes to crack overdoses. She had not been sued a single time for malpractice for anything that had occurred in the entire eighteen-month stint, and her reviews were nothing short of glowing.

Strictly on instinct, Spagnola picked up the phone and called a friend that he had met at a forensics seminar. His friend was the first assistant detective for the York County Police Department. York had been the first non-city department in the state to form a county police force and to go high tech.

Spags had no problem tracking down "Big Jim" O'Donovan. The county system was efficient to a fault, and had largely supplanted the state police presence that had investigated most major crimes in York County prior to its invention.

"Detective Jim O'Donovan here, how can I help you?"

"Hey, Big Jim, Spagnola from Chester County here. How are you?"

"Doin' well, thanks. How is crime in the big city?" Big Jim chuckled.

Spagnola feigned laughter at the attempted humor and went right on.

"Oh, we are holding our own, but you know those criminal types are getting smarter every day. Just ask them." It was Jim's turn to chuckle.

"Well, there aren't any out-of-town seminars where we can drink the place dry coming up, so you must be callin' on business. What can I do for you?"

"I need to know about any missing evidence at or near York County hospital from April 23, to October 14, last year Any way you can check on that for me? I have some evidence missing in a homicide investigation, and it might relate to a souvenir taken by medical staff."

"Well, you have come to the right place. It will take me a while because the wait for computer time is extended right now while we are upgrading our software, but we can track almost anything these days. We not only track homicides, but all deaths, the official causes of death, and whether there are any similar deaths within a five-year period in the county. We have abilities that make the Feds' mouths water.

"Seems that one of our state representatives, the DA, and our President Judge are all computer junkies. They got together, got all kinds of funds and grants, and now we can tell you how much change is in someone's pocket when they die, if you need to know. Just can't tell you who killed 'em is all . . . "

At this, both detectives laughed.

"Good thing or we'd both be waitin' tables," said Spagnola.

"Never looked good in a cocktail dress," chuckled Big Jim. "Give me your number and I'll be back to you as soon as I can."

CHAPTER 46

C ARMEN DID NOT like the way the patient looked. His chart seemed to indicate that he was recovering well, slowly but well. He was no longer in a coma but was for the most part unconscious. His temperature was still a little high, but with a gunshot wound to the abdominal area, that was to be expected.

Carmen put the blood pressure cuff on his arm and pumped air through the sphygmomanometer. She let the air out slowly, making sure the reading was precise. She was always precise.

"One forty-five over eighty-two," she said to no one.

It was her habit. She spoke the numbers out loud whenever she took the pressure of a sleeping patient. No rhyme, no reason; she just did, she always had. Nurse Rodriguez entered the reading on the chart and stood back from her patient. He just didn't look right. She knew something was wrong, but couldn't for the life of her put a finger on it.

Something else was wrong. There was a sound down the hall that was out of place. She knew every sound in these halls; she was said to have radar. At night it was even easier to pick up sounds when the hospital itself was resting. *The hospital never sleeps,* she thought, *but it seemed to rest at night when the pompous-ass doctors went home in their expensive vehicles and the relatives of the patients stopped hovering around the halls.*

She heard it again, softer this time. She walked calmly and quietly down the hall. She didn't make a sound. She moved like a cat. *People didn't realize that heavy people could be agile and quick,* she thought, quietly laughing to herself. At five foot three and one hundred and forty-five pounds, she had been subject to that discrimination, as well as being the object of other discrimination as a Hispanic woman.

The noise had stopped, but she knew where it had come from. She had no fear, just anger; anger that someone was creeping around her floor. She went straight from her station to the drug closet where all prescription class medications were kept.

The closet was supposed to be in secure lock up for the various medicines that were on a schedule with the state and federal governments, meaning they could only be dispensed by prescription. The closet had actually served that function exclusively for the first seven months after the hospital had opened. Eventually, the closet had been needed to store several file cabinets, then a portable EKG machine, then bandages, and the list went on and on.

Rodriquez found the metal closet door barely ajar. Technically, the locked glass cases behind the metal doors were sufficient to prevent people from dipping into the drug cookie jar, but protocol for good hospitals called for locked glass cases behind locked metal doors in order to keep the crazies from just smashing the glass. The addition of the locked metal doors also prevented those in charge from the temptation of medicating themselves for recreational purposes. She thought there was already far too much self-medication in the physician and nurse professions without making it any easier on those who were inclined to help themselves to prescription meds.

No light came from the crack in the door, but a small click emanated from inside. Not much of a noise, not something a person would notice, but Nurse Rodriquez noticed. Her ears were as sharp as her wits. She debated calling security, but she had a suspicion of who might be messing in Wonderland, the name given to the prescription room by the head nurse. Rodriquez weighed her options. She could barge in, or give a little notice before turning on the lights; she opted for the latter. More dramatic.

Carmen cleared her throat a split second before she pushed open the door and switched on the light. She was hoping for someone, a nurse, a physician, someone, to say, "Excuse me?" She was looking for some sign that this was routine, that an error had been made.

It took a moment for the scene to register in her brain. The cabinet in front of her was wide open and items had been strewn about the floor. The room at first glance, however, appeared empty. She stood stock still. The scene before her, though chaotic, looked like it had been carefully staged. . She looked all around the closet, but saw no one. She took a single small step forward because she wanted a better view of the mess, but most of all because she was scared. She paused, looked, listened, saw nothing and heard nothing.

She then took two quick steps forward. Carmen sensed her mistake before she was hit. When she turned, she sustained a forceful blow to the back of her head that drove her to her knees.

Carmen was able to get her hands out in front of her just in time to prevent her head from striking the floor, and she was already halfway into a push up when she felt a stab of pain in her neck and then another in her shoulder. Her right arm vibrated and suddenly collapsed under her, leaving her suspended by her left arm. As she tried to pull herself up on her left arm, a foot came into view and kicked her left arm out from under her. Her head cracked on the floor. She tried the other arm, with the same result. She softly breathed out her mouth, "What do you want?" The only answer she received was another stab of pain, and when she tried to ask the question a second time, her request was followed by another stab of pain.

Then Nurse Carmen felt warm; it was spreading all over her body and she thought, This must be a dream. You couldn't be in pain and feel so warm and so good at the same time.

I wonder if Eduardo remembered to let the dog out, she thought. It was her last thought as she lapsed into unconsciousness. Three minutes later, Nurse Rodriguez was dead.

CHAPTER 47

THE COATESVILLE CITY Police Department was the first one notified of the suspected homicide of Nurse Rodriguez. They in turn notified the county detectives' office. The police kept the crime scene clean until the detectives and forensics people could arrive and do their job. An assistant coroner arrived prior to the forensics people, but other than taking pictures, he disturbed nothing.

This suspected homicide was not a normal occurrence. In fact, the hospital had no records of a homicide ever being committed on its grounds. There had been several suicides over the years, but never a homicide.

All of the hospital administrators had been notified: those who were in the building, those who were at home asleep, and those who were on vacation, including many members of the board of directors. Every one of them was in shock; some of them were already looking to place, or avoid, blame. "Where was security? How did the intruder get into the hospital? Why wasn't the pharmaceutical closet more secure? Who could have done such a thing?"

Vision in hindsight was always twenty-twenty, Rogers Endersly thought. Endersly was a third generation hospital administrator and was very efficient at his job. He was not particularly well liked among the staff, but he was respected for running a no-nonsense operation. His hospital was not going to be purchased by a larger entity and wasn't going to be declaring bankruptcy either. Compared to the rest of the administrators, he was fairly nonplussed. He knew full well how difficult it was to maintain any real security in a hospital environment, unless you sealed off the wards and didn't allow visitors. Oh, yes, and closed the emergency room and the trauma center because, the good Lord knows, no one could keep those areas secure in the height of their chaos.

Endersly was about to be interviewed by the police. He had had just about enough of the police in the form of one Defective Spagnola and his obsession with the allegedly missing bullet from the previous weekend. Now this. He took a deep breath, straightened his tie, popped a breath mint, and punched the key for his intercom.

"Nanette, please have the officers come in now." His father had taught him to always keep people waiting in your outer office; it gave them a sense of your superior position and it gave you time to compose your strategy. Endersly had lived by those thoughts, but not always as successfully as he would have liked, Detective Spagnola having been his most recent failure.

Detective Richard Ayers was the first one in the door, followed by Sergeant Stoltan of Coatesville, and Corporal Reyes from the same department. Stoltan was a black man as big as a house, Reyes a five-foot-five-inch man of Puerto Rican descent, and Ayers was an average-sized WASP.

Ayers took charge after the introductions.

"Mr. Endersly, we have a series of questions we want to ask you. We understand you are the person who would have most, if not all, of the answers we need to certain technical and personnel questions. Would that be correct?"

"Yes, that is probably true. I am the senior vice president in charge of administration at the hospital." His voice betrayed his pompous nature.

"A preliminary review of the possible crime scene indicates that Nurse Rodriguez may have been killed in a secure area of the hospital, specifically a prescription narcotics closet. What are the procedures that are used to keep that area secure?"

Endersly was very nervous, but he hoped he was ready for this type of question.

"Officer . . ."

"Mr. Endersly, it's detective." Detective R. Richard Ayers did not conceal his annoyance at being referred to as officer instead of detective.

"Oh, yes, yes of course, my apologies, Detective, so sorry. Back to your question, this hospital has a protocol regarding all of its Class III and Class IV medications. It's part of our manual. Right here in fact . . . , " Endersly pointed to a page in a large three-ring binder entitled "Hospital Procedures Manual."

"The applicable section states as follows: all Classification III and Classification IV medications as well as any medications that are not clearly labeled Classification I or Classification II are to be kept locked in a secure area or areas, accessible only by physicians who are licensed to dispense . . . "

"I can read, Mr. Endersly, and I appreciate your providing us with this copy of the policy manual, but what we need to know is who actually has access to the closet in which Nurse Rodriguez was found dead. It would appear that the door to that closet was open and that she had no key. Your policy would not have allowed her to have a key. So I guess the question is, who was here at the time Nurse Rodriguez died? Who had a key?"

"Well, you don't believe that one of our physicians opened that door, do you?"

"Mr. Endersly, I have no idea who opened that door, but whoever it was may have murdered Nurse Rodriguez. I also know that you believe that only staff physicians licensed to dispense the drugs in that closet have a key. We'll need a list of all of the physicians who were here, say from 10:00 PM to 2:00 AM last evening, along with their addresses and home phone numbers."

"But wouldn't that be an invasion of their privacy or something for me to give that to you? I think I'll need to contact counsel to the hospital to get her OK on this." Endersly was clearly out of his element and he knew it; he couldn't let this hit the papers *and* have all of the physicians come down on him as well.

"Let us worry about the niceties, please. We have a homicide on our hands and unless you can convince me that someone other than your physicians has a key to that room, or someone shows me that the room was not locked or was broken into, then all I have is your physician list. I'm going to have that list in the next twenty minutes, or I'm going to pull you in for questioning and alert every newspaper in Pennsylvania that you refused to cooperate in a homicide investigation. Is all of this clear to you?"

Endersly was losing his internal control, but outwardly maintained his composed persona.

"Your threat is quite clear, Detective. We will have a list of the physicians who were checked in for any part of that time period." He reached for the intercom.

"Nanette, please get me two copies of our duty roster for physicians for yesterday, together with computer printouts of check-in and check-out times for all physicians during the hours between ten o'clock PM and two o'clock this morning."

"Is that all, detectives?"

"No." Ayers was now on a roll. "We are going to need to see personnel files on everybody who works here. We specifically need to know if you have any staff member, and I mean *any* staff member, who has had a drug or alcohol problem in the past. We also need to know of any disgruntled employees who have been let go or quit within the last six months. Finally, we need to have access to everybody who worked last evening. We are going to need a room to conduct interviews and a schedule. Figure fifteen minutes per interview until we are done. I'd like to start in an hour."

Endersly was now visibly shaken. He took a sip of water, scribbled some notes on a pad, all the while trying to regain his composure. To a degree he was able to do so.

"OK. Without a warrant or a court order I cannot, *not* will not, but cannot give you the personnel files. I've been through this before with our counsel. You can threaten me all you like, Detective, but we can't release those files to anyone absent a warrant or a court order. It's state and federal law. However, I will gather them all up so that they will be at your disposal as soon as you have the warrant or the court order. I presume you will have no problems obtaining one. I will call our counsel, Diane Jamieson, whose number is on this file card." Endersly fumbled with the card as he withdrew it from his drawer and handed it to Ayers. "She will work with you and the district attorney regarding release of the files."

Detective Ayers rose, stared hard at Endersly, and began to walk out of the office. At the last moment he turned, as if he had an afterthought. "We'll make the calls and get the warrant. Thank you for your cooperation."

CHAPTER 48

THINGS NEVER HAPPEN exactly the way that they are portrayed in the movies or in novels. Real life is never that clean, that precise. Critical events just don't fall into place, nor do the police or the detectives come to brilliant revelations after observing seemingly inane information or clues.

In the police world, more often than not, it's just staying after the details, interviewing the witnesses, and looking for the most likely suspect that leads to a good arrest. In real life crime, more often than not, if one follows the money or the likely motives, he usually finds his perpetrator.

"Son of a bitch." Spagnola was in a foul mood. "We have the nurse who is looking after the victim of a potential double homicide killed twenty feet from him and no one thinks to notify me?" He was yelling at no one in particular. He was generally unhappy, but he was going to take it out on that mealy-mouthed hospital administrator Endersly first.

"I told him to call me if Mr. Kauffman so much as sneezed."

He picked up the phone, began to dial the number of the hospital, and then hung up mid-ring. "No, I'm going to see that son of a bitch first hand and find out what the hell he was thinking, if that little weasel thinks at all," he said, again to no one.

The drive from the police station to the hospital was relatively dull. Left on 113 to the 30 bypass then stay on the bypass until the hospital exit.

Spagnola exited, taking the curve at forty-five. He realized that he needed to focus or he was going to be the subject of his own homicide investigation. He couldn't believe that neither the detectives nor the Coatesville Police nor this administrator thought there was anything strange about the coincidence of the nurse dying near the victim of an attempted double homicide.

Spagnola had phoned County Detective Will Smoren about the incident earlier that morning and had received a terse response.

"It's just a coincidence. Nothin' in common with your case, man. Just bad luck on Nurse Rodriguez's part," Smoren had said.

Spags didn't believe in luck, good or bad.

CHAPTER 49

A NY GOOD CRIMINAL investigator from the police to the FBI will tell you, "I don't believe in coincidence." Spagnola was no exception. He felt the word coincidence must have been invented by a lazy bastard looking for a way to explain the universe without doing any work. He didn't know Smoren. Didn't need to. He held Smoren in contempt just for using the word. How could someone say something was just a coincidence *before* they investigated the connections, the possibilities? In a word, Spags felt that coincidence was bullshit.

Despite his erratic driving, Spagnola arrived at the hospital without killing anyone, including himself. As he stepped out of his car, he noticed Arthur Dietrich, Elaine Kauffman's brother walking into the hospital fifty feet ahead of him. The word coincidence never crossed Spagnola's mind.

"Mr. Dietrich." Spagnola was cool and professional.

"May we have a word, Detective?" Dietrich was controlled but agitated.

"Is there anything new in the investigation?" Dietrich had an annoying way of enunciating his words.

"Nothing that I can share with you." Spagnola was professional if not cool.

"Detective, I know you are working hard on this. My problem, frankly, is that I have to return to work soon. I need to make some burial arrangements for my sister, given her husband's circumstances. I can't access her insurance until suicide is ruled out by the coroner. He said he can't help me in that regard because his findings are part of an on-going criminal investigation. You can surely see the circles I'm running in."

Spagnola did not want to seem surprised, so he stole a quick deep breath and asked, "Who are you dealing with regarding the insurance? Maybe I can be of some assistance there."

"Oh, that would be great. It's a Nationwide policy that Elaine took out last year. Apparently, it names her husband and me as the beneficiaries, equally. I have a card here for the agent. Name's Penrode, Deremis Penrode." Dietrich fumbled with his wallet and extracted a card.

Spagnola looked at the card briefly and then took out his notepad and wrote down all of the information.

"Policy number is on the back," Dietrich added.

"What prompted your sister to purchase the life insurance?"

"Don't know really. She just thought it was a good idea and a good price. I actually was trying to get her to invest in an idea of mine, but she declined."

"OK, well I'm on it. I'll try to call this guy today and get back to you tomorrow. I have your cell phone number in my file."

"Good, anything you can do would be helpful. And please keep me updated on your investigation." Dietrich walked away.

"Yeah, sorry for your loss," whispered Spagnola. His feeling that Dietrich had a hidden agenda was now stronger than ever.

CHAPTER 50

"I VISITED WITH MY brother Bill just last week," he said. "I had a good business opportunity for him."

The patrolman dutifully scribbled on his pad. He wasn't sure what to ask Bill Kauffman's brother next, but he didn't want that guy to know that so he scratched his chin looked around and looked back at his pad.

"This is all preliminary information we're gathering about your brother's death. You know? Did your brother seem nervous or upset when you last spoke with him?" the patrolman asked.

Bill's brother paused, feigning a struggle over recalling his brother's mood, knowing deep inside he had paid his brother's mood no attention at all. Bill's brother had only one concern; he was looking for some money.

"Uh, no, not that stood out, you know?"

"Was everything OK between your brother and his wife?" asked the patrolman cocking his head to one side as he did so.

Bill's brother didn't hesitate. "Yeah sure, they were lovebirds, you know? Married for life and all that stuff. I wasn't planning on staying here very long." He shrugged.

"Oh, why not?" he asked acting surprised. The patrolman had the feeling Bill's brother was an asshole.

"Just wasn't a social visit, that's all. I just stopped by, didn't stay for dinner or nothing, strictly business . . . I'd tell you the details but it's confidential stuff."

There was more scribbling by the patrolman and then he looked up and asked, "Where are you staying, Mr. Kauffman?"

"Oh, Red Roof Inn, on Route 100. Room 306. They have a killer buffet breakfast."

The patrolman continued to scribble and didn't look up. "I am sure the detectives will want to talk to you so please let us know if you move." He continued to scribble. "When is the funeral service?"

"I don't know, I haven't really heard anything about that," said Bill's brother, looking perplexed by the question.

"Are you helping your brother out with the funeral arrangements seeing as he is laid up?"

Bill's brother visibly squirmed, and he ran his finger under his collar as if his chest were on fire. He looked around and said, "Wouldn't there be insurance for that sort of thing? I mean . . . "

Now it was the patrolman's turn to look perplexed. He stopped writing and looked up.

"I meant are you helping with the arrangements to bury your sister-in-law and all . . . not were you paying the bill." He shook his head slightly.

"Oh sure," Bill's brother said, "yeah, whatever they need, I'm here for them."

The patrolman just stared at Bill's brother for a time. "OK. Detectives will be in touch."

CHAPTER 51

ON A BRISK but sunny Friday, Keifer awoke around noon and carefully exited the culvert, replacing the brush in front of the entrance and stepping on logs and debris to keep from leaving footprints or trampling down the now-dying waist-high weeds. He gave this procedure no thought; it was mechanical in nature, probably something he had picked up in the military.

The culvert had been designed as a flood drain by a long-forgotten engineer. The engineer had believed that the Rhonda building project on the east side of Route 100 would cause localized flooding and that a culvert was necessary to carry water from the eastern side of Route 100 underneath to the western side, where the runoff would drain into the wooded area that was later to become Marchwood Shopping Center. He was wrong; the water had never come and the culvert was mostly forgotten.

Over the years, the culvert had been the source of local rumors, particularly at Lionville Junior High School during the 1980s. Many students bragged to have traveled under Route 100 through the culvert, but in actuality, few of them had. The drainage pipe was almost 280 feet from one end to the other. Because it lacked lighting, it provided the perfect retreat for bats, an occasional furry animal, lots of insects, and Keifer, who called the culvert home. None of the vermin fazed Keifer, who liked the culvert for its quiet inconspicuousness and the shelter it provided against the elements.

Keifer walked casually passed the front of the Marchwood Hardware Store through the Marchwood Shopping Center doing his best to avoid attracting attention. He thought about whistling, but at the last minute, decided against it. It was late afternoon, that lull when moms needed to pick up their children before dads got home from work. Keifer encountered a few people as he crossed the parking lot. Thinking about all those dads working and moms picking up their kids reminded Keifer of his own childhood. He knew that nowadays, most families had two working parents and that children often grew up on their own, in daycare centers or in front of televisions and computer games. But Keifer didn't care one way or the other how families had changed over the years. The memories of his own childhood were mostly vague and fragmented.

Keifer was a hopeless alcoholic and had been for many years. Other than sweeping an occasional floor, shoveling a little snow, or doing a day's labor, Keifer's income was strictly from the Welfare Department and an occasional stint at panhandling. From odd jobs such as these, Keifer had twelve dollars in his pocket at the moment. Keifer, hands in his pockets, realized he was thirsty and decided to casually stroll over to the state liquor store. The employees of the state liquor store were not too keen on Keifer because he had a tendency to stay inside the store a long time and his bathing habits were legendarily unhygienic. Keifer had a feeling he wasn't liked there, so he decided to make a quick entrance and exit.

Keifer stopped in front of the cold case, which contained myriad sweet wines and liquors that he favored when he had the money. A bright orange substance caught his eye. It was called Trelouise. While he didn't know exactly what it was, it looked sickly sweet and chock full of cheap liquor, just the way Keifer liked it. When he pulled it out, he saw that the price was $7.95—out of his price range that afternoon. He put the bottle back, strolled down an aisle, picked out a $5.75 bottle of Jacquins Brandy and headed for the counter. After handing the clerk a ten, Keifer was puzzled that the change he received didn't quite add up to the ten dollars he had given the clerk, less the cost of the bottle. This particular clerk was kind enough to point out to him (perhaps for the hundredth time) that the purchase of liquor carried with it a 6 percent sales tax.

Keifer mumbled something about the government always getting his money and walked out. The man behind the counter mumbled something about Keifer being on welfare so his money was the government's, but Keifer never heard a word of it.

Keifer's plan was to parlay some of his brandy for some beer, wine, or maybe a little pot, and still keep most of the brandy for himself. If he was really lucky, he might get some potato chips and pretzels or even a couple of bucks from the deal. He walked back behind the Marchwood Hardware Store, took a couple of quick belts on the brandy, and then tucked the bottle inside of his pants, zippering up his coat jacket. In the haze of thoughts that were Keifer's damaged mind, he recognized that walking around with an open bottle in Uwchlan Township would in the best case land him in township lock up, and in the worst case attract the attention of some big strapping police officer who would undoubtedly pour Keifer's brandy on the ground in front of his crying eyes. The first prospect was bad, but the second was awful, so he started the long walk to Township Line Park.

CHAPTER 52

TOWNSHIP LINE PARK had been created in 1994. It consisted of roughly four acres of land not large enough for a little league field, way too small to support soccer, but just right for a little bit of open space, a small picnic pavilion, and a tot lot. The park had been created as a compromise between a developer who wanted to build houses and the township's need for more parks. Although the township had hoped to use the space as an active park, it really needed to add some passive park spaces to the inventory, particularly for the elderly and the very young, and this piece of ground seemed ideal for those purposes.

What the park had become, unbeknownst to most township residents (except a few neighbors and the local police), was a great place to make out, a great place for underage drinking, and an even better place to buy controlled substances (particularly marijuana) and to share a few tokes with friends. Almost every afternoon, a variety of groups gathered there for these seemingly harmless behaviors.

The skateboarders and inline skaters stayed in the parking lot. Despite what the police believed, these kids weren't usually involved in any of the drinking or drug activity. They were usually too busy trying to develop their stunts before it was time to go home.

The second group varied from day to day. They were armed with small, soft footballs, Frisbees, an occasional hacky sack, and once in a blue moon, a soccer ball. They were a mixed group comprised of boys and girls from a variety of ethnic backgrounds. It was rarely the same group two days in a row. Mostly non-athletes, they spent most of their time throwing the Frisbee, trying to make athletic moves, laughing, and basically having a good time. Occasionally, some of them went off into the far corners to smoke a little dope or have a couple of beers, but most of the time they were just out in the sun enjoying each other's company.

The third group was quite different. They weren't out in the sun much and they didn't care about anything but themselves. They often came to the park, even when it was raining or snowing, and they rarely entered through the parking lot. There were about six different ways in and out of the park, only two of which had been designed by the township. The other pathways had been invented predominantly by this third crowd.

Most of this group was the same day after day. Occasionally, one of them would go off to college or get a full-time job to be replaced by someone younger, but their numbers usually fell between twelve and fifteen, mostly high school kids who really didn't have anything in common with or want anything to do with the other two groups.

Members of the third group stayed to themselves. They did their best to stay out of the parking lot when the occasional police car entered. When one did, they slowly melted into the woods and either stayed there or exited on one of the four other paths out of the park.

Keifer didn't worry about such things. Keifer walked straight through the parking lot, around the people playing Frisbee, several of whom made unkind comments about him, and headed for the corner of the park where his "friends" were hanging out.

On his long walk to the park, he had cut through several backyards and tried a few garage doors. One had been open. Inside the garage he had found a case of beer. He commandeered a six pack and did his best to hide it under his coat. This would make him a big hit at the park.

When Keifer approached, several of the assembled members of the third group stared at him and shook their heads. One of the girls asked, "Hey, Keifer, bring us any goodies?" Keifer felt at home here more so than any place else in the world.

CHAPTER 53

KEIFER BARNEY HAD been a casualty of the Vietnam War. He had not been shot, he had not been wounded, he had not been physically hurt in any conventional way. His unit had lost its way on a night patrol and had almost been overrun by the Viet Cong. The members of his unit had distinguished themselves by killing three times more of the enemy than they themselves had lost. Tragically, however, Keifer's unit lost 50 percent of their men; and Keifer, who performed well according to all accounts, had been returned to his commander safely, but without any ability to function as a soldier. After numerous tests and arguments among the doctors who treated him, it was determined that he was in fact shell-shocked. The army doctors had decided that if he were to recover at all, any such recovery would occur over a long period of time with intensive therapy and medication.

The armed forces of the United States were not fond of recognizing Barney's Post-traumatic stress syndrome, and even less inclined to pay his benefits after the end of the war that everyone wanted to forget.

Returned to the real world in America, Kiefer often forgot to pick up his benefit checks, rarely remembered his doctor's appointments, and usually sold his medication to a buddy or simply lost it.

The army tired quickly of the Kiefer Barneys of the world for several reasons, not the least of which was the inability to confirm or deny if Kiefer (or guys like him) was actually suffering from shell shock or just looking for a way to tune out of the world, at the government's expense. Consequently, most of Kiefer's benefits had been terminated.

He had become homeless because he had forgotten to pay his rent for his portion of Section 8 housing for several months and had been evicted. He failed to make his appointments with the Veterans Administration so that he could find substitute housing and, left to his own design, he had found the tunnel. He had spent almost five weeks scouring the landscape for such a hiding place. When he found his new home, he cleaned out the inside and purchased hornet spray to get rid of the bees' nests. He had also set traps for the small rodents and chased the cats and birds away, although they hadn't stayed away for long.

Keifer had found his mattress on Concord Avenue. It had taken him four hours to drag it to the tunnel. He had accumulated other knickknacks from the dumpsters behind the Marchwood shops, conveniently located near the culvert. His favorite bar, the Fox Den, was also a relatively convenient three-mile walk from the tunnel he now called home. The Fox Den was one of the only bars where Keifer could get service. It was there that he often met up with his friends like Injun Joe. It was a quiet, out-of-the-way place.

The Fox Den only served hotdogs, hamburgers, kielbasa, and hard-boiled eggs. When the deep fryer wasn't broken, they served french fries. Everything was reasonably priced. The proprietor and bartender, Shea, was a not-so-cagey, seventy-three-year-old ex-veteran who would rather serve a bum than a police officer and was known to keep strangers waiting a long, long time before he got them a drink, in order to let them know that they weren't welcome.

However, if you looked downtrodden, were dirty like a workingman, or wore your union shirt, bowling shirt or coveralls in, Shea gave you your third drink or beer for free. This was a custom from his hometown of Brooklyn, New York. Shea saw no reason to comply with the Pennsylvania Liquor Control Board's regulations that said free drinks were prohibited.

Shea made a nice little profit, drank a fair portion of it away in the wee hours of the morning, and occasionally extended a little credit to a veteran of the "real wars."

He rarely had any problems in his place. When something did break out, he had so many wizened, old tough guys that they took care of it without any need for the police. If a guy caused trouble more than one time, he wasn't welcome back. This was an unwritten and unspoken rule that everyone there understood. Shea didn't like the police, from anywhere, and he never had. It was that way where he had grown up, and he saw no reason to change.

When Shea "the boss" announced last call, whether it was 10:30 PM or 3:00 AM, everybody knew that was it. Take out a six pack if you wanted to, but no begging, no pleading, no arguing. The night was over; time to go home.

Keifer was thinking it might be a good night to go down there. He had remembered to pick up his government check from the post office yesterday and had cashed it at the National Penn Bank. He loved the National Penn Bank. They always smiled when he came in, never asked him if he had an account (they knew he didn't), and always honored his check.

In the beginning, the bank employees had asked him for some type of identification. After a time they realized that he had no idea where it was located, and stopped asking.

He reached into his pocket and fingered the few bills and coins he had left. After some initial confusion over where all his money had gone, he finally realized that he had used a portion of his check to buy a pizza, egg rolls, and a liter of Coca Cola yesterday after leaving the bank. He had eaten like a king with no needs. Today, he thought, he still had no needs and no plan. What he did not know was that he was part of another's plan.

CHAPTER 54

K EIFER HAD BEEN able to make his way from Township Line Park to the Fox Den Tavern. To the extent that he could feel at all, he felt sad. The park had been a great deal of fun. He had shared a six pack and his brandy with his young friends. He was truly pleased that they were his friends and that they enjoyed seeing him as much as he enjoyed being with them. In reality, this illusion couldn't have been farther from the truth.

The young men and women at the park were there because they didn't fit in. Most of them abused drugs. All of them drank booze. For the most part, they were underage, underachievers, loner types looking for an identity. They found their identity in the park with the other "losers" who were not into the social scene at the local high school, and as such had formed their own little social clique.

For the most part, they thought of Keifer as an idiot. It never dawned on any of them that they could end up like him. Once upon a time he had been like them, feeling alone and depressed, unathletic, unpopular, and anxious in most social situations.

They had shared marijuana with him that afternoon, and he of course contributed four of his six beers and about half of his brandy to them in return.

They knew Keifer was no good at buying marijuana. In fact, they doubted that he could even figure out the process. Keifer certainly had no idea of its value or that he had traded four or five dollars' worth of very hard-to-obtain alcohol for about a third of its value in marijuana.

Keifer felt sad because the fun was over. His young friends had gone home. He still had some money in his pocket, so he headed for the Fox Den. Now, as he neared its doors, he had a concern. He wasn't sure what it was, but there was a nagging feeling in the back of his neck or perhaps it was his head. He wasn't quite sure.

What he couldn't remember was that the last time he had been at the Fox Den he had been flagged. He had not given the owner a hard time. Once he was flagged, he was out of there. In the back of his mind, he still wasn't sure if he was welcome there. He walked in through the front door and inhaled the familiar smells: stale beer, cigarette and cigar smoke, hamburger grease, and kielbasa. Despite the familiarity of the place, Keifer couldn't place his finger on the cause of the nagging sensation that something was wrong.

He fumbled in his pocket, pulled out what little cash he had left, plopped it on the bar, and waited for the owner to shuffle down to his end of the bar.

The owner gave him three sideways glances before he finally walked down to the end of the bar.

"So how do you be, Kiefer? Have you been behaving yourself?"

Kiefer was slightly stunned. He was not much at conversations and the question about him behaving himself made the hair on the back of his neck stand up.

"Yeah, sure," he said. "I'm doing real good today, real good. You can believe that."

The owner smirked, gave him a small wink, and said, "So what will it be, Kiefer? A pony of blackberry brandy and some Miller from the tap?"

"Yeah, yeah, that would be really good, thanks."

The owner gave a slight shake of his head, shuffled to the other end of the bar, took the blue blackberry brandy bottle, and poured a generous glass. As the dark liquor filled the glass, Shea couldn't help but think he was pouring the favorite of down-on-your-luck drunks. At the same time, he poured a seven-ounce beer glass and held it under the Miller tap. He was proud of the fact that he had Miller, Miller Lite, and even Miller dark beer on tap. Although only a few people ordered the dark, the owner fancied it himself and drank it in copious quantities on Mondays when the bar was closed.

He set the beer and the blackberry brandy down in front of Kiefer, pulled the proper amount of money from the small pile of cash, and deposited it in the strong box under the bar. He had a cash register, of course, but rarely put money in there. Usually he just rang up the food to keep track of what he needed to order. He thought there was no sense in paying the Pennsylvania sales tax on unnecessary income.

A strange guy who had been sitting in the back by himself listening to the juke box and drinking bourbon on the rocks, got up, laid two dollars on the bar, and said, "Thanks, see you soon." Shea nodded and grunted, unaccustomed to receiving tips as the owner. The stranger added, "I'm heading down toward Exton. Does anybody need a ride?"

This actually caught Kiefer's attention. He turned and said, "Naw. If you were going on down later on, I could use a ride, but not just now."

The stranger looked down the bar for a moment and said, "Sure," and slowly walked out. An hour later when Kiefer had run out of money, he regretted refusing the stranger's offer. He knew it would be a long walk back to Marchwood and he knew that trying to hitchhike up Route 100 was going to be useless.

CHAPTER 55

AFTER THREE BLACKBERRY brandies and two beers, Kiefer had run out of money. He didn't want to get in trouble again so he left the Fox Den Tavern and began the long walk home. Somewhere in his brain he realized that he shouldn't be out on Route 100, so he stuck to backyards, back roads, and parks until he came out on Devon Drive in Marchwood. It was quiet and cool. Keifer had no idea of the time. He gauged time by how many cars were in the parking lot in front of Wesos restaurant. He only knew that his day was done and it was time to hit the mattress.

He arrived at the woods in front of the culvert and stopped to listen. Hearing nothing, and seeing nothing, he worked his way into the woods and moved the brush away from the entrance of the tunnel. He stepped inside and pulled the brush back across the front of the tunnel, making the entrance and his home virtually invisible to the outside world. He scraped his feet along the ground until they hit his mattress and he reached down to take the plastic cover off his blanket.

A sound echoed from down the deep in the culvert and Keifer froze. His consumption of alcohol, his use of drugs, and his mild mental illness had served to mute most of his instincts. However, fear is the last instinct an animal loses, and Keifer had not lost his fear. He strained to listen over the buzzing in his ears caused by the drugs and alcohol. He heard the unidentifiable sound again. He remembered that there had been a time when a raccoon had found its way into his living area, but Keifer couldn't remember how he had resolved that. He was really afraid now, and his inability to remember how he had scared off the prior intruder made it worse.

Now there was another sound, and a pinpoint of light so brief that Keifer was not sure that he had actually seen it at all. In spite of his haze, he recognized that the sound had come closer. He thought he saw a tiny flicker of light, like a reflection off something shiny, but he couldn't be sure.

"OK, motherfucker, I have the sharpest-ass knife . . . " Kiefer drooled and lost his thought momentarily as spittle ran down his cheek. "I'm bad at this, motherfucker. Gonna have to stick your ass . . . " Kiefer paused, breathing hard now.

He heard something scrape against the concrete wall; it sounded very close to Keifer and he moaned. "Aaawwrghhhh."

He could hardly believe the sound was emanating from his own mouth. He fumbled around to find his knife. He realized that he had left it where he always did, on top of the mattress. He reached in the dark, but he couldn't locate it.

"Hey, come on now, don't be fuckin' with me . . . just leave me the fuck alone . . . come on now, ya hear?" Kiefer could hear the fear in his own voice, which went from a question to a plea.

There was no response. Keifer could hear no sounds inside the tunnel. Outside of the culvert, he heard the wind, which seemed to be picking up. He strained his eyes to see. Unfortunately, the only light coming in was a faint glimmer from the parking lot lights in the Marchwood parking lot, and they did little to penetrate the gloom. Keifer stood with his back to the light, giving him no real light with which to see.

Suddenly, he felt a stinging in his right hand.

"Ouch," he cried out. He felt like he'd been stung by a bee. "Shit!" Just as suddenly as he'd forgotten about the raccoon, Kiefer remembered his BIC lighter. That's what had scared off that furry little bastard, he thought, the lighter. He reached into his jacket pocket and felt another bee sting, this time on his forearm.

"Owwww . . . damn what the hell is going on?" As he reached into his pocket, his hand felt sticky. He brought it up to his nose and smelled his own blood.

He thought that he saw movement out of the corner of his eye, and as he did, his left shoulder was stung. This time it really hurt and he screamed.

"Ahhhhhhhhhhhhyeeeeee." This scream ended in a tormented cry that faded into a whimper. "Please, stop . . . stop." Keifer started to back up and stumbled over a beach chair, falling to the ground hard.

There was no answer to his plea. Only silence. Nothing moved in the culvert. Even with dulled senses, Keifer could hear his own breathing, smell his own sweat. He pulled himself up on all fours and began to turn toward the entrance to the tunnel. As he began to move, his head struck something hard, something that didn't belong in the middle of his home. He slowly reached his hand out and felt a boot. He pushed at it, but it didn't move. He vaguely remembered that the last time he had been in this position and felt a boot, the next thing that occurred was that the boot had struck him in the head. He pulled back and brought his face to his hands in order to protect himself. However, much to his relief, the anticipated blow never happened.

Being homeless and frequently drunk, Keifer was used to getting a good physical beating now and again. There was an endless variety of mean people in the world who gained some satisfaction in kicking dogs while they were down and trying to humiliate people whose lives had moved far beyond any humiliation a beating could give.

Keifer struggled to his feet and staggered toward the entrance. He felt a piercing pain in his left shoulder, forcing him to recall the sting stabs that had caused him to stumble initially. Before he could reach the culvert's opening, he felt more stinging stabs, this time in the middle of his back and then in his other shoulder. The blows were so great and the pain so searing that he couldn't get enough air in his lungs to cry out.

Once on the ground, a strong hand grabbed him by the hair and forced a rag in his mouth. It caused him to gag, but not enough to cause him to vomit. He could feel blood tricking down his back, his shoulders, and his wrist. He could smell it as well and it caused him to release his bladder, adding to his discomfort as the warm urine soaked his underwear and pants.

He felt a knee on his back and braced for another blow. Instead, he felt a faint prick in the back of his neck, not quite as painful as the earlier bee stings. The pain was virtually lost in his other miseries, but the pain was there nonetheless.

Before long, Keifer retreated mentally back to Vietnam. He saw only pitch blackness except for the illumination caused by the firing rifles and machine guns. The gunfire and exploding mortar shells mixed with an occasional command or scream, sometimes in English, other times in Vietnamese. The Viet Cong column and Kiefer's patrol had walked right into one another and the fighting was fierce.

Fortunately for Keifer and his men, the Viet Cong had initially believed that the Americans were a full column and had attempted to fall back, regroup, and mount an offensive. This had proved costly for them. In the dark, it was hard to tell who was who. This was further complicated by the fact that almost all of the soldiers on both sides were using the Russian-made AK-47, so that the sound of friendly gunfire was the same as the sound of the enemy.

It took the Viet Cong commander nearly nine minutes to figure out that the force he was facing was only a patrol. It took him four minutes to get the word out to mount a counterattack. It took exactly one minute for the Viet Cong soldiers to overrun the position they thought the Americans held. It was only then that they discovered their mistake, and six more of their own soldiers were dead from their own friendly, but deadly, fire. The next thing the Viet Cong knew the Americans were on their flank, firing directly into the now-consolidated Viet Cong force.

The Viet Cong commander made his last mistake when he rallied his troops and headed into the right flank, believing the Americans, in smaller numbers and severely outgunned, would retreat. The Master Sergeant was dead. The Americans had the misfortune of having taken a position in front of a tangle of growth so thick, they could not retreat. Their choices were to fight or surrender, since escape was impossible.

Several of the Americans were wounded. No one in the American patrol knew where the radio was, and essentially no one was in charge. Since the patrol couldn't move, its members simply fought. Private Keifer had wedged himself under a log. The dead body of a Viet Cong soldier had landed on Keifer's legs after being blown into the air by mortar fire. In Keifer's position, he could not bring his weapon to face the enemy, but only train it back on his own soldiers. As luck would have it though, he was also virtually invisible to the Viet Cong because of the dead solider upon him.

As the Viet Cong passed over him and beyond, he would simply fire his weapon point-blank at their backs and kill them. In the confusion, the Viet Cong forces never did figure it out and eventually retreated. They did not retreat, however, until Private Keifer had killed or wounded nine of their soldiers, a number of whom ended up on a pile until they actually covered Keifer's entire body, and he was no longer able to shoot. Keifer estimated that he lay in the pile of dead and half dead bodies for six hours before another patrol had dug him out.

Keifer had never had another thought of that night until now. His mind was drifting and he no longer felt any pain. He had completely lost touch with reality and had no knowledge that he lay bleeding in his home in Marchwood. He began to lose consciousness. He never knew he was a hero. He never knew that the twelve men who had survived the nightmare in Vietnam all owed their lives to him. He began to feel peaceful. His last thought was that he had never wanted to be in the army, anyway.

CHAPTER 56

LIONVILLE PARK WAS practically deserted. It was Sunday morning. Township rules and regulations prohibited the organized use of the park before 1:00 PM on Sundays. A solitary individual was throwing a Frisbee to his dog at Pipeline Field. Other than that, Detective Spagnola and Corporal Kevin Maloney were alone. They rode their bikes through the park.

Spagnola liked Maloney. Maloney was a no-nonsense ex-military kind of guy. He was excellent at defusing drunks intent on beating one another to a pulp, domestic violence situations, and other similar confrontations. A large but not particularly tall man, Maloney had a good sense of humor and was a cop's cop. Although Maloney had started with a GED that he obtained in the military, he later graduated from Nelson Junior College and was attending school part-time to obtain a bachelor of science in criminology. He aspired to be a detective some day.

They pedaled together at a leisurely pace. Maloney was on duty, but Spags had come along just for the heck of it. By the time they returned to the station, they would have covered twenty-six miles of roadways, parks, and trails as part of Maloney's bike patrol rounds.

They both knew that by 1:00 PM, the park would be teeming with activity; boys' and girls' soccer, women's field hockey, and intramural girls' lacrosse games on Pipeline Field. For now, it was quiet and empty. Spagnola had felt the need to get some exercise, and at the same time he had been interested in hearing what Maloney might have to say. Nobody in the department actually knew it, but

Spags and Maloney relied upon one another as sounding boards. Occasionally, on the way home, they stole off for the proverbial cold beer at the Malvern Meeting House. Policemen in Uwchlan Township were prohibited from drinking in public, even at public restaurants within the township limits; so the Meeting House, which was located in a nearby township was "cop friendly," and was the place they frequented.

"Anything in the criminology courses that sheds any light on why someone would do this to another human being?" asked Spagnola. Maloney smiled. Spagnola was constantly making little jabs at him for the fact that he was taking courses in criminology even though he was an experienced police officer. They both knew that was the only way to the top. Attaining the title of detective wasn't as easy as it appeared on TV; you didn't solve some big case and automatically get a promotion. Promotions were based upon seniority, education, and, last but not least, internal police politics.

"The textbooks say that serial killers don't react the same way as normal people. Although there has been a great deal written about them, I think most of it is bullshit. If there was truly a pattern to them, why is it that the United States has nine times as many serial killers as the rest of the world combined? Psychologists say they do not feel the way we feel. The professional psychologists' thinking is that serial killers don't understand love, affection, or almost any emotion other than anger. Sometimes they don't even experience anger. That's how they are able to do what they do. That's why they are so hard to catch.

"Some of these guys have actually been married with families. They lead seemingly normal lives, are relatively intelligent, and have no problem holding down jobs because they can look around and see how other people act and imitate it. At the same time, they are quick and savage because they have no morals to cause them to hesitate in anything that they do." Maloney paused. "Great, now you've got me sounding like a psychiatrist."

Spagnola mulled it over for a few minutes. They rode out of Lionville Park and behind Clemens Shopping Center heading for a little known trail that connected the back of the shopping center with the Wyndham Development. It would take them through a couple of nice fields and past a small pond. They both knew there would be empty beer bottles by the pond because it was a favorite spot for underage drinkers on Saturday night, some of whom didn't bother to clean up.

"Why pick these lowlife bums? Why not go after a real citizen, someone who gave them a struggle, someone who gave them a challenge, someone who might fight back? How much of a thrill can it be to kill a guy like Injun Joe?"

"Maybe he's not looking for a challenge," said Maloney as they passed by the pond, scattering three deer that had been drinking by the pond's edge.

"Maybe we're his challenge. Maybe the cops are his game. Maybe being smarter than us, being able to shove it in our faces, is what he's looking for. Maybe that's the kick to this guy. Maybe it's about the messages. I know, I know. I'm not supposed to know there was a message, and I wouldn't be telling anybody, but maybe that's this guy's thing. He might be leaving the messages to throw us off. Could be that he just sits back and watches us scurry around trying to figure out messages that don't have any meaning or bearing on the murders themselves."

The cyclists moved into another development along a road that would eventually lead to Uwchlan Trail.

"Well, we don't know if he's serial; we're guessing that. We're going on the instincts of the medical examiner, but this does smell of a ritual killing. The problem is that there is no indication that there was more than one person involved, which seems unlikely. The docs estimate that the mutilations must have taken up to an hour and a half. No one can figure out how one person hauled that guy up into the tree. One of the officers thought it might have been done with ropes and pulleys.

"The docs are still trying to figure out why there aren't any rope burns if that's what happened. They think if it was done with ropes and pulleys that this son of a bitch actually brought padding along, put the padding under Injun Joe's armpits, the ropes around the pads, and hoisted his sorry ass up into the tree.

"If that's the case, we not only have one sick sonofabitch on our hands, we have someone who travels with all the right party gear. This guy would also know a fair amount about anatomy, a fair amount about police work, and just how to get Injun Joe in the car without any apparent struggle and without anybody noticing." Spagnola had been running this over in his mind since the previous day when the body was found.

"Not a party I'd want to attend," Maloney added.

Maloney then turned left out onto Dowlin Forge Road where the sidewalk ended, and they had to cycle onto the street. They both increased their pace so they'd miss the Sunday morning church crowd as they raced to make it to 10:30 AM mass.

CHAPTER 57

S PAGNOLA AND MALONEY continued their bike patrol until Maloney had completed his rounds. It was now break time for him. Spagnola, despite his day off, went to the locker room, showered, changed, and fifteen minutes later was at his desk. He checked his voice mail messages first, his e-mail second, and his reports last.

He listened to the phone messages. Nothing. He checked the e-mail quickly, deleting all the advertisements and responding to the more important ones with one-line answers. The reports turned out to be the most intriguing.

A supplement to the initial medical examiner's report had been faxed to him the evening before. There had been additional findings in the morning with regard to the murder of Injun Joe. Despite the mutilation, the medical examiner's office had determined his identity prior to calling it a day on Saturday and had transmitted this information telephonically to Spagnola the preceding evening. The supplemental report indicated a possibility that Injun Joe had been subdued chemically and anesthetized prior to his murder. A nick, consistent with that of a hypodermic needle, had been found in the bi-section of his left quadricep muscle. Unfortunately, Injun Joe had used a lot of hypodermic needles in his day, so it was also possible that he had recently injected himself with a chemical substance.

As the medical examiner had put it though, "For a person who was mutilated and tortured prior to his death, there was very little indication of restraint (handcuffs, tape, rope, or the like) and no defensive wounds." This was a sure indication that Injun Joe had been unconscious at the time that the killer had done most of his gruesome acts.

The more intriguing matter was the fact that a trace of seminal fluid had been found at the scene. The sample was small, however, and the medical examiner was concerned that testing it would destroy it.

As any good cop knew, if you tested a sample and destroyed it, defense counsel could successfully argue that the test itself was inadmissible in court because the defense had no way to contradict it and no way to independently test it. Luckily, he thought, that was not Spags's decision to make. The dilemma would have to be resolved by the district attorney's office and consultation with the medical examiner. In the meantime, the seminal fluid would be held by the medical examiner, tagged, dated, and preserved, protecting both the sample and the chain of custody.

It could become important, Spagnola thought to himself, but only in the event we have a suspect. At the moment, they did not have anything and based upon his examination of the scene, the medical examiner's findings, and the reports of the other officers, there was no suspect on the horizon.

Detective Spagnola reviewed the facts in his own mind. The killer had known Injun Joe personally or known about Injun Joe. It didn't seem possible that this was a random act against a random person.

The killer (or killers) was familiar with the area and knew that he would be undisturbed for several hours in the park, so long as he didn't make noise, light a fire, or leave a vehicle conspicuously parked in the parking lot. That one troubled Spagnola. Where did the killer(s) park the vehicle? There were no tire marks in the fields around where Injun Joe's body had been left. If a car had been parked in the parking lot for any length of time, the police in Upper Uwchlan would have noticed it and investigated. The park was closed at dusk, and the rules were strictly enforced by the township. The township refused to allow people in the parks after dusk because it created problems like underage drinking, narcotics, sex, vandalism, and unwanted noise. He made a note on his handheld dictation device to contact the Upper Uwchlan police, check their logs, and see if in fact the park had been secured on rounds during the course of the evening. Between the medical examiner's reports and the police reports regarding the park, perhaps he could put together a good timeline and make further conclusions from there.

Spags continued to make mental and verbal notes. He knew that the killer had come prepared. He must have had ropes and pulleys, a method of transporting an unconscious or semiconscious person from a distant location to the middle of the park, tools to torture and mutilate the victim, gloves, a mask, perhaps even a water-tight outfit so as not to become contaminated with the victim's blood. Contracting AIDS was definitely a possibility in picking on someone like Injun Joe. The blood reports had not come back yet, but there was a good chance Joe had contracted the HIV virus through his use of drugs.

The killer (or killers) had been strong and resourceful. With the use of ropes and pulleys and perhaps a wheelbarrow to transport the body, the actions of the killer or killers had required significant strength and determination.

Spagnola glanced at his watch. Time had flown. He'd been sitting at his desk for over two hours and recognized it was time to move on. There wasn't much to be done with the Injun Joe case at this point. He hoped there would be some more forensics, hoped that the officers canvassing the neighborhood would find someone who had seen or heard something that would give then information from which they could gather more details. He knew this is how it worked, how it always worked. Now he had to move on.

He neatly tucked his notes into a folder, pulled the tape from his dictation device, and put the folder in a filing cabinet drawer on the left side of desk inside of another folder. It was larger and thicker than the case of Elaine Kauffman. Spagnola was good at compartmentalizing. He compartmentalized the Injun Joe case, putting it on hold, and automatically began thinking in terms of Elaine Kauffman, William Kauffman, and the events surrounding the robbery, murder, and attempted murder within their home.

Three new police reports had been placed on top of the file. He scanned them briefly and found nothing interesting. He picked up the phone and called Brandywine Hospital. He was able to get through to the fourth floor ICU and spoke with the nurse in charge.

"Good afternoon, this is Detective Spagnola from the Uwchlan Township Police Department. I'm the homicide detective investigating the murder of Elaine Kauffman and the attempted murder of William Kauffman. The case is Code Glenmoore-K." There was a pause on the line as the nurse pulled up security codes on her computer. Once she had done this, she matched the security code for information with the security code words just given to her by Spagnola to make sure she had authorization to release information.

Satisfied with the security code, she came on the line. "OK, Detective Spagnola, what would you like to know?" she asked.

"Can you tell me whether or not Mr. Kauffman has regained consciousness and if he is able to speak with me?" There was another pause as the head nurse scrawled down through the information going to the last entry.

"The last entry was at 8:00 AM. The physician reports that Mr. Kauffman had briefly regained consciousness but was slightly delirious, in all likelihood from the effects of the morphine drip. I can't tell you whether he is awake right now, but if you're asking me, if he's on a morphine drip and in and out of consciousness, talking to him might not make a lot of sense right now. Do you want to speak to a staff physician?" asked the nurse.

"No. I think I'll just stop by. It's 12:45 PM, who should I see when I get there?"

"Nurse Wadkins," she responded.

"And just who is this Nurse Wadkins?" he asked.

"Me," she said coyly.

CHAPTER 58

PAUL GARDINER HAD loaded his dog and his two children into his Jeep Cherokee to complete his "honey do" list at the Marchwood Shopping Center. Everything was open on Sunday morning. His daughter had completed her first year of soccer and was excited to get to her game because her team was doing well. His son, Kevin, was six, playing LYA soccer for the first time, and he was so excited he always slept in his uniform the night before a game and awoke at 6:30 AM ready to play.

The children's games weren't until three o'clock in the afternoon, but their mom had already fed them, and Paul knew the hardware store would be open before the game. The family dog was a golden lab named Rufus, and he was always excited about getting a ride with the kids in the car. He was seated in the front passenger seat, and the children were securely strapped in the back. Paul had picked up a cup of coffee for himself and juices for the kids at the local Wawa, and Rufus had his artificial bone to chew on, so everyone was happy.

Paul turned left into a parking spot to the far right side of the hardware store, where they kept the sale items out on the sidewalk. Before Paul had completed his turn, Rufus dropped his bone and began to growl. This startled Paul as he had rarely heard the dog make such a noise. Rufus usually only growled like this at night when something with a smell he didn't like approached the house. Paul's first instinct was to check the backseat and make sure the children had not thrown anything at him or hurt him in any way.

The children were busy with their juices and hadn't even noticed the growl. Paul looked back to the dog and saw that his tail was down, the fur on the back of his neck was standing up, and he was pressing his open mouth against the window.

"Hey, what is it Rufus?" Paul asked the dog as if he expected an answer.

The dog whined.

Paul exited the car and walked around to Rufus's side of the car. At this point, Rufus was beside himself and was actually jumping in place trying to get out of the Jeep.

"Rufus, sit, good dog, sit. Sit or this door stays closed."

The dog obeyed and sat wagging his tail, impatience in his eyes.

When Paul opened the door, Rufus wasted no time and ran through the parking lot straight into the woods, where he started barking frantically. Rufus jumped around like the ground was on fire and looked occasionally over his shoulder for Paul. He cracked the windows of the jeep, checked the children one more time, and locked the doors with his remote control.

"Be right back guys. Do not unbuckle your belts," Paul said. He put his coffee on the hood of the car and walked slowly toward the woods, where Rufus was showing no sign of slowing down in his frenetic behavior or his barking binge.

"Hey, Rufus, what do you see, boy?"

The dog whined in response.

When Paul arrived at the edge of the woods, he hesitated. Looking around, he saw no one nearby and realized that the closer he walked toward the woods, the farther Rufus went into the woods. Being allergic to poison ivy and scared to hell of bees, Paul did not look forward to stepping into the woods, even though he was wearing a pair of long jeans and a sweatshirt. He stayed at the edge of the woods and peered in.

Rufus was now a good twenty feet into the woods and his actions had not changed. He kept looking back expecting Paul to follow him, and apparently he was not willing to go much farther if Paul didn't back him up.

Paul glanced back at his Jeep and could see his children, still going after their juice with elongated straws.

"Come on, Rufus, time to go. Let the raccoon go, boy. Come on."

At this, the dog gave up waiting and ran twenty more feet into the woods. He began jumping about in a sort of semicircle, barking and whining alternately. Paul did not want to follow Rufus all the way in but was willing to go another ten feet or so, which he did. The leaves on most of the trees were still intact so the light did not penetrate well. Paul waited until his eyes adjusted and then strained to see what the dog was so excited about.

All at once, the world became very quiet. Rufus had stopped barking. He stood twitching and letting out an occasional whine, as if someone had stepped on his paw. Paul could hear, before he could actually see, a pair of hornets flying about the shoulders of the man standing, his back to a tree, directly in front of Paul. The man wore a hat and had one foot propped almost in back of him, in a pose reminiscent of one of those black cut out figures Paul had seen leaned up against a tree in his neighbor's yard. Despite the morning chill, a bead of sweat ran down the side of Paul's head.

Paul stared straight at the man, but the man did not react. With the sun filtering through the back of the trees and both Paul and the man standing in the shade, it was difficult to make out details. Paul's eyes tried to adjust to the strange lighting.

When Paul's eyes finally adjusted, they fell upon the figure of Kiefer Barney. Kiefer stood some twenty-five feet away from Paul, back against a tree. Kiefer's hands were at his sides and his shoulders slighted slumped. He stared straight ahead, just to the left of Paul. Keifer neither heard Rufus's whining nor saw the man in front of him.

Paul instinctively began backing up. As he did so, he took furtive glances over his shoulders to assure himself that his children were still seated safely inside the Jeep. Once he had reached the car, he extracted his cell phone and dialed 9-1-1. Less than three minutes later, the first police car arrived, siren wailing and lights blinking.

Kiefer saw none of it. Kiefer heard none of it. Kiefer was dead.

CHAPTER 59

PATROLMAN BART DEGEN was dispatched from the station and raced across Route 100, turning left into the shopping center and coming to a controlled, but screeching, halt. He got out of his car slowly removing his sunglasses in the process and surveying the scene. Despite regulations, he did not don his hat.

His instinct to run toward the scene was suppressed by his training. At the police academy he had been trained by a wily old sergeant who had few rules, but one of them was, never run, unless you're chasing somebody. He had been taught that far too many police officers raced into a situation, failing to register potential danger and ended up injured or sometimes dead, when a slow walk and a good look around might have avoided just that.

"If you walk slowly and look careful . . . might just go home to your family at night . . . every night," Sarge had told him.

A man stood by a jeep with a leashed dog at his side, the dog obviously perturbed.

"Sir, would you mind putting the dog in the back of the Jeep? He seems pretty upset, and dogs don't always take well to strangers, especially ones in uniform."

Paul looked a little confused. Finally, he mumbled something and put Rufus in the back of the Jeep. His children had gotten out of their seatbelts and hung outside his driver's window, while he reached over and patted them on the head.

Sirens wailed in the distance, the sounds coming from the north on Route 100. Paul said, "You know, the dog was barking like mad, I just never thought . . . he was acting really crazy."

"Are you the gentleman who called 911?" asked the patrolman.

"Yes. He's over there, in the woods. I think he's . . . " Paul turned and looked at his children. "I think he's finished."

"OK. You just take it easy. There'll be several officers along in a minute and an ambulance too. You just stay here with your children and I'll take a look."

The officer continued his slow walk, looking left and right and attracting far too much attention. Shoppers were congregating in front of the Marchwood Hardware Store, and those people at the food market began to walk toward the officer as well.

He turned slightly, and using his most authoritative voice said, "Everyone, please stay back. This is an official police investigation. Please obey my orders and do not come any closer."

The curiosity seekers stayed where they were, but almost as soon as he turned his back and headed toward the woods, the bystanders began to creep forward. Patrolman Degen undid the snap on his holster and put his hand on the handle of his gun. His other hand held his radio as he made a transmission.

"This is Patrolman Degen. I am at the Marchwood scene. I am satisfied that there is no immediate danger, and I am approaching the woods to see the condition of the man reported to be injured or dead. I am going to keep this line open until backup has arrived."

Degen stepped into the woods, scanned the area around him, and listened. Other than the buzz of flies and the chatter of the crowd at his back, there was only the sound of approaching sirens. Nothing else moved, not even the dying leaves on the trees. He could make out the form of a man ahead of him and to his right, who appeared to be leaning against a tree. The man wore a small hat and his hair appeared to be matted.

"Sir, I am Patrolman Degen of the Uwchlan Township Police Department. I am here to give you assistance. If you have any kind of a weapon, please put it where I can see it and drop it to the ground. Please answer that you understand me."

There was no response.

"Sir, if you are injured and unable to talk, please move your head up and down to signal that you can hear me and understand what I am saying."

Patrolman Degen took three short steps closer to Kiefer. There was no response. Patrolman Degen removed his pistol from his holster and clipped his radio onto his belt. He slowly raised the pistol, stepping two paces to his left and three more paces forwarded, bringing his left hand over so that both of his hands were now on this gun, which was aimed at Kiefer's feet.

"Please don't make any sudden moves, sir. I'm here to help you." Degen moved two steps closer and aimed the gun at the ground. At this distance, it was clear that Kiefer was not conscious. Two steps later, it was clear that he was dead.

"Shit." Degen took a deep breath. Just to be sure, he carefully stepped forward and put his hand on Kiefer's cold, dead throat. "Goddamn. Goddamn." He backed away slowly, trying to be careful not to upset the scene any more than he already had. The sirens were close and sounded like they might have pulled into the parking lot, but Degen, being slightly stunned, couldn't tell for sure. He instinctively reached for his radio, forgetting that he had left it on and the line open. "Don't think we'll need that ambulance. This guy is dead . . . and cold."

CHAPTER 60

S PAGNOLA WAS HEADED toward the Route 30 bypass when the
call came in that the situation in the Marchwood Shopping
Center appeared to be a homicide.

"Hey, Detective," called the desk duty volunteer, a retired
cop from Pittsburgh. "They got a cold one for you over at the
Marchwood Shopping Center. Looks like a homicide crime spree.
Somebody must think we're in the big city out here."

The volunteer's sense of humor was not only poor, but thirty
years in the city police force had made his humor dark as well.

Spagnola was not amused. He carefully turned around, pulled
over, put his light on top of his vehicle, and sped back toward
Marchwood, his mind racing.

What the hell was going on? Spags thought. This isn't goddamned
North Philly!

CHAPTER 61

D ETECTIVE SPAGNOLA STOOD in the parking lot staring into the woods. After taking a cursory look at Keifer Barney's corpse and the surrounding area, he'd made a judgment call to bring in the state police. The state police had crime scene investigators in a special homicide unit and they had arrived less than an hour after his call. The crime scene investigators were now walking the grid. They were carefully placing little flags with wire-tipped endings at various points in the woods itself and all the way out to the parking lot. They wanted to be sure that every area within fifty feet of Keifer, in every direction possible, was being carefully walked, examined, marked with flags, and photographed.

Detective Spagnola knew that Uwchlan Township did not have the resources to create a grid, and he felt it was absolutely necessary to have one done under the circumstances.

Unlike the homicide involving Injun Joe in the park, this wooded area seemed ideal for a good thorough crime scene investigation. It was highly unlikely that anyone had walked through this crime scene from the time that Keifer had been literally nailed to the tree and the time of his body's discovery. In addition, unlike the park where deer, dogs, raccoons, squirrels, and birds were evident from their droppings, the proximity to the parking lot kept most animals and birds away from the little culvert. Kiefer himself had kept the rest away.

It was now close to one thirty and it had become rather warm. Spagnola had removed his windbreaker and placed it at the back of his car. The crowd had grown from about four dozen people when he arrived to over three hundred now, and the township police's main focus was on crowd control and were currently trying to get the general parking unsnarled so that people could actually access the stores in the shopping center.

Detective Spagnola managed to get wooden horses in place to keep the crowd from encroaching on the scene. Men, women, children, and dogs had flocked to the barricade in hopes of getting a view and, in some instances, a picture of the homicide scene, or better yet, a picture of the deceased Keifer himself. In life, Keifer had attracted very little attention. He tried to be inconspicuous and he thought he had done a good job. Now he was the center of a tremendous investigation and controversy.

The coroners had been alerted that an autopsy would be necessary, the sooner the better. The body had not yet been released to them, but a technician from the coroner's office had come to the scene and taken measurements, body temperature, and four rolls of film of Keifer's body before retreating into his van and leaving the scene. In his adult life, Keifer's picture had only been taken three times, two by newspaper reporters and one by accident. Before he was laid to rest, his fame in death would result in hundreds of pictures being taken of him, as well as a movie of his autopsy.

It had not been difficult to identify Keifer because of his clothing. A number of the people who had gathered in the parking lot told the police that they knew who he was and had given the police his name. It was interesting that no one had any idea where he lived. An off-duty Uwchlan Township police officer who had picked up Keifer a few times for public drunkenness (but had never arrested him) had come to the scene and identified the body. The officer was unsure whether or not Keifer had any relatives or anyone else who could identify the body officially for the coroner's records.

Kiefer didn't appear to be carrying a wallet, and although they had not investigated his home in the culvert, Spagnola's suspicion was that he had no form of identification.

The younger of the two crime scene investigators strolled over to Spagnola and nodded.

"We'll probably be here for another two to two and a half hours, but the body can be moved anytime you want. We've moved the grid out to about twenty-five feet from the body and have all of the information that we need. We simply ask that whoever goes in and takes the body is accompanied by one of us so that we can account for the footprints and any trace of evidence they might leave accidentally. We'd ask that they not be allowed to smoke, chew gum, or bring any food or beverage with them when they remove the body."

"I understand," said Spagnola. "These guys are professionals too, but I'll remind them and I'll make sure that one of you guys is present anytime they go in or out of the woods."

Spagnola knew that the removal of the body was going to be problematic. Whoever had done this had used a combination of bailing wire and concrete nails to secure Keifer to the tree. From a distance it gave the appearance that he was simply leaning up against the tree, one foot forward of the other, knee slightly bent in the other leg, staring out and away from his position. In reality, nails had been secured to the middle of the tree in a triangle with the spikes facing outwards. Keifer had been impaled upon them. Pulling Keifer off the spikes was not going to be easy or pleasant, Spags thought.

In order to keep his shoulders straight, a small strand of wire had been run around his chest and the back of the tree, concealed by his jacket. His left foot had been placed up against the tree with his knee bent, and his foot had been nailed to the tree with what appeared to be a six- or eight-inch spike. His other foot was securely on the ground where it had been wedged between two small stakes, and then his foot nailed into the ground at the toe and at the heel of his shoe. The nails had simply been nailed right into the dry earth. A small hat had been placed on his head at a cocked angle as if he was trying to obtain a look. A scarf had been placed around his neck to conceal the other string of bailing wire. The other wire had been ran around his neck and then nailed to the back of the tree.

In essence, whoever had done this had spent a great deal of time and effort to stage the scene. Although the scene was quite different from that of Injun Joe, Detective Spagnola sensed that the same forces had been at work here. The question that kept coming through his mind was, why? Why would anybody do this? What, if anything, did it all mean? Spags admitted to himself that he had no idea.

CHAPTER 62

DAVEY HARRIS WAS sweeping the parking lot around the Exton Eatery. He took furtive glances down at the scene below in the Marchwood Shopping Center as he observed Detective Spagnola.

"Hey, hey, Davey," called a customer getting into his car with his wife and children after a Sunday morning brunch. Davey turned and gave a half wave and said, "Hey, hey, hey." He liked the way that sounded. He had heard it once in a movie about a mentally challenged man and thought it fit his persona perfectly.

Davey Harris was not what he seemed. In fact, he was not Davey Harris at all. He had been born forty-four years earlier as Richard Leelund Walsh. He had received an undergraduate degree at SUNY Albany and his MBA at New York University. He had worked his way up through the ranks of Trimble, Kobal, and McFearson, one of the least well-known and one of the most successful small brokerage firms on Wall Street. But that had been a long time ago.

For the past four and a half months, he was a mentally challenged middle-aged man who cleaned up at the Exton Eatery and lived in Section 8 subsidized housing, two blocks from the bus stop in West Chester.

He had chosen the Exton Eatery over four other restaurants for his employment so he would be close to the police station. His choice of location put him close to public transportation. He would be close to the Pennsylvania Turnpike. At the Exton Eatery, he would be close to disappearing again if he needed. Keep your friends close; keep your enemies closer, he thought.

Davey didn't like all of the attention that was going on below. He didn't like the apparent crime wave that had hit the area. He had chosen this area because it had a low crime rate. He had chosen not to have a car and to take the identity of a mentally challenged man, as there was very little chance he would be stopped, arrested, or identified in any manner. He was just a harmless retarded man making a living sweeping floors and cleaning up with his trademark "hey, hey, hey" when anybody called his name.

There was one problem, one large problem. Davey had seen Keifer Barney the night before. He knew where Keifer Barney lived. He had actually followed Keifer Barney at one point to see where he lived and what he was doing. He could be retarded and inquisitive at the same time. People very rarely noticed him. He hid in plain sight.

The problem was he had seen someone else too. Davey had little doubt that the other person had killed Keifer Barney. He did not recognize the other person but he probably had seen things that would help the police catch the killer. Unfortunately, he couldn't do this. Prior to coming to Exton, he had spent eighteen months living in his own cave in the forest preserve just north of the Indiana University of Pennsylvania. During this entire period of time, he had no contact with his wife or children. He had no contact with his previous employers. He had no contact with his parents, friends, or relatives, save one. Davey had only communicated with Kenny Silverman. He and Kenny had gone to grade school together and then junior high. Kenny had gone on to go to a private high school in Connecticut, and they had not seen each other in a number of years. He thought for that reason it would be ideal to contact Kenny for the purposes he needed him.

When he had called Kenny and said, "This is your longtime friend," Kenny's response was quick and measured. "You're not a longtime friend, you're a friend I had a long time ago," he said.

Despite the rough beginning, Kenny had agreed to do what he asked. Every three months he would call Kenny and assure him that he was alive and doing well. Kenny would then place a small ad in the *Baldwin Citizen* the last week of the month. It was in the personal section and read simply, "Missing you, the Turtles."

He had set this up with his family before his departure and let them know that he was alive and doing well, and could not communicate with them without putting them in serious jeopardy and himself at risk with both the law and the bad guys.

He was, in fact, between a rock and a hard place, and had been for years. He was not a bad person but a victim of circumstance and, at least for now, was left to live out his life pretending to be a retarded man sweeping floors.

He felt guilty, not about what he had done, but rather what he had seen and was unable to communicate. He'd figure it out. He was good at figuring things out.

"Hey, Davey, how's it going?" came from another young man about to get into his car.

"Hey, hey, hey," Davey called out as he gave a half wave. *Hey, hey, hey, indeed,* Davey thought. It was going to be another bad day in a long line of bad days. He knew he had to make the call, regardless of the cost.

CHAPTER 63

DAVEY DIALED THE phone number of the Uwchlan Township Police. He had looked it up in the yellow pages because he did not want to get involved in using the 911 number. He was as nervous as a school kid about to give a speech before the class. He wasn't sure if it was the fear of getting caught or the fear of not helping catch a killer. Either way he was committed to seeing it through.

Davey had put together a small bucket of semicooled grease from the trap behind the grille. He didn't know how much the police could find out about him from his use of the cell phone, even if he wore gloves and wiped the phone down when he was done, but he believed that the grease would do the trick. His plan was to make the call, turn off the phone, drop it in the bucket, and put the bucket in the dumpster. It would have to do, he thought, it would have to do.

Davey walked behind the dumpster and positioned himself where he could see if anyone was coming, but no one from any angle (except directly above) could see him. The parking lot was always noisy, not just because of the cars coming and going, but it was positioned next to Route 100, and the noise of the trucks never let up. He took a deep breath, pulled the phone out of his pocket, and flipped it open. He pressed the red button, was sure to mute the sound, and waited for a signal, which seemed to take forever. His heart was pounding and he began to sweat. Every noise was magnified in Davey's ears, and he resolved twice to walk away and toss the phone, before he finally got the signal.

"Uwchlan Township Police," the voice stated, with a slight tinge of menace and a dash of boredom.

"You are looking into the murder of a young man at the Marchwood Shopping Center." Davey made no attempt to hide his real voice.

The sound of an electronic beep came through the line, reminding Davey that the call was being recorded, as was the practice with all police departments on incoming calls.

"Yes," came the police officer's response, now interested, no boredom, trying to restrain himself so as not to cause the caller to hang up.

"I need to give you some information and I would like you to write it down. Please don't interrupt me or I will lose my nerve and hang up, OK?"

"Yes, sir," the officer responded, not sure if he was required at this point to tell the caller that the conversation was being recorded, or if the fact that the caller wanted him to write it down made the warning unnecessary. The officer decided that he might well frighten this guy off the line if he pointed out the recording aspect, so he decided to take his chances and remained quiet.

"I'm listening and I'm writing. Go ahead and take your time."

The comment about taking his time made Davey wonder if they were in the process of tracing the call, and he wasn't sure how that worked with a cell phone. He decided to go forward, be quick, and take his chances.

"I saw a person, dressed completely in black enter the woods where they found Keifer, about ten o'clock the evening he was killed. The person was not very big, looked like maybe five foot ten but definitely not six feet tall. The person in black had something mechanical with him. I can't tell what it was, but I think it's important. Let them know that. OK?"

"Yes, sir, is there anything else you would like to tell me?"

Davey looked at the phone as if in disbelief.

"Uh, no, like what?"

"Do you know the name of the person in black or where they live?" asked the officer in a very calm and matter-of-fact way.

This was the last straw for Davey; he felt like a caged animal. He fumbled with the cell phone, finally got it turned off, dropped it in the cooling semi-liquid, semi-solid grease, took a glance around the lot, and dropped the grease can in the dumpster. He carefully removed his gloves, put them in a plastic trash bag, and stuffed them into his apron for disposal when he got back to the room he called home.

Heart pounding, head spinning, he became Davey again. He saw Mr. Belvedere exit his car about fifty feet away.

"Hey, hey, Mr. B!"

"Hey, hey, yourself, Davey. You behaving yourself?"

I'm not sure, Mr. *B*, I'm really not sure, Davey thought.

CHAPTER 64

THE CRIME SCENE investigators from the state police determined quickly and conclusively that there were three separate and distinct sets of footprints within the grid after eliminating Officer Degen, Paul Gardiner, Detective Spagnola, and themselves. The one set of footprints belonged to Keifer. They matched his shoes; they matched the shoe prints leading to the culvert and away from the culvert, apparently made the preceding day when Keifer left his home.

The other two sets of footprints created a problem for them. One set was clearly a pair of sneakers. They were either a size nine in a male or a size ten in a female. The other footprints were made by a work boot, wide print, thick sole, multiple grooves. Determining the size foot of a work boot was much more difficult.

The crime scene investigators knew that many people wore heavy socks with work boots and often times wore no socks at all with sneakers. This could affect an entire shoe size difference between a conventional sneaker and a heavy-duty work boot. This boot apparently had a steal toe and from its brand name, would be very popular among workers and potentially even hikers in the area. The work boot appeared to be a size eleven male or twelve female. They told this to Detective Spagnola and said that they would need to do some testing to see why the boot prints appeared odd in their configuration.

The younger of the two crime scene investigators, Walter Hoops, thought it might be possible that the boot print belonged to someone with one leg significantly shorter than the other, or a person with a disability that caused the person to walk in an odd fashion such as a person with back problems, a knee injury, or suffering from rickettsia.

Detective Spagnola, as usual, was skeptical of all of the explanations. He was also skeptical of the crime scene. He felt deep down that this was the work of the same person who had tortured, brutally murdered, and disfigured Injun Joe. While it was fully possible that this was the work of more than one person, there was no proof from the original crime scene involving Injun Joe of multiple sets of footprints. Spags knew that could mean that the killer had enlisted the aid of a second person; that someone had come upon the scene before, during, or after the act, or that second person had been present at the first crime scene but they left no traces that they had been able to find. If this person was in fact a serial murderer, it was odd that they would act in concert with a second person. Not completely out of the question, but odd. If they were ritualistic killers, it would make sense that there was more than one. The question was, what messages would there be on or about the body of this victim?

When the crime scene investigators had packed up and left, Detective Spagnola walked the grid three more times. He did so as slowly and methodically as had the investigators, but he did so at different angles and different directions and with a different pair of eyes. He was looking for something that stood out. Something out of the ordinary. Something left, something dropped (purposely or by accident). While he did this, every inch of the culvert was being searched by the Chester County detectives' office. They had sent two detectives over to assist and they had been there for four hours. The detectives had first set up in the same fashion as a grid; had their photographer take pictures of everything in there from the moss-coated concrete ceiling to the articles of furniture and clothing that Keifer had placed in there to make it his home. Each item was then catalogued, tagged, bagged, and taken out to the evidence van. The uniformed police of Uwchlan Township had been given the task of interviewing the owners of stores, persons in the parking lot, and surrounding homes to determine if anyone had seen or heard anything unusual. The interviews had proven fruitless over the first five hours. They would continue on interviewing for several days until everyone in the area who lived or worked in proximity of the culvert had been interviewed. Detective Spagnola would then determine if anyone required a second interview, and he would conduct the second interview himself.

With Keifer's body now removed and on its way to the coroner's office, Detective Spagnola walked around the tree three, four, and then five times. He stopped at different locations, looked up, looked down, stepped back to the side, and tried to determine exactly how Keifer had been attached to the tree and whether or not it was the work of one or more people. Keifer was not very heavy. Spagnola guessed that he weighed less than one hundred fifty pounds.

Once again, he thought, the question was, why?

CHAPTER 65

S PAGNOLA SAT AT his desk shuffling police reports. There were details in the Kauffman homicide that made no sense. There were other details that fit the theory of robbery/murder too neatly. There were a number of things that troubled him.

He had learned a long time ago that spouses always have two prime ingredients to be a homicide suspect: 1) motive and 2) opportunity. One of his professors at Quantico had said all spouses have motive, you just have to find out what it is. Spagnola had thought that this was just cynicism from a guy who had been divorced three times. Having been divorced himself, Spagnola recognized it wasn't cynicism; it was a cold hard fact. Might have to dig for it; might have to probe for it; might never even find it, but motive was just below the surface in any strained relationship.

Putting the impossibility of Bill Kauffman's involvement aside, the theory of a staged robbery in order to commit a murder had holes in it as well. Ordinary citizens didn't commit burglaries and had no clue what the difference was between a burglary and a robbery, and clues that they created in the staging of these crimes were usually fairly obvious.

The break in at the Kauffman's involved the breaking of an outside window located in a door and the turning of an improperly located dead bolt switch to gain entrance. Most people trying to stage a robbery would break the glass from the inside, leaving the shards outside or perhaps the smart ones picking up pieces and putting them inside the house. Of course the scatter patterns from the window itself would show the blow came from the inside. In the Kauffman home it was quite obvious that the glass had been struck with a hard object and probably fairly large, and that all of the glass had landed inside the house. The burglary (burglary being the act of entering the dwelling place of another with the intent to commit a crime) seemed to have gone bad when the burglar awakened the sleeping Mrs. Kauffman and shot her.

From the illustration of Mr. Kauffman, who lay in the foyer critically wounded, it appeared that the ill-fated burglary turned into a second opportunity for homicide when Bill Kauffman entered his home and surprised the burglar a second time.

Certain facts didn't fit the pattern. People who committed robberies have nothing in common with burglars at all. Burglary is not usually accomplished by someone with a weapon. To the contrary, most burglars want to get in and get out unseen, unheard, and without confrontation—their livelihood and freedom dependent upon it.

In the case of a burglary, there are no witnesses. Usually the burglar or burglars get in, get out, and have a pre-arranged fence to purchase what they've stolen for $0.20 to $0.30 on a dollar. Jewelry, small stereo systems, guns, and silverware are the common items for the thieves.

Robbery is a little bit more personal. The robber assaults the victim face-to-face with a gun, knife, or sometimes just by bludgeoning them to the ground, and literally runs away with their personal property. Burglaries gone bad are marked by the burglar being identified. Robberies gone bad, on the other hand, often result in serious injury or even death to the victim.

Spagnola knew that most burglars were not robbers; most burglars were not murderers; most burglars were not rapists. On the other hand, many robbers were murderers and many robbers were rapists. Robbery is a severe act of violence even when the victim was physically unharmed. The trauma of having a knife pointed in your face or a gun stuck to the side of your head was about as violent as it could get, short of assault or rape.

Burglary victims often felt betrayed. They often felt violated because someone had gone through their personal things in their houses. They are often depressed from the loss of valuables that couldn't be replaced. Robbery victims needed psychotherapy. Their world has been shattered by a stranger who caught them by surprise for no godly purpose and held their lives in criminal hands.

Spagnola knew all of this and it bothered him. It was not as if every crime fit a certain pattern, but this one was out of kilt.

From an inventory of the known items in the house, it was clear that jewelry, a DVD player, and a silverware set had been stolen. It remained to be seen whether or not any cash or other items were missing, and until Bill Kauffman recovered, there was little hope of discovering that. Even when he recovered, it was doubtful he would have knowledge of the household items as deep in detail as his very organized wife, Elaine. They had gone through her papers and she had kept things such as warranties for appliances, televisions, VCRs, DVDs, and the like. From a recent receipt, it was obvious that a DVD player was missing. From the same set of documents, they had determined that some jewelry were missing but couldn't determine whether or not other pieces were held in a safe deposit box, hidden under a bed, or had simply been sold or traded for other jewelry.

There were approximately two dozen known fences in Chester County. There were a dozen other businessmen suspected of fencing items from time to time. Most of the fences were businessmen. They owned small appliance stores, hardware stores, machine shops, or did repairs on stereo equipment and the like. Two of the known fences operated shops from which they sold lawnmowers, tractors, and the like. Most of them were not career or full-time criminals. Most of them were businessmen who saw opportunity in buying low and selling high.

Society did not view them as dangerous. What society didn't realize, Spagnola thought, was that without these business guys, the bad guys, the robbers, and the burglars of the world would have a difficult time plying their trade. You couldn't just sit on a park bench and say, "Hey, bud, want to buy a VCR?" Sure, he thought, with smaller items like watches and jewelry a thief could do a certain amount of that, but that type of sale also took a big city mentality for both buyer and seller.

On the sidewalks of Philadelphia, the fences were roaming all the time. In New York, it was even worse. You could buy watches, rings, uncut stones, guns, or anything else you needed in broad daylight.

In Uwchlan Township, it was very difficult. One would stand out like a sore thumb. There was no true town of Uwchlan or Lionville, just a collection of residences, restaurants, banks, schools, and parks—suburban America.

Spagnola knew that most people did not keep their receipts, did not write down the serial numbers of their VCRs, DVDs, and stereo equipment. Most people did not photograph their jewelry or have it professionally appraised by someone other than the person they bought it from. Most people had no idea about security, their windows, their locked doors, the places behind which they felt safe and warm. Elaine Kauffman was a perfect example.

It was obvious that the Kauffmans, or the builder of their residence, were smart enough to have a dead bolt. Unfortunately, they were not smart enough to have a good solid door. They were not smart enough to have a key entry-only system so that the burglary could not have occurred in the manner it occurred.

Their windows were secured by inside locks. However, it was a simple thing to break the glass and reach in, unlock the window and open it, had the burglar decided the door wasn't going to work. It was an all too common pattern.

People in suburbia left their garage doors open. The garage doors, of course, led to a garage which had an opening into the house. The door into the house usually was flimsy and unlocked. People hid keys to their homes by the front door where anyone with a little bit of imagination would find them. In the case of the Kauffman's, they had done all of these things. A search around the house revealed a key at the front door and a key at the back door. If the burglar had the time and inclination, he would have found he could have opened the doors and walked into the house.

Apparently, he did not feel he had the time and certainly did not have the inclination.

One of the questions that continued to trouble Spagnola was, how did the burglar know about the house? How did he know about the jewelry? Why did he mistakenly believe that no one was home? These were mistakes professionals rarely made, so it had the feel of an amateur. Amateurs didn't usually carry guns, so where did the gun come from? Something that was found at the residence and used in panic? Or had the user been smacked out on PCP or cocaine, giving rise to the disastrous result?

And what about Mrs. Kauffman's affair? So far there was little evidence that Mr. Kauffman was fooling around other than the fact that he didn't love Mrs. Kauffman anymore, and he wasn't home very often. There was nothing else to indicate he might be having an affair of his own. Inane records such as credit card receipts and matchbooks were the best method of beginning that type of investigation, and he already had an officer on it. If Mr. Kauffman was fooling around, they'd know about it soon enough.

Thinking about the matter for hours gave Spagnola a severe headache. He closed up his paperwork and headed home for a sandwich.

CHAPTER 66

S B STOOD OVER Kiefer Barney in the main theater of the autopsy facility. He was not alone. On his right stood Chester Fairbrook, MD, Chester County medical examiner, and across from him stood his assistant Kevin Moan. SB liked to just look at the deceased for a period of time before starting the formal autopsy. He would stand and stare, move a few paces left or right, back or forward, and do this until he was ready to begin. Neither the cameras nor the microphones were on. He had determined not to use the video cameras for this autopsy anyway. Too many problems later on.

SB was a cynic. SB was a lover of the conspiracy theory and despite having spent a good deal of his time in the service of one branch or another of the government, he was skeptical of everything involved in government and politics. With good reason, SB thought. He knew from practical experience that the old line from *Dogpatch*, "What's good for General Motors . . . is good for the USA," was one of the only truths one could discern from politics. Big business, big people, special interests, and money decided what was good for America; what (and what not) the common masses could hear, read, and even know about.

He wouldn't let any of his beliefs interfere with his work; he never had.

Chester Fairbrook was a dyed-in-the-wool Republican, in a bastion of the Republican Party in Chester County, Pennsylvania. There was suspicion that Chester had changed his name so that he could be even more associated with the county. It wasn't true but made for good folklore.

Chester was a "yes man," the kind his party loved and cherished. Chester had very little imagination. He rarely read a novel, never a poem, but could put in hours a day reading medical journals. He had never had an original thought in his life and, yet, liked to think of himself as a forward thinker. He believed that everyone was guilty of some crime. Although he couldn't articulate why his theory had any plausibility, he would tell anyone who was willing to listen that most people had never been arrested simply because they had not been caught. It wasn't really his theory anyway, just something that he'd heard an old police sergeant say. He picked up on it and used it as if he'd invented it.

Chester had a cop's mentality when it came to his job. He believed that every death was a homicide, but that the police (and his own office) simply didn't have the time, money, or manpower to pursue everything they needed to pursue. Chester would have been a terrific worker in a police state. Chester would not actually put his name on the autopsy report. Instead, he would wait to see if the autopsy proved to be important to the investigation and, if so, would make it very clear to the press that his participation had been key. If things did not work out, his name would not be involved.

Kevin Moan was a study in contrast. He had inherited six million dollars when he was twenty-three years old, a third year medical student at the time. His parents were both dead at the time and his grandfather had never gotten around to changing his will to a living trust, or providing that his young grandson would not get all of the money at the same time.

When the estate had closed and his check had cleared, Kevin took a leave of absence from medical school and headed to California. He dabbled in a variety of things while there, including a small T-shirt company, a beach shack restaurant that sold Thai food, event planning for amateur volleyball, sex, and drugs. Mostly drugs. One morning he woke up in the county lock up and was taken before the local magistrate. It was his fourth trip to court for minor criminal offenses, but his first trip before ex-police chief

Quatro "MF" Barnes, now known as Magistrate Barnes. Moan was still just a bit stoned when they lead him into the courtroom.

When Moan finally focused his eyes, he was looking up at Magistrate Barnes, a six-foot-eight-inch, three-hundred-pound black bear of a man in a black robe, with tiny little bifocals resting on his nose.

"And what brings you here before me, Mr. Moan?" the magistrate inquired.

Not thinking very clearly, and not even sure he was awake or that this scene was real, Moan responded, "These officers brought me here, sir . . . I'm pretty sure I wouldn't have come any other way."

Barnes leaned back in his swivel chair thinking that maybe he had himself another smart-ass, rich white boy in front of him, looked straight into Moan's bleary eyes, realized this knucklehead was genuine, and roared with laughter.

"That is the best one I have heard today, young man, but I must say that the day has just only begun in earnest."

"Officer, what did this young knucklehead do to bring the wrath of the Santa Monica Police Department about his person?"

It was all that the officer could do not to laugh, but he knew better. Magistrate Barnes was tough but fair, and you tried not to laugh in his courtroom no matter how funny things got.

"Sir, he was publicly intoxicated, had no identification, and was carrying a small amount of a controlled substance when he was arrested," answered the officer.

Barnes rubbed his chin and stared at Moan. "Priors?"

"Mostly the same kind of thing, three arrests, one plea of guilty, two other dispositions."

"Did he give you a hard time, resist arrest?" Barnes asked suspiciously.

The officer couldn't help but chuckle. "No, Magistrate Barnes, he was passed out in the middle of a parking lot near the park, damn near ran him over."

Magistrate Barnes had given Moan a choice: thirty days in rehab or thirty days in the county prison. Barnes carefully outlined the downside of prison. He also put Moan back in the holding cell with orders that he was to be put on suicide watch and given plenty of fluids and food whenever he wanted until he made up his mind what he wanted to do. And, oh yeah, call the public defender and let them know he was in the cell, just for the hell of it.

Moan wisely chose the rehab. The public defender declined representation when it turned out that Moan still had 3.4 million dollars in the bank, despite being one of the great young spendthrifts in California history. It took him two tries to complete the program, but after that he was drug-free. He completed his medical education (with honors), volunteered for clinics in his spare time, and married a wonderful religious young lady, Pam Beiner.

Moan carried some baggage through his life, but it wasn't drugs. He opened a small family practice in Phoenixville which ended up growing into a large family practice with four other physicians. He was well liked and well respected, and his lifestyle did not bespeak the fortune he had amassed in the twenty-six years since completing his rehab. Nor did it speak to his other side. Unbeknownst to anyone but his wife, Moan had also amassed an unbelievable large collection of pornographic material.

Moan had a special room built into his house, on the inside with no windows where he housed a literal theater for watching movies and rooms for looking at porno displays from all over the world. This was an addiction he had not been able to beat. His wife of many years had simply begun to accept this and watched movies now and again with him. Other than an occasional glass of Pinot Noir, this was Moan's vice. Deep down Moan knew that the porno, like the drugs, could be viewed a lot of different ways, but the bottom line was, drugs were destructive to those who used them and to society, and so was porno. He knew deep down that he had traded one addiction for another, but was unwilling and unable to let go.

SB looked around the room. SB was the foremost forensic pathologist in Pennsylvania. He did not specifically work for the county but was stationed there as his headquarters. In fact, he was an employee of the Commonwealth of Pennsylvania and only answered to the attorney general's office.

He was ready to begin. He recognized that this team had been assembled with several purposes in mind. SB and Moan were probably the best team of coroners in southwestern Pennsylvania for doing a complicated autopsy. Chester was probably the least qualified in that regard, but he would be very grateful for having been invited to participate. Later on, that would mean access to money, men, and materials if the investigation widened. Chester wouldn't think twice about calling upon his political buddies if asked, because that was the way that he thought that his world worked.

SB activated the microphones.

"This is Dr. SB. It is Sunday, October 3rd, at 4:00 PM. We are at the Chester County Morgue. I am pleased to report that Chester Fairbrook, MD, county coroner, and Kevin Moan, MD, have joined me to assist and observe this autopsy. Thank you for attending, gentlemen. We have before us the body of one Kiefer Barney, adult male, age unknown, who was discovered dead at the Marchwood Shopping Center, Uwchlan Township, this morning at approximately nine thirty. The body was turned over to us by crime scene investigators and the Uwchlan police at one o'clock this afternoon."

CHAPTER 67

BILL WAS FREEZING. *Sweat dripped from his brow. He shivered. It made no sense. How can I be sweating and freezing? he thought.*

Someone was kneeling over him. Whoever it was couldn't be seen, but that person was ripping his shirt. Then he remembered that he had been shot.

Of course, they need to rip my shirt off, just like in the movies . . . so they can get the bullet out.

Something smelled funny, not bad, just different. He had never smelled it before. He thought about it and was sure he had never smelled that smell before. Bill knew there was pain somewhere in the distance, but it was going to be all right. He had been promised it would be all right, hadn't he?

He could hear the doctor humming as she worked on his stomach. He could hear rock and roll music in the background. He knew he was safe. He had thoughts of running and falling.

He faded back into oblivion.

CHAPTER 68

S PAGS HAD RECEIVED the call from SB at 10:00 on Wednesday night. They decided to meet for lunch the following day. SB had promised to have a preliminary report on the autopsy of Keifer Barney so that they could move that investigation along.

Now they sat in a booth at the far end of the Hello Bob Deli. SB, as always, had a voracious appetite. Spags picked at his sandwich, waiting for the story to unfold. You couldn't rush SB, that's why it was important to dine with him over anything important. "A man needed his nourishment," SB was fond of saying, as he patted his stomach and ignored the fact that he was a good thirty pounds overweight.

"I'm not so sure that they were tortured. I mean, I have found some indications that a powerful but hard to detect drug was used to anesthetize them prior to someone administering catastrophic wounds. I know that sounds crazy, but I'm beginning to think that whoever these people are, they are more interested in the reaction to what they have done than they are into torturing these guys. Don't get me wrong, there is possibly an enjoyment factor here, there is just too much torture not to be. However, I think some of it is for effect. Maybe most of it is for effect."

It looked like Spags was going to speak but SB raised his hand, "Let me finish."

"It's not like on TV, Detective." Spags knew it was getting serious whenever the good doctor called him detective. SB didn't usually deal in titles any more than he expected anyone to call him doctor.

"It's not like there's a single classic serial murderer out there. There are different shapes and sizes. They all have different motivations. Most of the stuff that has been written about serials is pure bullshit. Most of the guys who've written it claim to be profilers or ex this or ex that, but have had very little field or practical experience in dealing with serials. The guys who do have experience are mostly with the FBI and aren't out there writing books.

"You may not remember him, but a good friend of mine, Dr. John Gallen IV, was with the serial murderer unit of the Federal Bureau of Investigation for quite a few years. He, in fact, headed up the forensic group for many years. He was in charge of overseeing the autopsies of the victims and the criminal investigations on some of the most renowned and some of the least known serial murderers in America.

"Before his disappearance, he cataloged twenty-one different classifications of serial murderers just from the cases he had alone. It was his belief that the number of categories might exceed one hundred. He knew that his information would blow away everything that everyone believed they knew about serial murderers. It would turn most local investigations into shambles. The problem is, we only think we know something about these people. In truth, serials may be killing fifty or even a hundred times as many people as we think they are on an annual basis in this country alone.

"Although it has always been presumed that serials are white, male, middle-class, well-educated, smart, cunning, middle-aged murderers, who begin to spin out of control after a period of time, that may be only one profile out of the more than a hundred that we have to look at.

"Worse yet, the idea that they can actually spin out of control is probably not correct. Sure there are some serials whose actions are sexually related. Perhaps they are unable to feel true emotions like love and hate. This group may have a sexual dysfunction, and they may heighten the experience of committing murder by doing it more often. To assume that this happens, in even a small percentage of the cases, is an error. A fatal error, no pun intended.

"Let me tell you a story. It's just that, a story, but keep it in mind whenever you might need or think you need information on how a murderer thinks or acts.

"I'm going to tell you John Gallen's story. The FBI says it's all fiction of course, but it's his story nonetheless."

CHAPTER 69

"GALLEN WAS A well-respected forensic pathologist," SB continued. "He was head of an elite unit inside the FBI whose job it was to investigate serial murders. It is unquestioned that his unit had accumulated the largest database of serial murder information in the world. As head of the unit, he was in fact, the guardian of that information.

"Through cooperation with a variety of state and local police departments, Gallen believed they had pinpointed a serial murderer whom they could tie to six individual murders and the murder of an entire family of four. Unfortunately, all of the evidence was circumstantial, and there were was no forensic smoking gun. Worse, get this, the person was ex-US government. Let's just say that the person under investigation's name was Carl. Carl was a former CIA agent.

"Carl had been under surveillance for almost three months. During that time, he had committed at least one murder virtually under the noses of the FBI and a local law enforcement agency. The flaw in the investigation was that they believed that Carl was tracking a young lady who would be his next victim. The FBI concentrated its efforts on being able to respond almost instantaneously if he was to approach her or enter her apartment. While it is still believed that he was in fact keeping her under surveillance as a future victim, the cold and calculating Carl apparently planned his murders two or three persons in advance, and she was either number two or three on his list, not number one.

"What appeared to be a robbery-related homicide of a young and upcoming Wall Street broker at a Long Island railroad station was almost assuredly the work of Carl. The fact that it occurred on the FBI's watch and under their noses had the team in Gallen's office in a frenzy to find evidence against Carl. That evidence would not be forthcoming.

"Suddenly and out of the blue, Carl stopped his surveillance. He stopped his late afternoon walks through Central Park and at some point apparently destroyed his Blackberry.

"He stopped taking photographs with his telephoto lens and whatever film had been in the camera he had destroyed rather than developed. He destroyed his digital images. Carl began spending a significant amount of time outdoors where he could be plainly seen and not within his apartment, as had been his previous routine. The FBI believed that somehow Carl was on to them. A no-knock, no-warrant search of his apartment on one of his many newfound long walks produced nothing. He had apparently replaced the hard drive in his computer, not erased it as some people would, but replaced it in its entirety so that there were no telltale signs of any files his computer may have held. To this day, they have never found the original hard drive and it is suspected that on many of his long walks he had disposed it.

"From that point on, decisions rolled easily, if not carelessly. It became somewhat of an obsession with the unit to put this guy away. After a while, there was very little thought given to legality, just results, and with virtually no oversight of this unit, things began to run out of control.

"The FBI files began to change radically to show that Carl was a suspected purveyor of child pornography. Evidence from three other child pornography cases from years past were surreptitiously gathered and reworked to provide ammunition against him.

"A series of computer disks were created of known child pornography Web sites with encryption codes to later be dumped into his hard drive.

"You don't know where this is going, do you, Detective?"

"Not a clue," said Detective Spagnola.

"Well, I'll go on then.

"It happened quickly. One day, Carl came back to his apartment and within two minutes the FBI followed him in. You can imagine the look of shock on his face as he stood there holding a magazine replete with child pornography, as the FBI charged in, arrested, and handcuffed him for possession of that magazine. Of course, on his hard drive, they found vivid images of boys and girls in various states of undress, committing various sexual acts, with no question that those boys and girls were under age.

"Not surprisingly, the only magazine in his apartment that contained his fingerprints was the one that he was holding at the time of his arrest. His lawyer tried to make a great deal of hay out of that. His lawyer was a tough son of a bitch from the Bronx who had been a prosecutor and knew a rat when he smelled one. Despite this, the US Attorney's Office held firm and prosecuted Carl to the full extent of the law, convicting him of possession of child pornography. The charges of possession of child pornography with the intent to distribute and various RICO counts against him with unknown conspirators were dismissed by the good legal work of his attorney.

"Carl was sentenced to eight years in a federal penitentiary. Gallen had been a key witness in his trial because of his knowledge of fingerprints and was called as a counter-expert witness to Carl's expert. Carl's expert testified that it was nearly impossible that Carl could possess those magazines and keep from having his fingerprints show on any of them, no less on his hard drive. Gallen had shown the jury very ordinary techniques to prevent Carl from leaving fingerprints on the porno material, including but not limited to the use of latex gloves. Conveniently, there had been three boxes of lightweight latex gloves found in Carl's bathroom at the time of the search.

"Knowing that Carl was a serial murderer and knowing that someday he would be out of prison, a series of checks and balances were set up so that the FBI, all witnesses who testified at Carl's trial, and Dr. Gallen's department would be notified a significant period of time prior to Carl's release.

"Frankly, no one believed he would live for eight years inside a penitentiary. He had been convicted of child pornography. Child pornographers and rapists didn't do well in prison back then, especially federal prisons where macho drug lords took offense to people who abused women and children, despite the fact that the lords did the same thing to women and children in a different venue.

"Carl turned out to be more formidable than anyone believed. Carl, a pig named Lipsy, and a Hispanic rapist named Raphael had become the targets of a certain drug lord inside the penitentiary. After a number of beatings had been administered to Lipsy and Raphael, they were transferred out, but for some strange reason, despite numerous threats against him, Carl was not moved by prison authorities.

"One morning, the guards opened the cells at 6:00 AM to do a head count and found the drug lord dead in his cell. He had, of course, been murdered. No one ever determined how, but the rumor in the prison was that it was Carl. From that point on, nobody went near him, nobody threatened him, and he served his sentence in peace. His nickname became Casper. He was named this because they believed he had become a ghost, gone to the drug lord's cell, killed him, and gone back to his own cell. There seemed to be no other explanation either from the prisoners, the guards, or the video cameras.

"Eight years tends to be a long time. There were presidential changes and changes in the Justice Department, the US Attorney's Office, staffs, protocols, and priorities. Somewhere along the line, the fail-safe system to notify everyone when Carl was released from prison failed itself. Due to overcrowding and the nonviolent nature of his crime, Carl was released from prison after having served six years and four months of his sentence. In Last year, Carl without any fanfare became a free man."

CHAPTER 70

SB's SANDWICH CAME. He took a couple of bites, sipped from his chocolate egg cream, and continued on.

Shortly after Carl's release, Dr. Gallen left work, got into his green Ford Taurus, and headed home to the Washington suburb of Bowie, Maryland. Neighbors saw him pull his car into the garage after opening it with his garage door opener and saw the garage door close. That's the last anyone ever saw of Dr. Gallen. No ransom note, no suicide note, no sign of forced entry, no telephone call, no body. In fact, the only clue, if you want to call it that, was a water stain next to his car where someone had cleaned up with soap, water, and Clorox."

"What were the official findings?" asked Spagnola.

"Too much pressure on poor old Dr. Gallen. His wife had left him and he was in the process of a divorce. He was estranged from his two children and his grandchildren. He worked long hard hours trying to track down some of the most heinous criminals in the United States history. Official story: he cracked, took a walk.

"There were problems with that theory, of course. Everything that was known about Dr. Gallen was closely monitored after his disappearance. The moment he disappeared, there was no use of his credit cards, no access to his bank accounts, no access to his pension or profit sharing plan. He had disappeared off the face of the earth.

"The unofficial view was that Carl had gotten him. Right there in Gallen's own garage. Either killed him or disabled him, cleaned up after himself with the soap, water, and Clorox; hell, maybe even left it there as some sort of sick joke so there would be something the forensic boys could look at and took Dr. Gallen or his body with him.

"There was no evidence of anyone breaking into the garage. At the same time, Dr. Gallen had no security at his home. He didn't even have dead bolts in the outside garage doors. It would be pretty easy to jimmy one without leaving any evidence. More importantly, he never paid any attention to his surroundings despite warnings from his colleagues at the FBI. He was always deep in thought and didn't notice what occurred around him. A neighbor across the street said that Dr. Gallen had a very set routine, which is a bad thing when someone is stalking you. His routine was to pull into his driveway, pop the garage door with his opener, get out of the car, walk back to his mailbox to check his mail. During that whole time, he would have his back turned. Someone in the bushes or around the side of his house could easily slip into his garage.

"It seems a little foolish at first, but think about it. The would-be murderer slips into the garage. He knows almost immediately if he's been seen or not. If the good doctor doesn't come into the garage, the murderer sneaks out the back, locking the door behind him, and takes off. There is no evidence he's ever been there, and there is no way they are going to catch him. On the other side of the coin, if Dr. Gallen doesn't notice him, he's inside, catches the doctor by surprise as he gets out of the car. He either disables him or kills him before Dr. Gallen is able to do anything else. In my story, they just hope he's dead."

"What do you mean they hope he's dead? Are you telling me they still haven't found a body?" asked Spagnola.

"No. Absolutely nothing. Detective, there is a moral to this story. I've been called into a few investigations myself. I've read all of Dr. Gallen's materials, which consisted of thousands and thousands of written pages. Despite all that material, he wasn't even close to completing his work. Do you know what the public perception is of a serial murderer? Don't answer, I'll tell you what it is.

"One: middle-aged, white male. Two: fairly smart, works in your community. Three: sexually impotent or at least possessed with serious sexual problems. Four: spinning out of control and trying to get caught. Five: psychological issues with his parents and home life. Six: certain trait characteristics when they are young, such as torturing animals, being excited by violence. Seven: little or no emotional feelings.

"Do you know why they have that profile? Do you know where it came from? It came from the FBI. It is all bullshit. It was created because the FBI realized they had no idea of the magnitude of the situation. People like Dr. Gallen started to open their eyes and it scared the crap out of them. If the public knew the real story, they'd panic. It would hurt the government, the economy; it would hurt everything. Citizens would be arming themselves, shooting each other. There would be chaos in the streets. Sounds like some silly doomsday scenario. Well, I for one don't think it is. I think it is pretty close to the truth."

Even though he stated it with an even keel, it was pretty obvious that SB was worked up about this issue, but Spagnola couldn't figure out for the life of him as to why.

"SB, I really appreciate all of this. I do. I'd even like to read up on the stuff you've read up on. What does it have to do with those two unfortunates that got killed on my watch?"

"Everything and nothing. At the time of Gallen's disappearance, he clearly identified twenty-one different types of serial murderers. He would not allow for a classification unless he was convinced through pure, hard evidence that there were at least five serial murders that fit a particular class. If that's not scary enough, he believed that in the end, there would be over a hundred different types, and he began to catalog them. The really disturbing part is, for the most part, it showed that the FBI profile was wrong in almost every way. The most serious deficiency lay in the fact that these people were not spinning out of control. In most of the classifications that he came up with, he uncovered very few cases where the serial killer appeared to be trying to get caught.

"Think about it, Detective. Even if Dr. Gallen was wrong about how many more personalities of a serial murderer type existed, he clearly identified through empirical evidence twenty-one. Have you ever heard anything of this research? Have you ever read anything that suggested serial murderers came in twenty-one different flavors and were not looking to get caught?"

Detective Spagnola was not easily impressed. The thought that there were twenty-one different personality types who were not only capable of, but who had committed serial murder, was a staggering thought. His training had indicated that there were only four types and that all of them were seeking attention, and all were seeking to be caught. If those basic premises were wrong, then the statistical analysis of how many murders occurred at the hands of serial murderers, and how many serial murders were out there, were all wrong as well.

"If that's the case, SB, why haven't they released that empirical data? Why aren't there books and articles about this? How come the FBI hasn't jumped into the fray?"

SB shook his head and laughed. "Picture next year when the FBI releases its statistics on crime in America. Remember that lasts year's report would have said that one out of every sixteen people that is currently listed as missing is actually dead. Who would sign the new report if it indicated that three out of every ten persons listed as missing were in all likelihood dead and most of them had fallen to foul play? Picture the Americans' reactions to the idea that serial murderers were everywhere; that they were cunning, that they blended into the neighborhood, that they often kill and then move on, that they were bright and they were not the sadomasochistic sexual predators that the novelists, moviemakers, and yes, the FBI too, has lead us to believe are out there in limited numbers."

He continued, "What if we were to tell the public that a number of these serial killers had significant police training, whether through formal means or self-taught. What if we told the public that some of them were doctors or nurses. If I were a guy who believed in conspiracies, I'd wonder if our own government hadn't snatched Dr. Gallen. To some, he would have been considered the most dangerous man on earth. What do you think he was going to do with his research in the end? He was going to either publish it or bring it to the authorities. Either way, there would be no chance of burying it. Why not bury him instead?"

CHAPTER 71

"THE FEDERAL BUREAU of Investigation classifies serial murderers in two categories, organized and disorganized. Both categories carry with them the basic premise that the killings are consciously or subconsciously linked to sex. The FBI mantra is that some killers are overtly linked to sex, such as the killer who rapes his victim before (or often after) he has killed them. Some killers are linked covertly because of their behavior. The link is often drawn through subtle signs regarding how the body was dressed by the killer, or how the body is arranged by the killer. Finally, the categorization is often linked by the reaction the body (and its dressings) is supposed to make when the body is found by the authorities.

"According to the FBI book on serial murder, organized serial murderers plan their killings well in advance, usually are performed against victims who are strangers, and are usually ritualistic in nature. According to the FBI, the killer makes an effort to conceal the body and to disassociate himself from the crime scene. This serial is statistically a white male, middle income more often than not, with a troubled childhood.

"The disorganized serial killer acts on impulse. The disorganized killer kills randomly and makes little or no effort to conceal the body or leave props at the crime scene. The disorganized serial often kills persons that they know. This serial is statistically white male, middle income with a troubled childhood.

"Only one problem, Detective . . .," said SB putting down the summary that Spags had been reading regarding serial murderer.

"What's that?" asked Spags.

"It's pretty much nonsense. The profilers know it, so does the FBI. It's way too neat, way too clean. It lulls the population to sleep because if there is an organized serial out there, most of the public believes that they would never be the target of such a person; what would the odds be? If there's a disorganized serial out there, he's going to be caught or maybe even killed; so why worry? What are the odds? Everybody believes they would know if someone in their social set was a serial murderer.

"The FBI claims that there are 1,026 known serial murderers in the United States. Let's face it, the statistic is needed to have the FBI funding. At the same time, that is only one out of every 306,000 Americans. According to the FBI, we lose three hundred times more people on the highways annually than we will ever lose to serial killers. So the Feds tell the public that things are all well in hand while at the same time requesting continued funding to keep things in check." SB paused for effect.

"In actuality, the FBI has no idea how many serial type murderers are out there. They have no idea how many people these serial murderers have killed. Their own statistics show that an enormous number of Americans go missing every year. If just 10 percent of those people have been killed by serial type killers, the number of serials would range closer to ten thousand rather than one thousand. If that's the case, serial-type killers are making great headway in the race to be America's top nonmedical killers along with the automobile industry."

SB shook his head.

"Dan. The bastard we have here is smart, strong, and has been at this a long time. We're going to need everything we have, and not a certain amount of luck, to bring this one down before he moves on.

"Believe me, there is nothing disorganized about this one. No psycho-sexual fantasies, no lack of breastfeeding, no bed-wetting freak . . . no, this one kills with a purpose. I know you can't fathom the purpose and neither can I, most likely this one hides the purpose, and God knows we may never know what that is. The rest of it, the theatrics, the staging, the brutality, is all meant to fit the FBI mold like a serial killer doing a caricature of himself.

"Be careful, Dan, be very careful. This one is playing with us."

CHAPTER 72

S B FINISHED HIS sandwich. Spagnola had already done so, devoured his pickle, and was working on the complimentary miniature package of potato chips. As the waitress walked by, SB asked for a Pepsi.

"Only got Coke," was the reply, and SB nodded his consent. Spags knew that SB was pulling his thoughts together, and he wasn't about to interrupt him.

When the Coke had arrived and SB had finished his sandwich, he wiped his lips, reached into his jacket pocket, and extracted a set of photographs. They were five-by-sevens, taken in the forensic lab and taken close up. SB handed them to the detective and sat back.

After thumbing through them, Spagnola whistled. He went through them again and looked straight into SB's eyes.

"Let me guess. You found this little ditty on our most recent victim?"

"Yes, in fact, it was in a plastic package stapled to his back. Fortunately for Mr. Barney, it appears that the stapling had been done post-mortem. As I had suspected from Injun Joe, we're dealing with a serial murderer here. I know that the classic Gallen test is three murders of a similar type, but, as I've said, he hadn't cataloged everyone, and from his notes he was well aware that serial murderers don't always follow a particular pattern either in who they kill or how they kill them. I'm not even sure that we have a single murderer here or a group. As you know, we haven't been particularly successful in catching individual serial murderers, no less groups."

"So what's the deal?" asked Spags.

"Take a look at these," said SB as he passed to Detective Spagnola two more photographs neatly laminated.

Detective Spagnola looked at them and dropped them back down on the table. He took a swig of his Coke and waited. When SB said nothing, he said, "So?"

SB raised his hand. "That's your official Uwchlan Township detective card. The little 'd' I showed you first was written on that, placed in a plastic pouch, and stapled to the victim's back. I have no idea what it really means, but it could mean that you are next. That's why I'm here. That's why I'm telling you the story. You need to start being careful, and I think I can tell you how."

"Wait a minute . . .," said Spags. "How in the name of hell did he get a hold of that?" Spags was now both angry and uneasy.

SB shrugged, raised both hands upward, and said, "Once I got deep into this type of criminal behavior I became paranoid. Maybe paranoid isn't the right term, but I began looking at things in a different light. What I do on a daily basis, what kind of routine I have, who might be watching or filming me, or who has access to my personal information, how my home and car are secured. Remember, in 1997, there wasn't a great deal out there on the Internet compared to today. Now if you Google your own name, you find out things about yourself that maybe you didn't even know. I'm concerned, Dan, really concerned that whoever is doing this, that person or persons is messing with us in particular. You and me. In my own paranoid way, there's just too much that points in that direction.

"I'm sure you wouldn't know this, but according to his data, the classic serial murderer is not even in the top ten that Dr. Gallen identified. In fact, according to the empirical data he used, the absolute best information available, the classic serial murderer only ranks fourteenth in terms of the number of murders committed by serials in this country. The guy who's playing with us ranks much higher, and historically has been next to impossible to catch."

"Well, let's start with the obvious question: what is it that this guy is looking for, what's his motive for killing? Is it the bums themselves?" Spags asked.

"Could be, could be his dad was a bum, or even his big brother, uncle, grandfather, best friend's dad, you name it. The problem is, Gallen believed that we had caught so few of these monsters that we really didn't know much about them. Worse yet, he believed that when we did finally catch one, and there was no way out, the serial might well play the role of one of the FBI stereotypes, just to be treated specially."

Spags coughed, a phony cough. "So we have nothing . . ."

"Nothing but caution," said SB. "We really have to be very careful with this one."

CHAPTER 73

S PAGS WAS A quick study. He wasn't convinced that SB was right, but held him in high enough regard to do some independent reading on the subject, and was surprised with what he found. As SB had told him at their luncheon meeting, the FBI (and law enforcement in general) publicly held to the theory that there were only a smattering of serial murderer profiles, and all known serial murderers fit into one or another of these.

Serial killers could be broken down into four categories and two essential types, the organized and disorganized. The concept actually dated back to the nineteen sixties with the studies of Wolfgang and Feruuci.[1]

Spags scrolled through numerous articles and treatises on crime looking for as much quick information as he could obtain. He noted an early study that suggested that the victim was one of the causes of the crime by Hans von Hentig, and later expanded upon by Mendelssohn.[2] If Gallen (and SB) were right, the FBI's methodology and conclusions would produce very little useful information regarding serial murders in general because their basic premises were incorrect.

---

[1] The categories had been pronounced by the FBI and each category had a number of subcategories.

[2] The FBI, of course, scoffed at this investigation of an unsolved homicide. The FBI did not believe it was helpful to perceive the victim as in any way provoking the murder, but rather they attempted to be aware of how the offender thought.

At the same time, the FBI had done a study identifying 134 variable's pertaining to deaths of 109 at the hands of convicted serial murderers. The study also included 9 persons who had survived their attacks and added valuable information from the victims' standpoint. Unfortunately, Spags thought, the information from the living victims was largely ignored in the findings section of the report. It didn't seem that the perpetrator of the killings of his two victims fell into any of the FBI categories. In the FBI organized killer scenario, the murderer generally had sex with the victim while the victim was alive. In the disorganized scenario, they most often had sex with the victim after they were dead or while they were dying. He thought of what SB had said about Gallen. If SB was right, they had a very smart, opportunistic killer, who was toying with them, probably hoping they would look for similarities between the murders and the victims. This would only add confusion to the investigation. Add to that the chaos of the Kauffman murder, the missing bullet, the possible connection to hospital personnel, and it added up to a terrible headache for Spagnola.

Spags knew that this was only the beginning of his problems. If he tried to get the FBI involved, they would most assuredly assume jurisdiction over the matter, and he would be out. After what SB had told him, he didn't have much faith in the FBI investigating this serial, not if they read their own manual. In the worst case scenario, they would poke their respective noses into the case, declare the killing was not that of a serial killer, and move on. This would leave Spags with a worse situation than he already had, and no closer to catching the killer.

It didn't take long to make the decision; he would do without the FBI's fabulous database and forensic teams, in favor of good detecting.

And if that doesn't work, Spags thought, well . . .

CHAPTER 74

FOLLOWING LUNCH WITH SB and his quick search of data on serial murderers, Spagnola used his cell phone to access his voice mail at the police station. There were three messages all related to the Kauffman case.

The first message was from the township's day-shift sergeant whose patrolman had rounded up the information on the life insurance policy on Mrs. Kauffman. They had found that the life insurance company itself was doing an investigation into Mrs. Kauffman's death because the policy had only been taken out within the past two years. Her murder had occurred within what the insurance company called the "contestability period." It was apparently standard procedure for life insurance companies when the amounts exceeded one hundred thousand dollars to conduct such investigations. The patrolman had left a name and phone number to contact at the insurance company.

The second message was from Endersly, the Coatesville Hospital administrator. As always, he sounded shaky. The information he left was that the Coatesville detectives had contacted him about some unusual information regarding Nurse Rodriguez's husband. They were looking into it, but Endersly had nothing else to offer and decided to share this information with Spagnola, so that he didn't get another tongue lashing. Spagnola chuckled at that one.

The third message was more intriguing. It was from the state trooper that he had spoken to regarding Dr. Evans and the incident on I-95 in Maryland. The message was brief, terse, typical of a state trooper, and even more typical of this one, Spags mused.

The trooper stated that there was one thing more that had come to his attention when he was kicking this matter around with his partner. His partner recalled that one of the deceased had shown significant signs of blunt force trauma. His recollection was that it was not the kind of trauma that could be inflicted by a foot or a hand. "Remember," the trooper said, "the theory was that the two of these truckers had literally beaten each other to death. We found the blunt force trauma to be perplexing because no blunt force instrument was located at the scene."

The trooper's follow-up telephone conversation with Dr. Evans who had discovered the scene was unhelpful. Her recollection was that there was no weapon around either of the deceased truckers, or within her line of sight in the immediate vicinity. A follow-up search of the area by the troopers had uncovered nothing either. The statie's partner had presumed that the doctor had taken the blunt instrument as a souvenir. The use of the word "souvenir" made the hair on the back of Spagnola's neck stand up, and he got the feeling that he might be just unraveling a thread.

Spagnola believed that good cops had good instincts, which is what they drilled into him at the academy and later at the homicide division in Philadelphia. He knew, however, that instincts don't get search warrants and there was no way to know whether the doctor had stolen the bullet along with whatever blunt instrument she had come across on that bizarre day at the rest stop in Maryland. If he could get a few more strings to attach this case together or put a little pressure on Dr. Evans or on Endersly, there might be something there.

Spagnola really didn't give a rat's ass about the doctor or whether or not she collected trophies or souvenirs. He did need the bullet, however, to make a match and be sure that he could eliminate the idea that, 1) more than one gun was used, 2) there were more people involved in the incident, and 3) that someone might have removed a weapon from the scene. Spagnola flashed to the scene of the Kauffman's house when he arrived: chaos everywhere, authorized and unauthorized persons tromping around the house, no one keeping track of who was coming or going, their status, their shoe wear, their clothing, their identification, or perhaps the fact that they were removing things from the scene. Unfortunately he would never know, but finding the bullet would help him backtrack into a more comfortable theory regarding Mrs. Kauffman's death.

He immediately dialed up his good friend from York County. The phone was answered on the third ring. "Hey, Spags, how are they hanging?" The sergeant chuckled.

"I hate caller ID," said Spagnola. "I'm trying to get a phone that reads out 'President of the United States,' so everyone will answer when I call."

"Two calls in one week. You must be into some really deep stuff. What can I bail you out on now?" asked the sergeant.

"I need you to take another look at our Dr. Evans. I know, I know, I know. You're going to say you've looked at everything you can, but I still want you to look again. What I'm most interested in is souvenirs or trophies of crime scenes. Forget about the hospital records, we've already looked at those. I need to know if there have been any homicides during the period of time she was at York County Community where officers had a suspicion that a knife, blunt instrument, a gun, a bullet, a hatchet, you name it, whatever, was removed from a crime scene with the possibility that it was removed by a third party for a souvenir or a trophy." Spagnola laughed. "Let's see how good your damn computer is now. Let's see if you twinkle-toe tech kinda guys can actually do some police work."

The sergeant was laughing as well. "Why don't you give me something easy? How about the location of Judge Crater and Jimmy Hoffa? Wait a second, while I'm at it, I may as well find out whose glove that was that wouldn't fit on OJ's hand." They were both laughing hard now.

"OK, OK," said Spags. "You can solve those any time. Let's just see what you can find out about my lady, and I use the term lady loosely. She's a bitch on wheels."

"I'll see what I can do. I'm going to actually need to get somebody with better technical experience than I have because I'm not sure how to run that search. I'll find out and I'll get back to you. Watch the comments about twinkle toes. I happen to be a very sensitive guy." They both laughed and hung up without saying good-bye.

CHAPTER 75

S PAGS RETURNED TO the office at 3:00 PM. He was still full from lunch at the Hello Bob Deli and was unable to shake his thoughts about SB and the Gallen matter. He checked his phone messages again, all four of them new. Nothing of interest, he thought.

He pulled up his e-mail. Despite the police force IT and his best efforts, he had four ads for Viagra, two for antacids, one for Prozac, and another which looked very much like an introduction to a pornography ad. He deleted these along with two well-hidden vitamin ads, leaving him with two interdepartmental memos (both of which he reluctantly saved).

He scanned what remained on the screen. The third message stood out because it was from the Maryland State Police Barracks in Bel Air. The message also contained an attachment. The e-mail itself read:

> Detective: Found this supplemental report after my voice mail to you. Thought it might be of interest since it references your subject inquiry, Dr. Evans.
>
> Sgt. Phillips
> Md. State Police
> Bel Air, MD
> 410-555-1212

The attachment was in PDF format. Spags was impressed. That meant that after his voice mail the sergeant had taken the extra time to follow up on the matter, had found something interesting, had scanned it into his computer, encrypted it so it could not be altered, and forwarded it as an attachment to his e-mail. Most older cops (Spags assumed the sergeant was older just based on his attitude) couldn't turn a computer on and off, no less pull off that stunt.

Spags had trouble opening the attachment at first, but on the third try it popped up on the screen. The attachment appeared to be a state police form used to supplement an original report. The document looked like it was set up as a report to be filed by the assisting officer but could be used by any officer (except the primary) to supplement a file. It was signed by a Corporal Devyn, giving his badge number and a large amount of internal operations information, as well as code numbers which meant nothing to Spags. It appeared to have been completed and forwarded to the file well after the original report had been made. It obviously postdated the original report of the state trooper who had received the 911 call and responded to the scene of the double homicide.

Spags scanned the four pages noting nothing special, until he got to the second to last paragraph on page four. It read:

> Victim James Denmore appeared to have been hit with a short metal pipe or tire iron. The injuries indicated that he had been hit several times with this instrument across his neck, right shoulder, and head. The victim Burt Kansas was also struck with an instrument (most likely a blunt object), directly across his face, perhaps a two-by-four piece of lumber or even a glazed brick. The object was smooth. No foreign objects or weapons were recovered from the scene.
>
> The witness, one Dr. Evans, had already left the scene when the search was conducted and no other witnesses were forthcoming when this trooper arrived at the scene. It would appear that someone removed some evidence from the scene because the victims/perpetrators could not have done so on their own.

That was the end of the report. There had obviously been no follow up. Two truck drivers beat each other to death . . . who cares?

Souvenir hunters were not unheard of, in fact they were well known to police and forensic personnel all over the world. They ranged from teenagers looking for a kick, out to impress their friends, all the way to beat reporters and even, sadly, cops themselves, Spags thought. And doctors? Spags had known nurses, hospital orderlies, and even security guards who snatched the odd scarf, comb, or even knife now and again, but he had to believe Dr. Evans was his first doctor.

Spags knew that this solved one problem, only to create three more. Dr. Evans was smart, tough, well heeled, and highly respected. She was not going to be bullied into admitting that she had taken the bullet, and it was entirely possible that someone else had done it, or that the bullet was in fact lost. He knew he would need a search warrant but he was going to have to be really clever with his probable cause. He also knew who he had to call, and wasted no time in doing so.

CHAPTER 76

I T STOOD BEFORE a bathroom window and gazed at itself. The last rays of autumn sunlight drifted over the tops of the trees in the backyard and filtered through the bathroom window. Everything was turning gray. The only true color left came from the skylight where a brilliant blue sky belied the fact that the sun had already set and within minutes it would be dark.

As always, It was highly aware of the need to be cautious, extremely cautious. It began its examination by taking a good close look at Its sneakers. One after another, It hefted the sneakers up and looked at them inside and out. It pulled the tongue down and loosened the shoelaces. The sneakers were a size ten, New Balance 609s. The sneakers were medium-priced cross-trainer sneakers with a very distinctive design on their sole. The design of this sole was identical to the soles of the New Balance 508, 605, 503, and the new 411 New Balance sneakers. There were virtually hundreds of thousands of these sneakers in circulation in the United States alone.

After It had examined each sneaker in turn, It began the process a second time. The sneakers had been dyed black inside and out. The shoelaces had been removed and they and been dyed black as well. The white plastic tips on the end of each shoelace had been removed and replaced with black plastic tips. The black dye was a dull black and created no shine or reflection even on the shiny surfaces of the sneakers.

The mirror was only a half mirror. There were no full-length mirrors in the empty house. It knew that this usually meant that the owners/occupants did not like to view the lower portions of their bodies. It knew that people with large hips, large rear ends, varicose veins in their legs, and the like, rarely had full-length mirrors in their homes. Whoever had lived in this house had a least one person (or maybe more) who fit this pattern.

It's socks were black wool, a black as dull as a fabric softener commercial. It carefully examined the line where the socks were covered by the black nonreflective Under Armor tights that It wore in lieu of pants. It took out a penlight and flashed the light around the seams, in order to be assured that no reflection would occur.

It wore a pair of lightweight diving gloves, black in color, which were a good match to the black of the Under Armor long-sleeved shirt that It wore to complete its body outfit.

It had donned a neoprene mask which covered It's hair and neck, folded underneath the Under Armor shirt, and allowed only openings for It's nose, eyes, a small portion of It's cheeks, and It's ears.

Simple and plain, Halloween black, nonreflective makeup covered the rest of It's exposed skin. It was careful to shine the light on the exposed areas and make sure that nothing reflected light and that no skin was exposed. As the daylight outside continued to fade, so did the reflection of It in the mirror. It was literally as black as the night.

Satisfied that It had taken all of the proper precautions, It placed the penlight in the black plastic pouch that It secreted in a side pocket of the pullover shirt which closed, and was further secured by a black Velcro strip.

It descended the stairs to the first floor and worked its way to the dining room where several windows faced the backyard. It sat down on the floor and began to focus. It started by closing compartments in its mind one by one. It then began to direct its thoughts strictly on the reconnaissance planned for the evening ahead. It made last minute adjustments to its sneakers. Although they were size ten, It clearly wore something more akin to an eight and a half. It owned numerous sneakers in numerous sizes shapes and brands, and had early on determined diverse ways to make use of them. In this instance, having a larger footprint was part of the plan. It had shored up the rear areas of the sneakers with soft black fabric in order to make the sneaker fit, unlike most people who would stuff the toe areas to make an oversized shoe fit. It knew that having its weight forward would allow it to run, whereas a stuffed toe would inevitably cause the wearer to stumble over the toe, inhibit their speed, and probably cause them to trip and fall. On the contrary, It had developed a wedge in the back of the sneaker made of a combination of black plastic and died black sponge, which allowed It to have its foot in the front of the sneaker and to run and walk as if it were wearing a size eight and a half. It did not anticipate it would be required to run very far this evening, nor that it would leave footprints that would be meaningful anywhere, but caution was always It's watchword. It was a predator and predators did not leave things to chance.

It continued to focus and close compartments of its well-ordered mind. Having completed this task, It took one last look around the empty room. It appeared that no one had lived in this house for some period of time. It was sure that no one had lived here in the past six weeks. The "For Sale" sign had been up for a while, and It had even called the realtor upon occasion to inquire about the home's availability for sale in one instance and the house's availability for rent in another. A third call had been made to the same realtor (under a third name), simply looking for information about the neighborhood and the school district.

The house had worked as a perfect staging area. The neighborhood was perfect for It's purposes. It opened the back dining room windows slowly and quietly and crawled out into the night. It was careful to close the dining room window after exiting, a black bag wrapped in black plastic in its left hand. It left nothing in the house, and there was no reason anyone would ever suspect It had been there.

In the event that It had to change its operations or move suddenly, there would be no trace that this house had ever been used. It slipped through and behind the bushes, completely unseen. It worked its way through the neighbors' yards and beneath some short trees without incident. It had scouted the neighborhood long in advance and knew that only two residences in the five-hundred-yard, long cul-de-sac housed pets. In the third house down on the left the residents had a dog which was very old and appeared very ill, and the fifth house on the right sported a six-toed calico cat. Neither pet would make any noise or in any way alert the few neighbors that an unwanted presence was afoot.

The neighborhood had been carefully selected. There were three houses for sale out of twelve. The fact that so many houses were for sale was strictly happenstance. In one of the houses that was for sale, an elderly widow had died, and the estate was in probate. In the second residence, the individual who owned it in his own name had become estranged from his second wife, and they were now separated, both living in other residences in other states with new beaus. The residence that It used as the staging area was owned by a couple who had to move quickly when the husband's job had transferred to Houston, with barely enough time to pack. This was a perfect neighborhood, It thought.

After exiting the neighborhood and working its way down Ship Road, It meandered its way behind the township building, storage building, and finally to the woods just behind the police station. It stopped there for at least fifteen minutes without moving anything but its eyes. During this period of time, It surveyed the area by sound and limited eyesight as it had done three times previously. It was interested in cameras and listening devices. It had been surprised in its first reconnaissance to find none, but as It suspected, the police here never had a reason to believe that they would ever be the ones under surveillance. It wondered if, when all was said and done, the police would feel differently.

CHAPTER 77

S PAGS HAD PLACED his call to the DA's office. He spent a significant amount of time explaining, without detail, his dilemma. Spags was torn between protecting the assistant DA, his case, and the need to the get the search warrant. He knew he'd only have one shot, if that, and that he had to be able to answer the district justice's questions without officially collaborating with, or having the judge call the district attorney's office for advice.

Spags had no delusions. The DA had a good, clean, albeit conservative office. They would not sanction the warrant based on what Spags had as evidence and to a lesser extent, they would not want to tangle with a person such as Dr. Evans without a lot more evidence than normal. Spags used his connections with a guy at the DA's office (actually a woman he occasionally dated) who promised to make him a better lawyer if he would make her a better detective. It was a good and honest relationship, Spags and the assistant DA used one another for their own ambitions. His lady friend gave him some valuable insight into the district justice and the types of question the district justice would want answered. Spags listened like a charmed school kid and wrote everything down.

"Bic pen," Spags said to no one, "sixty-nine cents, inside information, priceless!"

Spags knew that the biggest gamble was getting the warrant without the information getting back to the hospital before the warrant was served. Searching the residence before Dr. Evans got to her father (or her father's lawyers) was the key. Even though there was technically nothing they could do to quash a search warrant after it was served and had been . However, after its execution in full, they could apply not-so-subtle pressure at the county, state, and even federal level to get a judge involved, seize any items from the search, put in a gag order, and crucify Spagnola. Not a pleasant thought. At that point the DA's office might officially withdraw the warrant and everything went back to ground zero, except Spags's head which would roll a long way before it stopped.

Timing would be the key, he thought. His next call was to Nurse Eleanor Watkins. He informed her that he had some routine follow-up questions for Dr. Evans and her crew.

"Nothing urgent," he told her. "Routine, couple questions, some forms to complete, in and out in fifteen minutes." He lied.

Nurse Watkins actually sympathized with him. She knew the difficulties with forms, what with Medicaid, Medicare, MediGap . . . She knew the drudgery of the system of forms. She told Spags that the hospital had special crews for staffing the trauma unit. At any given time, one of the crews was on alert.

This meant that the crew had to be awake, dry, and alcohol/ drug free. It also meant that the crew had to be no more than a twenty-minute ride from the hospital, even under bad weather conditions. High alert required the entire crew to be present at the hospital.

There were three standard crews, Gold, Blue, and Green. Gold crew received the best schedule, Blue the second best, and Green the worst. Obviously everyone aspired to be in the Gold crew, and it had always been that way as long as trauma units had existed.

There was always a backup crew. The backup crew was required to be alcohol- and drug-free, but not necessarily awake, and could be as far away as a one-and-one-half-hour drive in bad weather conditions. All crews were on duty for twelve hours and then off for at least twenty-four hours. There was actually a fourth trauma team available in the event of a catastrophe. They were always off but could be called up on eight hours' notice, whenever the need arose.

Spags learned that Gold crew was the official name for Dr. Evans's crew, and they were physically at the hospital as he spoke.

Figures she'd call her group the Gold crew, Spags thought. Dr. Evans and her crew were tending to a group of construction workers who were literally buried alive when the trench they were working in collapsed. The nurse assured him that it would be quite a while before the Gold crew came off of their shift.

Spags quickly but carefully typed up the probable cause section of the search warrant, word processed (cut and paste) Dr. Evans's personal information from the records disk secured from the hospital, and ran the warrant off the printer in rough draft form. He gave a copy to the desk sergeant who read it and then chuckled.

"Has a nice ring to it. I'd give it a seven for creativity, but . . . a word to the wise, don't damage the ladies' furniture." The sergeant more chortled than laughed and handed the draft back to Spags.

"Any helpful hints?" asked Spags.

Sarge scratched his head. "Yeah, bring His Honor an iced cold Diet Pepsi when you go see him, oh yeah, and a Snickers bar. Don't ask me why, but the man loves his calories in his Snickers bar and would kill for an iced cold Diet Pepsi. He lived off that stuff when he was a cop."

Spags shook his head. "I meant with my wording, not with the judge."

The sergeant laughed out loud at the revelation.

"Detective, with that crock of you-know-what in your affidavit, you have a better chance with the Snickers bar and the Diet Pepsi."

Spags returned to his desk, spell-checked the document twice, ran it off in final, made three copies, and strode out of his office on a mission.

CHAPTER 78

T HE DISTRICT JUSTICE was amused by the Diet Pepsi and immediately dug into the Snickers bar.

"Used to live on these things in the old days. Never could stand donuts, and coffee made my stomach a wreck, but Diet Pepsi and a Snickers, that was livin' large."

The warrant was another issue altogether.

"Detective, you sure what you're laying out here is even a crime? Never saw one of these when I was wearin' blue."

Spags knew that the key to being successful in front of any judge was knowing when to talk and when to keep quiet. He chose to keep quiet at that point.

"Let's see, you cite 18 *Purdon's Statutes*, 29-1(d) and 4112," the judge muttered, still chewing on a huge chunk of the Snickers bar. He spun around and extracted the three volumes of *Purdon's Statutes* (18: Crimes and Offenses) from his bookcase. He fumbled with volume 1, set it aside, and opened volume 2.

"Hmmf. 2901 (d): the intentional removal of evidence of a crime scene as defined below is a first degree misdemeanor. If the removal is by reason of gross negligence the act of such removal shall be a misdemeanor of the third degree."

The judge tossed aside the second volume and picked up volume 3. After he found the right pages he mumbled to himself several more times and then dropped the book, staring at Spagnola.

"It appears that what you have alleged constitutes a misdemeanor. Why the hurry here? What's the DA's office think?"

Spags tried to remain calm, but his heart was beating at a pretty good clip. He consciously tried not to squirm and to keep his voice under control. He knew the next couple of minutes were critical.

"Judge, I really don't care if this lady collects crime scene memorabilia. I honestly don't want to file any charges against her. Hell, I don't care what we find in her closet. I need to see if the missing bullet matches the one they took out of poor Mrs. Kauffman. If it doesn't, then I have two different weapons and a completely different investigation. If they match, then I know where I'm going. I don't care if I find Jimmy Hoffa in the closet; all I want is that bullet. If she doesn't have it, that's the end of it; if she has it, that's the end of it."

The judge didn't blink. "Can I have your word on that?"

Spags didn't hesitate. "Judge, you have my word on that."

Against his better judgment, District Justice Merion L. Beible signed off on the warrant.

"I'm giving you eight hours to get it served, conduct the search, and file your report. Not a minute longer, even if Jimmy Hoffa is in there! I assume that's enough time for you?" said the judge, raising an eyebrow.

"I'll admit that's a little tight, but if we can skip the report part of it, no problem at all," Spags countered.

The district justice hesitated, but he knew Spags was a straight shooter, a good cop, no politics, and of course there was the Snickers bar. He handed the signed warrant over to Spags, checked his watch, and took a long pull on the Diet Pepsi.

CHAPTER 79

Detectives Ron Mayer and Preston Barnett had worked together as a team for ten years. They each had over fifteen years experience in police work, and, like an old married couple, argued about just about everything. They were a very successful, well-respected team, and though they appeared casual in their approach to their profession, they were very thorough and fed well off on one another's strengths and weaknesses.

They were both divorced and remarried. They did not socialize together, except once every three months they went out together for a couple of beers (Preston actually drank Scotch) following work with three assistant district attorneys at a bar in the middle of nowhere. They all agreed that they liked that particular bar because: no one knew them, no one cared about them, the bartender didn't like to chat, and "Whiter Shade of Pale" and "Hotel California" were both on the jukebox. The five of them made an odd group, but no one at the bar cared, so it worked well for everyone.

The detectives drove up to the doctor's residence slowly and casually. They parked out front, not in the driveway. They didn't want to take the chance of someone coming out of the garage and ramming their ride. They always followed procedure; following procedure made them sure they would go home to their families at night.

On the way to Dr. Evans's house, Mayer and Barnett had placed a call to her unlisted phone number, which went unanswered. They knew that didn't necessarily mean no one was home, but at least no one was home who was answering the phone. They had a caller ID block on their cell phones so they couldn't be identified and lose the element of surprise.

There wasn't a car in the driveway or in front of the house and the garage door was closed. The neighborhood itself seemed quiet enough. There were "For Sale" signs on two of the houses, and no one was parked on the street. They opened their windows, turned off their radio, and just listened. No sounds of lawn machinery, no idling automobiles.

Without a word between them, they both began to focus on every detail around them. They had served warrants like this many times and the failure to be alert could get you seriously injured or killed. Only responses to domestic disputes were statistically more probable to get law enforcement officers wounded or killed than serving search or arrest warrants.

Mayer and Barnett both noted that it remained very quiet while they sat there. There were no dogs barking in the neighborhood. There were no cars on the street, and no sounds of people working or playing in their yards. The neighborhood was middle class and appeared to be fast asleep. As they got out of the car, they noticed that two houses had "For Rent" signs on them, and the weeds were starting to get high, indicating that the houses were probably not regularly occupied.

It was not a typical suburban neighborhood, they thought, it was way too empty and way too quiet. They both checked their weapons and their radios.

They both noted mentally that the houses were reasonably well kept but nothing special.

Strange place to live . . . for a doctor, Mayer thought.

CHAPTER 80

MAYER RANG THE doorbell and they stepped to either side so that neither detective was left standing directly in front of the door or the two glass panels on either side of it. They waited for a long count of ten and rang again, with the same result. After another count of ten, Barnett stepped forward, quickly opened the storm door, and knocked very hard and loudly on the wooden door.

"Police! We are here to serve a search warrant. I am informing you that if the door is not opened within fifteen seconds we will be forced to break it down!" Barrett had the loudest voice in the Chester County law enforcement family and always got the job of announcing police presence. Nothing within the house, or for that matter within the neighborhood, stirred.

Twelve, thirteen, fourteen, fifteen . . . Nothing happened. Mayer reached into his jacket pocket and produced an odd-looking device that he had seized from a career burglar some two years before. It was like a one-piece skeleton key and worked extremely well. Mayer was never able to find out where or by whom it had been manufactured, but it always worked extremely well and permitted him the luxury of not having to actually kick most doors down.

In a matter of seconds, the dead bolt and the snap lock had been unlocked. The pair of detectives carefully followed procedures in entering Dr. Evans's house. Upon entry, Mayer went to the left and into a crouch, and Barrett went to the right standing up straight and using the balustrade to the second floor as cover.

"Police," Barnett yelled.

Mayer was looking to his left into what he figured was a living room. It had hardwood floors . . . and nothing else. Barrett glanced around the corner to the right, which appeared to be a family room with a fireplace and wall-to-wall carpeting . . . and nothing else.

They both noticed that, just like the neighborhood, the house was quiet as a tomb. There was literally no noise whatsoever, not a fan, not a chime, not a refrigerator compressor, nothing.

They utilized the hand signals that they had developed over the years, avoiding speech and keeping as quiet as they possibly could. They had called, rang the doorbell, knocked loudly, and announced their presence twice. At that point they figured that anyone in the house had bad intentions. They eventually met in the kitchen. There was no clock, no phone, the toaster and the refrigerator had been disconnected along with the microwave. The heat was set at fifty degrees and was not currently engaged. The only indication that anyone lived in the house at all was a large cooler by the sliding glass doors that lead from the kitchen to the back porch. Neither Mayer nor Barnett wanted to open it.

"Your turn, handsome," said Meyer.

"No way, froggy, I opened that box two months ago in Kennett, and you know what we found in that thing!" Barnett answered.

"OK, fancy pants, but if it's something dead, you get to carry it out."

Mayer slipped on a pair of latex gloves, pushed the container with his foot, and hearing nothing, he bent over and opened it. Inside sat a partially melted eighteen-pound bag of ice, a tightly-closed loaf of bread, and two jars of peanut butter, one smooth, one chunky. They both smirked and closed the lid.

After a brief discussion they also decided to call for backup. They both came to the conclusion that either the doctor had flown the coupe or she was upstairs waiting for a good, old-fashioned shoot-out. There was one thing they both noticed right after they closed the cooler, something smelled decidedly funny and the smell was apparently coming from the upstairs.

CHAPTER 81

A FTER WHAT SEEMED like an hour (it had been fourteen minutes), the backup finally arrived. Everyone on the team felt spooked. It was hard to imagine that standing in a residence occupied by a single female doctor with virtually no furnishings, four experienced policemen all felt spooked in the same way, but they did. In an interview with the state police psychologist a month later, one of the officers admitted that he had the feeling they were about to be ambushed and overrun, an experience he had suffered in the Vietnam conflict. Barnett called it the "heevie jeevies," but whatever they called it, they all felt it and none of them would ever forget that feeling again.

Unfortunately, they found no evidence of any wrongdoing. They took trace samples of the foul-smelling portion of the rug in the corner of the bedroom, but it proved to be a spot rug remover that had been improperly used on the rug and another substance that was initially unidentifiable and would have to go the FBI lab for analysis. They found no bullets, no weapons, nothing. In fact, they found no television, no radio, no stereo, no lamps, no dressers . . . nothing, except eight sets of clothes and eight pairs of shoes in the bedroom closet. Eight pairs of panties and eight bras were all neatly kept in matched sets hanging in the closet. There was a toothbrush, a razor, some deodorant, and lipstick in the bathroom; no towels, no soap, but a single sample bottle of shampoo.

The basement was another story all by itself. It appeared that there had been a large workshop on one side, a storage area on the other, and, at least now, smack dab in the middle was something that looked vaguely like a torture machine from the Spanish Inquisition. The concrete floor below and around it were stained a reddish black, with small areas that looked (and smelled) like urine.

Just standing and looking at the machine caused one of the uniformed officers to shiver, his imagination conjuring up all manner of ways a person could be hurt on the contraption.

For one thing, none of them could figure out how the machine had been brought to the basement; it appearing way too large, way too wide, and way too tall to come down the stairs. It appeared to be constructed around a single welded frame, and there appeared to be no places for screws, bolts, or springs to undo it to make it smaller or break it down into pieces.

From one angle it looked like a sled. It appeared to have a wheel in the center and a chair, but it also had what appeared to be footpads on either end and symmetric bars protruding in three different directions.

They agreed to take multiple pictures of it and called the lab guys to take scrapings of the unit, the floor, the surrounding walls, and even the ceiling above it for trace evidence. It was a long process compared to the search of the rest of the residence and, in the end, they put police tape on it and walked out. It was pretty evident that this machine could have little use outside of stretching someone like a rack or pulling them a number of ways that seemed slightly inhuman in their design.

Then, after seemingly having searched every possible hiding spot in the house, in the back of a drawer in the kitchen with nothing else in it, they discovered a small case like something that you might store prescription medicine in.

The team all thought the same thing, that Dr. Evans's had decided to take a hike and that all the stuff that they found, she simply decided to leave behind. They were all quite embarrassed when they checked with the hospital only to find out she had reported to work on time, and was operating on a patient at that very moment. The good news was that the pillbox contained three things, all of which made the day a little less hard to swallow: a tooth, a mangled bullet slug, and a grayish brown substance that no one dared to guess what it was. In any event, the slug made it all worthwhile because they all agreed that maybe, they really did have a doctor who collected trophies, and maybe these were some of them.

When Barnett informed the district attorney's office that they had found something and had left a report to that effect on the doctor's kitchen table, there was stony silence at the end of the line. Despite the findings, for some reason, they all knew this was a precursor to something bad, they just didn't know what.

CHAPTER 82

BILL KAUFFMAN LAY in his hospital bed as he had for the previous four days. For all intents and purposes, he appeared to be sleeping peacefully. In reality, he was unconscious as a result of a number of forces. The first of which was his wound, the second of which was his surgery, the third of which was the painkillers administered to him by injection every four hours, and the last, but not the least, was a low-grade infection which was festering in his intestines.

Bill had an intravenous tube attached to his left arm. This was to provide him with a steady stream of nutrients as he was unable to eat. His team of physicians knew that the danger of peritonitis was much greater than the gunshot wound to the abdomen or than dying from the wound itself.

His right arm was attached to another intravenous tube. This provided his body with a combination of antibiotics designed to combat possible infection from the bullet itself, and as a precaution against peritonitis. Denise Wells stood at the foot of Bill Kauffman's bed. It was Sunday morning at 8:35 and the hospital halls were as quiet as they ever got. Denise read the chart from the previous evening and frowned. The patient's temperature had been checked twice during the night; once at 2:15 and again at 5:45. In both instances, the fever was recorded at just below one hundred degrees, 99.9. Denise Wells couldn't understand why his temperature wasn't being taken more often especially for a patient with an abdominal gunshot wound.

She checked the IV in his left arm first and that appeared to be in good shape, although she made a mental note to come back around 9:30 and check it again to be sure that the IV bag did not need to be changed.

She then checked the IV bag in his right arm and knew immediately that something was wrong. The amount of fluid that should have been gone from the IV bag had not been dispensed. She was not very happy with the efficiency of the weekend and night time nurses the hospital employed and swore under her breath. However, the code was simple: if it's a doctor who makes a mistake, file a complaint; if it's a fellow nurse, go see her and talk to her yourself. That is just the way it was and she made another mental note to find out who the nurse was, and make sure she got a good tongue-lashing for her lack of diligence.

Nurse Wells came around to the left-hand side of the bed and checked the flow on the IV. The flow was working fine but it was turned to about one-half of what he should have been receiving during the course of the evening. She goosed the cable, allowing a higher stream to enter Mr. Kauffman's blood stream. The antibiotics would be more in line with what the doctors had prescribed.

She checked the chart again and saw that there was a request for a morning injection of tzecololeal. This was to be administered an hour prior to the pain reliever. She knew the drug well. It was a powerful "chill" drug, which was extremely effective in bringing down a fever in dangerously feverish patients. She looked hard but couldn't discern the doctor's initials, and thought it a little bit odd that they would want to bring down the fever in a patient whose body temperature was as low as Mr. Kauffman's. Had to be a good reason, she thought. The staff was keeping a special eye on this patient because of the homicide investigation and the general ruckus that had occurred.

The tzecololeal had been placed in a locked drawer which only nurses and physicians had the key to. She extracted a new needle, tore open the bag with her teeth, put on her disposable nylon gloves, and set the canister of the drug into the syringe.

"If you can hear me, Mr. Kauffman, I'm going to give you an injection. It won't hurt, but you will feel a pinch followed by a little warm feeling moving up your arm. This is perfectly natural and to be expected. There are no side effects to this, and it should help bring your temperature down a little bit." There was no reaction from Bill Kauffman. Nurse Wells found a good vein, tied off Mr. Kauffman's arm with a piece of rubber tubing, and quickly and efficiently injected the fluid. She then put a cotton swab on the spot, covered the cotton swab with a band aid, and noted on the chart that the injection had been made.

She disposed of the syringe, her gloves, and the empty vial in a container marked "red waste." Before she exited the room, she checked her watch carefully and made a notation of the time on the chart and walked out. Inside Bill Kauffman, a terrible infection raged.

CHAPTER 83

S PAGNOLA HAD WORKED for eleven hours without a break. He decided it was time to go home, just let things sink in, have a beer, and listen to his jazz recordings. Spagnola loved jazz. His mind was at ease with jazz and sometimes, just sometimes, things that were bothering him straightened themselves out when he listened. He hummed "Drift Away" as he drove.

The station was only one and three quarter miles from his home. He liked living close to work; he liked working close to home. This was his township, his people. He shopped in the local supermarket and played tennis at the local high school on the weekends in warm weather. He was thinking about calling his friend, Ed Remembers, about a game for the weekend when he pulled out of the lot and onto Route 100. He headed south and turned his car left on Schoen Road. He was preoccupied with the details of his cases as he rounded the bend, oblivious to everything but the road in front of him and the questions yet to be resolved.

The SUV was sitting about forty yards up the road at a right angle to Schoen, looking down the hill with a clear view of the Route 100 intersection and the fish market on the corner. The SUV was parked, lights out, engine running, with the gear shift in drive. The parking break was set so that the driver did not have to use the foot brakes, thereby avoiding the brake lights going on. The driver's foot was carefully on the emergency break release.

As Spagnola hit the curve, he needed to look to his right to follow the curve. As he did so, out of his field of vision the SUV accelerated down the hill. The SUV was black, and the street light that normally would have illuminated Wren Drive had been shot out by a pellet gun the previous evening, leaving the street pitch black on the moonless, starless night.

When the SUV was less than thirty feet away and accelerating, Spagnola caught its movement out of the corner of his eye. It was just in time to begin to turn his head toward the movement and turn the steering wheel imperceptibly to the right. The steering wheel movement could not avoid the collision.

The SUV slammed into the side of the Crown Victoria with its huge front bumper striking three quarters of the way up the driver's side door, but at a slight angle caused by Spagnola's wheel adjustment just before impact. The impact crushed the door with the window shattering but remaining intact due to the nature of the safety glass.

Spagnola was driven sideways against his shoulder restraint so hard that it bruised his ribs. His head slammed first to the right and then back to the left, with the air bag deploying as the front end of the car struck a post and rail fence as it was forced into the front yard of 112 Schoen Road. The SUV continued into the side of the car, crumpling the sturdy reinforced door, sliding forward, and crushing the left front panel at the forty-degree angle of impact. The entire top of the vehicle bent upward, while the left front tire exploded. The sound of metal groaning and glass shattering reverberated throughout the quiet neighborhood.

The SUV did not proceed over the top or through the car only because of the angle of impact. Had the Crown Victoria continued on its original path resulting in a ninety degree angle collision, the damage to the car and the driver would have been more severe.

The Crown Victoria careened off of the SUV and slid on the lawn, but as it turned the SUV caught it again in the rear-quarter panel, crushing it and driving the front end of the car into a small tree where it came to rest. Upon the second impact, Spagnola passed out from the pain, unaware that his instinctive move had saved his life. He sat slumped against his restraint, bleeding from numerous cuts, but alive.

The driver of the SUV turned the ignition off, opened the door, and stepped out into the night. The driver surveyed the scene, threw the keys into the bushes, and calmly strolled away into the woods, never looking back.

CHAPTER 84

DETECTIVE SPAGNOLA AWOKE. Shortly after gaining consciousness, he heard the sound of sirens. He was dazed and unsure of where he was. He would not remember the actual crash until later. Once he was able to get his bearings in the crumpled vehicle, he began to remember where he was or what had happened. The pain in his legs, his side, his back, and his neck didn't compare to the pounding in his head.

He could feel that his right wrist was broken, and with his left hand felt the top of his head. He found his hair to be warm and sticky, which he knew meant that he was bleeding. He could only see out of his right eye and realized that it was the blood seeping down his scalp and into his eye that had temporarily blinded him on his left side. He tried his fingers and they worked. He tried his toes and was able to wiggle them. He repeated the test with his arms and his legs and everything seemed to work. Most of him just hurt like hell.

He could not reach his cell phone, but managed to get one hand on the steering wheel and began pressing the horn. Three dots, three dashes, and three dots. Apparently everyone in the neighborhood recognized the distress call and the 911 switchboard lit up like a Christmas tree in downtown West Chester.

Shortly before the ambulances arrived, a small crowd gathered to inspect the wreck. None of the assembled neighborhood people had any medical or police training, nor had any of them ever assisted at an accident scene. As a result, their help revolved around asking the detective if he was OK, and if there was anything they could do. There wasn't.

Suddenly a police car and an ambulance both arrived at the scene and skidded to a halt, scattering the onlookers. Everyone literally jumped from their vehicles and raced to Detective Spagnola's side.

Officer Richard Leiland was the first to speak. "Hey, Spags, can you hear me?"

Spags woke up and said, "I can hear you but can you get me outta here. I'm pretty banged up. Get me the hell outta here!"

An EMT brushed the policeman aside and looked around inside the collapsed interior of the vehicle.

"Let's try to open this door first. My guess is that it's not going to open, and we might need to look to extract him from the other side of the car," he said.

The EMT and one of the officers ran to the other side of the vehicle and quickly opened that door.

"Jesus," said the officer, which drew a sharp glance from the EMTs who were trained not to express their emotions upon seeing an unpleasant sight. The idea was not to panic the victim, thought the EMT.

"Detective, I'm going to need you to slowly and carefully describe for me how you feel, starting with your feet and moving up to your head. I can see you are bleeding from your forehead. It appears to be a superficial wound but you might have a concussion. Take your time. It's going to take a little while to get you out of here but we know how to do this, it's our job, and we've done it many times before. You are in good hands now and you are among your friends, so just try to relax as best you can and listen to my requests."

Spags felt lightheaded. For a moment he felt nauseous, knew that was a bad thing, blinked it away, and tried to focus on the questions from the EMT, and more importantly, the answers. Some of his dull pains were becoming sharper.

"I can move all of my toes. I can only move one of my feet, but I can feel the other one, don't think it's hurt. I think it is stuck underneath my leg. My right shin hurts. It's kind of a dull, achy hurt. I don't think it's broken, but it hit something or something hit it awfully hard.

"My knees seem to feel OK. My left thigh hurts but I don't think it's broken. Again, I think the door punched in on it, but I can move my legs a little bit and flex the muscles. Flexing the muscles in the left leg is really hurtful. My stomach feels OK and my back doesn't seem to be a problem. My left side is killing me. OK . . . " He drifted back into unconsciousness.

The EMT gave him a gentle shake to try and awaken him. "Come on, Detective, stay with me," he said. Spags's eyes opened.

"OK, I either cracked or broke some ribs when the door caved in on me. My neck hurts, think I sprained it. I'm feeling a little nauseous and there is blood dripping into my left eye."

As he finished speaking, the EMT was already dabbing at the wound on his forehead.

"I'm going to do two things right now. First, I am going to clean that wound and put a temporary bandage on it, and then I'm going to put an ice pack on your head to keep the swelling down. That will help alleviate some of the nausea, some of the headache pain as well. It should also help you focus on helping us get you out of there."

Spags just nodded, suddenly feeling too tired to speak.

CHAPTER 85

A SECOND AMBULANCE ARRIVED at the scene and the EMTs were surprised to find that there was no second victim in the SUV. The police at the scene began scouring the grounds of the residences in the neighborhood, presuming that the driver of the SUV had wandered off, was intoxicated, or was a juvenile driver with no license and in either event was trying to hide or at least get away from the scene.

The police examined the inside of the Tahoe and found no alcohol or drugs and no identification of any kind. The license plate had been removed.

The police quickly ran a search at the department of motor vehicles by computer with the VIN number off the inside of the front door and found that it belonged to a Jeffery Sedermin of Kent Place in the Marchrock Development of Uwchlan Township. A squad car was immediately dispatched to the Kent Place address to question the Sedermins. A telephone call to the Sedermin residence went unanswered save for the family's voice mail message indicating that they were not home.

Spags asked the EMT what happened to the other driver and was less annoyed than perplexed when he was told they couldn't find the other driver. They had given him a pain killer and, although mild in dosage, combined with his fatigue and the shock of his injuries, Spags's senses had become dull. He knew he'd have to give this situation more thought in the morning. He was just too damn tired and too damn hurt to think clearly right now. The EMT was doing his best to keep Spags awake.

At the Uwchlan Township building, a call went out to all the off-duty police officers notifying them that one of their own had been injured in a hit-and-run type of accident, and asking them to come and help. Every officer in the force responded and the station house was buzzing. The police in general took these things seriously. The police in Uwchlan Township were no exception. They were going to come to the aid of a fellow officer. If possible, they would quickly put a net on the person who had driven the Tahoe and throw the book at him.

Within fifteen minutes of the call, the accident scene was swarming with police, some from other departments, as well as a horde of ambulance core workers and firemen. Dogs had arrived on the scene to try and track the scent of the departed driver. A call had been placed to the Chester County Detectives' Office requesting a forensics team be dispatched to seize the Tahoe and check it for any kind of evidence that could link it to a driver. At the other end, Mr. Sedermin and his family were the current focus of the police portion of the investigation. It appeared that the Sedermins had two teenage boys, ages sixteen and seventeen, one of whom had been caught for underage drinking six weeks earlier and the other of whom had been caught the previous year driving without a license.

Unfortunately for the police, when they arrived at the Sedermin home, no one was there. A canvas of the neighborhood by the police did not produce any explanation as to the Sedermins' whereabouts, and the immediate neighbors had not seen any of the Sedermin family since early the previous afternoon.

The keys to the Tahoe were found the following morning in the bushes next to the woods through which the driver of the Tahoe had apparently fled. The police were able to identify eleven sets of footprints, all leading in the same direction with the right foot being a size nine and a half and the left size being a size nine. When the Sedermins returned home the following day, they were greeted by police before they even got out of their car. All four family members were in the same vehicle. They had verifiable alibis for the entire family which were quickly checked and rechecked by the police, to their ultimate satisfaction and disappointment.

CHAPTER 86

DETECTIVE SPAGNOLA WAS unconscious for almost ten minutes following the collision. Doris Schumaker had been sitting in her living room watching television when she heard the crash. She went over to her windows and looked outside but could see nothing from the angle her living room window afforded her. She went back to watching television.

After a few minutes, she decided that she should go outside to take a look. She carefully unlocked her front door and looked outside. Seeing no one but hearing a hissing noise, she carefully opened her screen door and stepped out onto the front porch. She knew she could see the rear end of a large black vehicle partially on her neighbor's lawn and partially in the street. Frightened by what she saw, she went back inside. She debated in her own mind if she should call 911 and finally did.

Unfortunately, Doris was flustered on the phone and actually gave the operator the wrong address, reciting the address she had lived at before she moved to Schoen Road. She had moved to Schoen Road five years earlier when her husband had died. The delay caused further confusion with the dispatcher, but eventually the police and ambulance arrived at the scene.

Although other neighbors had heard a noise, most of them simply turned to one another and said, "What was that?"

Absent Mrs. Schumaker's call, it might have been hours before anyone was on the scene. Had that been the case, Spags would have been dead. When Spags awakened and started hitting SOS on his horn, help was already on the way.

CHAPTER 87

BILL LAY ON *the floor in the foyer of his home. He could hear sirens outside and could smell his own blood. Only moments before he heard the door close, and since no one had come in after that, he assumed that someone had left. The person who left must have shot me, he thought. He knew he had heard a gunshot but he just couldn't remember what had happened. He was still groggy and dazed, but his thoughts were beginning to clear up. He began to notice little sounds even over the din of the approaching sirens.*

Bill heard the ticking of the grandfather clock that stood in the corner ten feet away from him. He could hear the droning of the air conditioning unit which sat outside on a concrete pad just behind the house. He was certain he could hear his own heart, but as he reached to feel his heartbeat, he could barely move his arms. They simply would not obey his commands.

Bill was puzzled. He felt as if he were looking into a fog, knowing something was in the fog but not being able to figure out what it was. He felt better though; he knew the fog was lifting, but at the same time that the fog was lifting, the pain in his gut was increasing.

Bill heard people outside now, or they appeared to be outside, but they didn't sound like police or emergency personnel. He thought he recognized the voice of one of his neighbors but he couldn't tell which one. There was excitement in the air since someone had heard the gunshot. Then suddenly the fog lifted. The fog had lifted because the pain had come through, terrible, terrible pain as if someone were standing on his stomach. The pain focused Bill's mind and he remembered.

CHAPTER 88

*E*LAINE KAUFFMAN HAD *been watching television and sipping a glass of wine. It was 4:40 PM and there was plenty of daylight left. Bill had asked her if she would like another glass and she had responded by saying, "That would be nice." Bill had gone to the kitchen with her glass, taken the sodium silicate XM pill that he had crushed up, and poured the wine into the glass with the reddish powder, just as he had done with her first glass. It was a full-bodied Merlot, and the pill had almost no taste according to the doctor, so he doubted Elaine would notice the difference in taste. She hadn't noticed in the first glass he had poured for her half an hour before. In fact, she didn't notice any taste difference, but she was feeling a little groggy.*

Twenty-five minutes later, Elaine got up off her chair and said to Bill, "Phew, I sure am tired. Gonna lie down and take a little snooze." Her voice was slightly off and she slurred the word snooze. Elaine only slept in bed and she didn't hesitate to make a bee line for their bedroom. It had always been that way, Bill thought. First sign of fatigue, headache, or stress and she was off to the bedroom for a nap. Bill had counted on her routine and Elaine had not disappointed him.

Five minutes after she entered the bedroom, Elaine was asleep. Bill picked up his cell phone, careful not to dial, and utilized the walkie-talkie feature. He depressed the button and said a single word, "Asleep." After a brief pause, there was a single-word reply from the other phone-turned-private-radio, "OK."

Bill walked to the garage and unlocked the side door. The door was wedged between some hedges and was rarely used by anyone. Within moments, what appeared to be a man of medium stature in a sports coat and a fedora slipped in the door and closed it behind. Bill waited in the kitchen, a bundle of nerves and nervous energy.

When the person emerged into the kitchen, Bill stepped forward to put his arms around the guest, and the person pushed him back. Taking off her hat and her jacket, Dr. Evans was all business. Concealed under the sports jacket were a variety of medical instruments, syringes, chemicals, gauze, and a slim case for a nine-millimeter automatic made by the German company Templar.

The doctor laid out the items on the kitchen table, along with four vials of Bill Kauffman's blood. The two of them had carefully donated some of his blood each week for four consecutive weeks, so as not to compromise his physical health, which would be vital in his recovery after being supposedly shot. It was important to give authenticity to what they were about to do.

Bill stripped off his shirt and handed it to the doctor. He then went into the garage and retrieved a small bucket of sand used to extinguish cigarettes in the backyard when summer required the occasional barbeque.

Using a homemade silencer, the doctor wrapped the shirt carefully in place on top of the sand bucket, moved the gun back three feet, and fired through the shirt and into the sand. There was a barely audible pop as the bullet ripped through Bill's shirt and wound its way deep into the sand before it came to rest.

The doctor placed the gun carefully onto a mat she had brought with her and placed on the kitchen counter, so as not to leave any trace evidence. She then handed the gun to Bill.

Bill donned a pair of latex gloves, accepted the gun from his guest, then went to his bedroom.

Elaine Kauffman was fast asleep. The combination of the drugs and the wine, together with her weekly tennis match, had put her in a deep sleep. Bill thought that this was both good and bad. It would have been easier if she was partially awake, and he tried to arouse her. Bill had a good deal of difficulty in rousing Elaine; she simply refused to wake up. The doctor grabbed her under her arms, pulled her off the bed, and laid her on the floor. The doctor raised her one hand, and Bill fired a bullet through it, which caused Elaine to jump into a seated position.

The last site that Elaine Ellen Kauffman ever saw was a bulbous contraption attached to the barrel of a Templar .44-caliber gun, staring at her with the face of Bill behind and above it. The second shot tore through Elaine Kauffman's heart and she was dead in less than twenty seconds. It didn't matter to Bill; he had hated Elaine for years. She was just a piece of furniture around the house that had not aged gracefully. He went back to the kitchen, careful not to remove his latex gloves.

Dr. Evans placed yet another set of plastic gloves on her hands and removed one of the syringes from her pouch. After carefully removing a vial of Dlantonisthel (a fast acting anaesthetic), she made an injection under Bill's fingernail and the substance quickly made its way through Bill's system. The Dlantinishtel was very new, not approved by the FDA, but lauded by MASH surgeons for its ability to anaesthetize battle-injured GIs quickly and efficiently, and could be administered in a number of different ways.

Bill walked over and positioned himself on the floor in the hallway. He began to get groggy. Before he could fall asleep, they placed his shirt back on him, buttoned the buttons, undid his pants, tucked the shirt into them, and lined up the bullet hole with a pin prick so as to mark a clearly identifiable spot where the surgery would occur. It was 5:47 PM and Bill and his accomplice both knew that they had about twenty minutes to accomplish the rest of their work.

CHAPTER 89

D R. EVANS PLACED *a small pillow behind Bill's head and pulled his feet forward so that he was lying flat on his back. This would not be the position he would be left in, but in this position it was easier for Dr. Evans to do her surgery. She reopened his shirt, trying not to pull it back out of his pants, but moved the shirt sufficiently to give herself good access to the pin prick where she needed to begin the surgery.*

Dr. Evans had been careful to remove the bullet from the sand in the bucket as soon as it had appeared to have cooled. It was not misshapen to any visible extent, and she carefully washed the sand from it. She did not want any forensic investigation to reveal that the bullet had been fired into the sand. She then coated the slug with a fine coat of blood to which she would add flecks of skin if she could get them to adhere to it. She determined it was unwise to attach a piece of the torn cloth to the slug, as there was no evidence of torn cloth inside the sand bucket. As it was, the bullet hole in the shirt looked great, she thought, and she began to make an incision.

She carefully cut away portions of the epidermis, subdermis, and fatty tissue. When she was done, she could make the hole in his body ragged, as if it had occurred from the entrance of a bullet. She deftly used clamps and an assortment of other items from her bag to prop the wound open and let it bleed. She was careful not to cut any main arteries or veins to keep the bleeding under control, and so as not to obscure her work.

Dr. Evans knew that in reality, the bullet might have passed directly through Bill Kauffman had it actually been fired into him at the range and the angle she was trying to mimic. There was nothing she could do about that inconsistency. She did not want to appear to have the bullet nick a bone, as this would complicate the surgery beyond the time limits that she had allowed herself. When she determined she had hit the proper depth, she picked up the slug with a pair of tweezers, rubbed the bullet in some of the subcutaneous flesh and epidermis, and placed the slug carefully inside of the cavity she had created in Bill Kauffman's body.

She knew that if all went well, she would be removing this bullet in a few hours at best. At worst, someone else would be removing the bullet, but the results would be the same. There would be no reason to believe that Bill Kauffman had not been shot. He was bleeding fairly significantly now, but nothing that would be fatal so long as help arrived within a reasonable period of time. She removed three vials of blood and placed them carefully by the wall. The doctor was strong and fit, and had very little problem in propping Bill against the corner of the wall, removing the pillow, and carefully soaking his shirt and pants with the three vials. The doctor then carefully replaced the caps on all of the vials and put them into plastic bags which she had arranged on the kitchen table. Once she was satisfied that she had left nothing behind, she took all of the small plastic bags, put them into a larger garbage bag, and folded it into a pouch that she would wear around her waist when she exited the Kauffman home.

She took off her surgical gloves, put them in a plastic bag, and put on a third set of gloves. The third pair came all the way to her elbows, as had the first pair.

The doctor carefully gathered all of the items, checked the entrance way, the kitchen, and the garage (twice). She then made a short call on her cell phone and exited the way that she had come in. She looked like an elderly man on an evening stroll. It was 6:28 PM.

Bill was stirring, the last parts of his dream fuzzy and confused . . . and his dream was over.

CHAPTER 90

S PAGNOLA DRIFTED OUT of his dream and into consciousness. His eyelids felt heavy but he opened them nonetheless. He dreamt that he was strapped to a gurney and was coming in through the main doors of the Brandywine Hospital. Endersly was standing there with a grin on his face in a Halloween costume. At least one hundred crows sat on a wire just inside the entrance to the room. Black balloons hung from the ceiling. The room was lined with people shaking their heads and murmuring. The dream was now over, and Spags began focusing on his room.

Just like in his nightmare, he was in a hospital. Unlike the nightmare, he was in a private room and he sensed that he was alone. He turned his head slightly to the side and could see the monitor on the left side of his bed. As he focused, he could hear the intermittent beep registering his own heartbeat. He was not flat on his back, but rather was in a semi-upright position and could look down and see the intravenous lines coming from his arm. In his groggy state, he thought it was his worst nightmare that he was in fact in Brandywine Hospital and at the mercy of Endersly . . . the clown.

He was aware of a dull ache in his right side, and he could see that his left arm was in a cast. He had a vague recollection of waking up in an ambulance and admonishing the team not to give him painkillers. Shortly after giving his tirade, he remembered being stuck with a needle and a warm flowing feeling going through his body while he submerged into unconsciousness.

His throat was incredibly dry and he looked around for water. A pitcher sat on his nightstand along with cups, but he was unable to reach either. After a few minutes, he became aware of an electronic button device that was seated neatly on his stomach. He raised his right hand and instinctively pressed the button. At that moment a red light went on at the nurses' station and a nurse was dispatched down the hall. At the same time, the nurse at the station paged Dr. Howard per the instructions on the computer regarding patient Spagnola.

Nurse Runyon was twenty-eight years of age, had a bounce in her step, and a great rapport with her patients. She strolled into the room through the open door of Spagnola's hospital room, smiled, glanced at the monitors, perused the chart, and said, "Finally awake, Detective, how are we feeling?" She also had the tremendously annoying habit of referring to the patients in the euphemistic "we" mode, which immediately annoyed Spagnola.

His throat was even more parched than he thought, as he was literally unable to speak. He mouthed the word "water." She complied and picked up the cup complete with straw, and held it up to his mouth so that he could drink. He sucked on the straw mightily, and he immediately began to cough as the cold fluid hit the back of his throat.

"Easy now, soldier, you've had a bit of a rough time. You need to be able to walk before you run. That goes for drinking fluids and eating as well. You were intubated briefly and that will cause soreness in your throat. It will go away shortly, but in the meantime, it will be a little more difficult to swallow any fluid, even cold water. Take your time. We'll get plenty of fluids into you. There, is that better?" she asked.

Spagnola nodded and took a slow, small sip from the straw. He glanced around the room and said, "How long?"

She glanced down at the chart and said, "You were admitted to the emergency room about three and a half hours ago. You've been here in this room for about two. We have instructions to notify Dr. Howard the moment you wake up, and I believe he has instructions to notify the police officers waiting downstairs as soon as you're able to be seen."

At that moment, Dr. Howard, a middle-aged male of what can only be called Euro-Asian extraction entered the room. He was no more than five foot four inches tall and barely broke 120 pounds. He wore farm-rimmed glasses and a short white coat that was as neat as a pin. Spagnola could tell from his demeanor that he was quite confident in his medical abilities.

"Detective Spagnola, I need to inform you that you have suffered the following injuries in your automobile crash: concussion, laceration of the forehead, strained neck muscles, two broken ribs, three bruised ribs, broken left arm, contusions of the chest, stomach, lower back legs, sprained ankle, and a variety of cuts and burns, some of which were caused by the deployment of your air bag.

"None of your injuries are life-threatening. Your injuries are going to slow you down significantly. You are going to hurt a great deal when you take deep breaths due to your cracked ribs, but your failure to take deep breaths will almost assuredly lead to pneumonia in one or both of your lungs. My advice is to breathe slowly but deeply. It is very important that you remain on your pain medication for the prescribed period of time, even though it may cause you some drowsiness." Dr. Howard paused. "Do you have any questions?"

Spagnola blinked, and then said, "Don't have the time, can't afford the time," and then made a motion as if he was going to try and sit up. Neither the doctor nor the nurse did anything to dissuade him from his movement. However, the look on his face told it all. A searing shot of pain ran down his right side despite the medication. It caused him a mild cough which brought further pain in his arm and his right leg, not to mention another wave of pain down his right side. He gently lay back, closed his eyes, and took three quick shallow breaths. All he could think of was that he was in total agony.

CHAPTER 91

T O ADD INSULT to injury, when he reopened his eyes, the chief of Uwchlan Township police, Art Diehle, an ex-military, no-nonsense type with great leadership capabilities and a strong police background, was standing on Spagnola's left, accompanied by his right-hand man, Sergeant Jake Reisenbach.

The chief started. "Don't talk, I'll do the talking. You were rammed by a black SUV owned by Joan and Peter Sedermin of Bel Air Avenue in Exton. They apparently were away and the vehicle was stolen. Whoever was driving it fled the scene, and so far we have no real witnesses. The SUV has been impounded. The county detectives are going to work it up for trace evidence. At first blush, it might have been a kid who stole it or several kids who went for a joy ride, but we are pretty sure that the SUV attempted to back up and smash into your car a second time. It is more likely that the driver tried to back up and get away, and it didn't work out. We've got to look into that. If it's the former, you must have really pissed somebody off. Are you behind in your alimony?"

Spagnola forced a smile. He knew the chief was trying to make light and appreciated the effort.

The chief started again. "You need to get some rest. We'll talk more tomorrow. Your buddy in York County sent us a message to tell you: 1) get yourself to a driver's ed class, you were always a lousy operator, and 2) he's got three incident reports from the eighteen months that you were looking at where evidence appears to have been removed from the scene of a crime and disappeared. He thinks maybe you're on to something with regard to trophies."

Spagnola visibly brightened at the news, but it was short lived as another stab of pain went down his right side.

The chief turned toward Dr. Howard. "Are you sure this guy isn't dying? He looks pretty awful."

Dr. Howard was totally bereft of his sense of humor, glanced quickly at the chart, at the vital signs, and down at the patient. He didn't understand the joke.

"I'm quite certain his injuries are not life threatening. I would suggest you leave him alone and let him get some rest. If he's in pain now, he will be in worse pain tomorrow, but things should improve in forty-eight hours. He should be able to return to work in about two weeks."

"Two freakin' weeks? You gotta be kiddin'!" Spags had to take four shorts breaths to compensate for the pain of expressing his displeasure.

The chief nodded at the doctor, turned to Spagnola, and told him, "Get some rest. That's an order. We'll be back tomorrow morning and we'll bring you your files. In the meantime, we'll keep trying to figure out what happened last night, and we're going to catch the bastard, whoever he is."

Spagnola drifted back off to sleep as everyone left the room. What he didn't know and had forgotten to ask was why he wasn't in Brandywine Hospital. He was in Berwyn.

CHAPTER 92

*I*N THE DISTANCE *Bill could hear a faint beeping noise. He could smell a number of smells, all alien to his nose, but none that were offensive. He could not distinguish one smell from another, but he knew they were there.*

His tongue was thick, heavy, and dry. He tried to move it and ask for water, but nothing came out of his mouth but a slight rasp. He tried to wiggle his fingers and was certain he was doing so but couldn't open his eyes to see. He thought about it for a while but could not work anything out.

He could tell that he was lying down by reason of a feeling of light pressure on his back and his calves. He could wiggle his toes and thought that this was a good sign. He couldn't remember much of anything and could not for the life of him figure out where he was. Even more distant than the beeping noise was the muffled sound of a telephone ringing, but it wasn't a normal ring.

He tried to focus on the ringing, thinking that understanding the ringing might help him understand where he was and what had happened. The ringing stopped and he thought he heard a voice but couldn't determine any words, and then the sounds of the voice went away.

Bill suddenly became aware of his own breathing. He could feel it rather than hear it and it had a soothing effect on him. He was breathing and drifting, breathing and drifting. He felt warm, not hot but warm. He wished that someone would turn down the heat. Maybe that's why his tongue felt so dry . . . maybe it was the heat. The expression "It's not the heat that gets you, it's the humidity" suddenly ran across his mind followed by the muffled sound of a gunshot which Bill found surprisingly did not startle him.

There was something in the back of his mind about a gunshot but he simply could not bring it forward. Bill was tired from his effort and drifted back into his deep slumber.

CHAPTER 93

I T WAS 12:15 AM. It was three hours and fifteen minutes after a black SUV with an unidentified driver had slammed into the side of Detective Spagnola's car. The night shift had come on at Brandywine Hospital, and the second shift nurse at the station for critical care on the third floor had been replaced. The replacement nurse, Mrs. Tyler, was a cantankerous, fifty-three-year-old malcontent woman. She didn't like the patients, she didn't like the nurses, she hated the doctors, and she had no time at all for the administrators. She complained about her salary, complained about her benefits. She was rude, unbending, and decidedly bigoted. She only moved up through the ranks due to longevity. She was well known and uniformly disliked.

She had barely raised her chin when the intern bypassed her station and headed down the hall, head engrossed in a textbook. She was supposed to monitor the comings and goings of all persons during her shift for security reasons, both for the patient's safety and for the safety of the drug cabinets. Everyone knew she did neither task. Most doctors had long since stopped checking in with her as they did not want to take her abuse. She always had something nasty to say and wasn't afraid to say it. Anything said back to her was always considered a racial slur or a discriminating remark regarding her body weight (at five foot six inches tall and 237 pounds, she was obese under any medical definition). She reported any comment made to her immediately to the hospital administration on the proper form (and on occasion to the

Pennsylvania Human Relations Board). If nothing else, Nurse Tyler knew all of the proper forms.

It registered in Nurse Tyler's brain that the person walking past her was an intern, name unknown, who was probably studying for an exam the next day and was preoccupied with his exam rather than the patients' well-being. She was big on patients' well-being. She pontificated on it whenever she had the opportunity.

At the same time, she very rarely got off of her stool and had no time for patient complaints. Knowing a doctor was in the house, she quickly glanced at the monitors, which showed that the hearts of all sixteen patients on her floor were pumping and that none of the patients had hit their emergency buttons.

She went back to reading her magazine and paid the intern no further attention.

The tall, slender, person posing as a young intern passed the nurses' station, headed to the side, and performed a slight limp in case Nurse Tyler was actually paying attention. The young intern had severe doubts about that. The young intern then made a bee line to Bill Kauffman's room, ducked inside, and quietly closed the door. The intern quickly checked on Bill's pulse, which the monitor indicated was just above seventy beats per minute. The intern checked the pulse manually and confirmed the machine. The intern then immediately turned off the IV drip containing the antibiotics and increased the pain killer. In addition, the intern removed a syringe from the intern's coat pocket, quickly and expertly extracted a drug from a sealed bottle that was meant to reduce fever, and injected Bill Kauffman with the drug just behind his ear. The syringe was then placed in a plastic bag which was placed in another plastic bag and placed back in the intern's pocket. The intern dabbed at the minor wound behind the neck until it was gone, and then covered it with a small quantity of lotion and Vaseline.

The intern took out a small tape recorder, more like a portable dictation device. The tape contained a recording fifteen minutes in length of the heartbeat of Bill Kauffman at approximately seventy beats per minute. Careful not to set off an alarm, the intern removed the cuff from Bill Kauffman's arm and placed the dictation device inside of it and pulled it tight. No monitors went off. There was no alarm and the monitor that showed the pulse of the patient both in the room and back at the nurse's station showed only a minor change. Nurse Tyler did not notice the change.

The intern counted to twenty, making sure that the increased dosage of the pain killer had entered Bill's bloodstream body. The intern then pressed down as hard as possible on Bill's still-unhealed wound. Inside Bill Kauffman, tiny perforations in his large intestine flowed with poisonous fluids from within his body. This action alone should have spiked his temperature, but the drug he had been administered kept his temperature down. His temperature remained steady at around ninety-nine. Bill was perspiring profusely.

Next, the intern pinched Bill Kauffman's nose. Kauffman began to breathe in a labored fashion through his mouth only. The intern began the procedure again and did so until their watch showed eleven minutes and forty-five seconds had elapsed. The intern gave Bill sufficient time to recover from the assault and for his heartbeat to come down just below eighty. The intern then removed the cuff from the tape device, placed it on Bill's arm, and monitored it carefully as his pulse came down.

Bill's immune system had been stretched to its limit. The nick in his esophagus made by Dr. Evans had not been properly repaired and the perforations in his intestines had caused him to develop a severe case of peritonitis. This, of course, was masked by a combination of pain killing drugs and the lack of a high fever. The recent administration of fever-masking drugs, and the fact that for ten minutes, twice daily, the intern would surreptitiously carry an ice bag to Bill Kauffman's room and lay it across his head to keep his fever down, would further mask his true condition. In combination, these efforts made a proper assessment of Bill's condition diagnosis highly unlikely. Peritonitis is an extremely dangerous condition. If not treated properly and promptly, peritonitis can result in a patient's hospitalization for a long period of time. If treated improperly or misdiagnosed, it will surely kill the patient. In Bill's case, the intern was doing what the bullet could not have. It was killing him.

The intern checked the chart. The nurse who was on duty was a good nurse most of the time, but on Sunday nights she had a habit of disappearing into the nurses' lounge and watching movies. Oh yes, she would check on patients, no question, but she checked on them immediately after arriving and usually didn't check on them again until 6:00 AM.

The intern knew that by 6:00 AM, Bill Kauffman would be in cardiac arrest. There would be heroic measures to save his life. There would be an autopsy. There would be fingers pointed and accusations made. The bottom line would be that no one would understand the nature of his death. First of all, they wouldn't investigate his death all that deeply. Second of all, the people who were looking were the same people who might be at fault. Third, the intern had been careful about when and how the intern had taken Bill Kauffman's life.

"Good night and good-bye, Mr. Kauffman," said Dr. Evans posing as the intern and then she quietly closed the door. Nurse Tyler didn't even look up as the intern walked by, nose buried in a chemistry book.

At 4:12 AM, the alarms went off. Bill Kauffman had gone into cardiac arrest.

CHAPTER 94

WITH THE CODE alarms pounding in the background at the nurses' station on the third floor intensive care unit, a team of doctors, nurses, and technicians sprang into action. Bill Kauffman was stripped of his gown, tubes were removed from his hands and arms. He was left with only his cardiovascular monitor still attached to him. The monitor showed greenish lights that indicated both his blood pressure and his heartbeat, which did not appear to be registering. The heartbeat was a flat line.

The first person who entered the room was a staff nurse who cleared the area around Bill Kauffman like a mine sweeper. The second person who entered the room was Dr. Trinh, third year resident of Vietnamese descent. This would be the twenty-first code response for him since he entered his third year of residency. Dr. Trinh, while diminutive at five foot three inches and 130 pounds, was catlike in his actions. He literally leapt upon the bed, called for and received a syringe filled with alvurocaine, located the proper spot on Bill Kauffman's chest, and delivered the 100 milligrams as expertly as it could be done, into Bill's heart. In almost the same motion, he jumped to the floor, quickly scanned Mr. Kauffman's torso, and, satisfied that there were no more objects or hookups that could create havoc, mentally noted a "well done" for the mine sweeper nurse as his feet hit the floor.

"Paddles," he called out. He was handed the paddles without having to look for them by an experienced physician's assistant named Grimes. He rubbed them together, spreading the gel between them and called out again.

"Clear."

He delivered the paddles against Bill Kauffman's chest, producing the smell of burning flesh, an audible snap and Bill's body came off the bed as if he were coming off a trampoline, a full four inches from the bed, from head to foot. A pulse appeared on the cardio monitor and the second nurse (Trinh thought her name was Kitmer) called out.

"BP ninety over seventy-five."

Dr. Trinh grabbed the chart and threw it across the room to the staff nurse, who caught it and flipped through the pages.

"Nurse, give it to me short and sweet, what's going on here?" Trinh barked in a not unpleasant manner.

Nurse Aronowicz, despite the urgency of the situation, almost smiled. She really admired the little guy; he was really good, really calm, really professional, and would make a great physician, she thought. Unfortunately, she realized that his English was straight from a *Pink Panther* movie. She always half expected Dr. Trinh to stammer a little and ramble on like Jackie Chan did in the movies.

"Gunshot wound to the abdomen ... six days ago. Bullet successfully extracted in ER, trauma unit Gold. No allergies, BP normal, no history of heart disease. All tests normal, running slight fever throughout his stay, high doses of intravenous antibiotics."

Dr. Trinh moved to the other side of the bed. He knew that something was terribly wrong and the chart's description of the patient did not fit. He instinctively checked the bracelet on Mr. Kauffman to make sure there was no error in his identity. Suddenly, the second nurse called out.

"BP one hundred over sixty. Heart rate eighty-six per minute."

Trinh glanced at the heart rate on the monitor. Way too fast for someone in this condition and with low blood pressure, he thought. He touched Mr. Kauffman's forehead with the back of his hand.

"Shit!" he muttered. "When was his last temperature reading?"

"Four hours ago, 99.2, can't read the doctor's name," Nurse Aronowicz responded.

The nurse thumbed through the chart.

"Well, he's got to be 102–103 now, get an accurate reading. He feels like he's burning up. Get the kitchen right now, get at least one hundred pounds of ice, stat. Get a fan on him right now, strip the bedding, and put cold compresses on all his pressure points. Jeez, he is burning up."

Dr. Trinh palpated the area around the wound. He found it was hard as a rock and hot.

"This man has a serious infection inside his wound, maybe peritonitis. Dial up the surgical unit and get a room prepped. He is going to need surgery right now."

The nurse was taken aback. She couldn't believe the diagnosis, but Dr. Trinh certainly sounded sure of his call. Before she could complete dialing, punching in the number, the cardiograph went haywire again and Mr. Kauffman flatlined. His blood pressure plummeted and Dr. Trinh cleared everyone away from him.

"Get me two hundred milligrams of atropine," Trinh called out.

He straddled Mr. Kauffman again. He was careful not to put any pressure on the wound or the surrounding area. Trinh pounded Mr. Kauffman's heart three times and then injected the heart with atropine.

"Blood pressure sixty over thirty, no heartbeat," called a nurse.

Trinh jumped down off the bed, took the paddles in his hands, and shouted, "Clear!"

Again the room resonated with a crack, as the electricity surged through Kauffman's body and it jumped a half a foot off the bed again.

"You are not going to die, you son of a bitch!" called Trinh, making several of the persons in the room giggle into their fists. Trinh didn't like to fail at anything.

The cardiograph kicked to life showing a heartbeat in regular pattern.

"Blood pressure eighty over forty."

"Ninety over sixty."

The orderlies came crashing into the room, secured Kauffman to a gurney, and raced out of the door, about one second after the nurses had disconnected him from all of his tubes and wires. They whisked him toward the OR and the awaiting surgeon by the name of Alexander Vaughn. All of the nurses and technicians raced behind them, leaving only Dr. Trinh standing alone in the empty room, his job done for now.

As they wheeled Kauffman into the elevator, he could just barely hear the nurse calling out the blood pressure. "One ten over sixty."

Trinh allowed himself a little smile . . . the patient was going to make it.

CHAPTER 95

THE INFECTION IN Bill Kauffman had begun in the cavity where the doctors had surgically removed the bullet. The bullet appeared to have nicked his duodenum. The nick had become a tear from Bill thrashing around in his hospital bed. The tear had released a variety of toxins into Bill's body. The intravenous antibiotics were neither of the type nor the strength to defeat the infections that the toxins had created. They were, however, masking some of his symptoms.

The antibiotics, coupled with the tetraceconol that had been regularly injected into his system (which did not appear on his chart), kept Bill's body temperature down and had done a fabulous job of masking the initial infections, the secondary infection which had eventually spread to his kidneys, and the peritonitis from which he technically had died.

The surgeon pronounced Bill dead at 5:30 AM. The operating theater was quiet. The sounds of the Moody Blues "Live at Red Rock Park" softly playing through the speakers.

In disgust, the surgeon threw his gloves on the floor and flung his gown in a corner. No one in the room moved. No one spoke.

"I don't have to tell you, gang, that this is bad, really fucking bad. I don't know how this guy was breathing when he got in here, but short of a new set of kidneys, a new set of intestines, a complete transfusion, a vacuum machine for all the crap that we found inside him, and some kind of miracle antibiotic that works in seconds, I don't know how the Good Lord himself could have saved him. This is bad."

The fourteen-year veteran of complex surgery just shook his head and walked out. Several minutes later, everyone else walked out as well.

CHAPTER 96

I T SAT ON the rooftop. In the west, It could just make out the dark gray clouds against a black sky, and the fading lights of stars in the distance. To the east, there was the faintest hint of what was to come. The skyline was tinted with a deep red, no yellows or oranges and no hint of blue. The sky remained a dull gray with dawn still some time away. There was no moon.

It enjoyed this time of day more than any other. While a fascination with sundown existed, as it did with every thinking creature on earth, the predawn was still It's element. Dressed head to foot in black, sitting on the black shingled roof, not even someone looking for it could see it stretched out on the rooftop of its home, relaxing after a fulfilling day, sipping water from a plastic container, and snacking on a granola bar.

With every moment, the sky changed. The sky was magnificent in southeastern Pennsylvania in October, and It never missed an opportunity to see it in the predawn hours straight through the dawn itself. As the seconds ticked away, there was a hint of white light developing on the high clouds just above the horizon, as the high clouds were witness to the dawn in advance of things on the ground.

Slowly, ever so slowly, the clouds at the horizon seemed to break up and streaks of orange and even yellow glanced off these clouds and up into the atmosphere. It knew that the time had come. It slowly stretched, unwound, recapped the water bottle, and finished the last bit of the granola bar before giving a final gaze at the unfolding of a beautiful morning.

CHAPTER 97

ALL SEVEN ATTORNEYS filed into Judge Amanda Greene's chambers when they were summoned. In the five minutes that they had waited outside her chambers, not a word had been exchanged. They had all introduced themselves earlier in the morning at the District Attorney's office and all the lawyers' posturing had been done at that time.

The first man into the chambers was Fitzgerald E. Harcourt, family attorney to Dr. and Mrs. Jack Fitzpatrick, the grandparents of Dr. Evans, flanked by his partner, Patricia M. N. Ryan. They were followed closely by District Attorney Paul Walsh and his first assistant district attorney of many years, Ed Crane. The DA was used to entering judges' chambers first and did not care for the fact that Harcourt had literally leaped through the door when they were summoned by the judge. The DA was used to holding the upper hand and didn't cow tow to defense attorneys no matter what their reputation. He had never even heard of Harcourt and that made him even more annoyed.

Local counsel, Thomas R. Wilson, followed the DA and was his usual confident and poised self. It was his presence that essentially allowed the others to participate in the Chester County courts as he was the only one on the defense side licensed to practice law in the Commonwealth of Pennsylvania. Wilson had the day before, hastily arranged for the other attorneys to be admitted to practice before the court pro hoc vicum and had filed the motions that were before the court this morning.

Wilson was followed by Eduardo Malateste Buanofito, a fast-rising legal star whose good looks, sharp tongue, and international connections made him an ideal successor to Evan R. "Duffy" McClary, a defense attorney extraordinaire, who had made his mark going to trial, all over the world, often winning the big ones. Duffy had first made his name representing low-level street thugs in Union City, New Jersey, but fast caught the eye of prosecutors, judges, and "big" law firms for his flair at the defense table. More often than not, he obtained a mistrial, which in the world of criminal defense put him statistically miles above most defense attorneys. He did not handle guilty pleas; that was left to the other members of his firm.

He walked in slowly, casually, and he was dressed impeccably. He wore no jewelry, save his unpretentious wedding band, and he was mildly tanned, nothing unusual.

The judge rose from her chair, greeted them all, and bade them to sit down. This made the DA very uncomfortable because, in his experience, you stood for Judge Greene, not the other way around, so she was showing some deference to these big shot out-of-towners, and he resented that.

What the district attorney did not (and would never) know was that Judge Greene had received no less than six phone calls the previous day regarding this matter. None of the phone calls inquired into the details of the case nor suggested an outcome, but all were clearly meant to say, "Don't make a mistake here!" Three were from political friends who had helped her gain her bench position, two were from members of the federal bench with whom she was friendly, and the last was from a colleague on the Supreme Court of Pennsylvania. All the calls were friendly and polite, all the calls were inappropriate, but neither unethical nor illegal.

What Judge Greene did not know (and never would) was that District Attorney Walsh had received three times that many calls in the past twelve hours, the last of which had occurred less than twenty minutes ago. His calls came from five state senators, two US congressmen, the head of a political party for the Commonwealth of Pennsylvania, a former classmate and friend of his who was now a sitting federal district court judge, and the attorney general, along with a number of political allies. Most of the calls were inappropriate. Some of the calls were friendly and polite. Some of the calls were downright unethical, and some were clearly meant to persuade him to proceed in a particular direction, and fast.

District Attorney Walsh was an honest, hardworking, unhappy prosecutor, and his scowl betrayed his feelings.

CHAPTER 98

ITH EVERYONE SETTLED, Harcourt, who stood a full six foot seven and courted a remarkable shock of white hair, attempted to direct the proceedings.

"As everyone knows, my firm represents the Fitzpatrick family and their many business and charitable ventures. As such, I would think—"

"Excuse me, Mr. Harcourt, but I am the presiding judge in this matter and while we are meeting informally to discuss how this hearing will proceed, it is still my proceeding and I will determine how and when we will go forward."

Harcourt did not flinch, but sagged a tiny bit, not used to being treated this way in his world of high finance and charitable endeavors. "But of course, Your Honor, I was merely attempting to cut to the chase, as it were. My apologies."

The judge held her hand up, it was her trademark. "Not a problem. What I have here before me are a writ of habeas corpus, a motion to suppress evidence, and a motion for return of personal property from the defense, and a motion to dismiss all three motions from the district attorney's office. From the number of visits to my chambers, phone calls, memoranda, a request for immediate hearing, and a request for a prehearing meeting, I can only surmise that someone feels that this matter is worthy of immediate attention, while at the same time avoiding public attention."

"As Your Honor appreciates," DA Walsh jumped in, "my office believes that the public has a right to know what is going on at all stages of a criminal proceeding, but only after an arrest warrant or indictment has been issued, neither of which is the case . . . "

The judge held her hand up again. "Counselor, do you have a written response to these motions to file? I know you are not required to do so until the time of the hearing, but if I grant their motion for an immediate review then you would be required to do so."

"Of course," said Walsh, motioning to Crane who produced three responses to the three filings and copies for everyone present.

"I must admit, except in my law school days, I can't remember the use of the 'Great Writ' when no one had even been arrested, and I believe the other motions may be premature as well. I presume that the defense has something they wish to share with us in the privacy of these chambers that they believe will put an end to this inquiry. Am I right, Counselor?"

The judge looked directly at Duffy, but to everyone's surprise, he just smiled and it was Wilson who spoke.

"Judge, we have here affidavits regarding the items seized in the search of Dr. Evans's residence. Without getting into the merits of the warrant itself, I think that these affidavits are sufficient to support a return of the seized items to Dr. Evans and to put an end to this inquiry. There is, by the way, a good deal of precedent for the use of the habeas writ under similar circumstances." Wilson handed the judge a short, succinct memorandum of law on the subject, and handed DA Walsh a copy as well.

The judge laughed; she had known Wilson for over thirty five years and was not the least bit surprised that he would have authority for the habeas proposition, though she was sure his interpretation of similar circumstances and hers would be quite different.

"All right, gentlemen, and lady, here is what we are going to do. I am going to dismiss the district attorneys' motions to strike the defense pleadings without prejudice to reassert these motions in the future. I am going to suggest that defense make a motion to conduct these proceedings in private, which I suggest be joined in by the district attorney so that the privacy issue is no longer on the table. I am going to suggest that unless I hear differently from defense counsel, the district attorney will have the right, subject to further review, to conduct whatever tests it deems appropriate on the seized items, without causing damage to them. Regardless of the hearing tomorrow morning, his office will be given at least ten days to conduct those tests, even if I order return of the property."

The judge paused for dramatic effect, confident that she had painted everyone into a corner from which she could make good, sound, and reasoned decisions without a lot of public fanfare or second guessing. "Do I hear a motion from the defense?"

Duffy responded this time. "I move that Dr. Evans's attorneys and the district attorney propose a stipulation that these proceedings be held in private with the record sealed, and that the district attorney have a maximum of ten days from the hearing tomorrow morning to examine the seized property regardless of the judge's ruling on its return to our client."

DA Walsh knew he was in a bind. The judge would certainly be unhappy if he refused, and that would not bode well for a situation that appeared to be heading toward a hearing in the morning.

"I will join in the motion and stipulation so long as it also contains the stipulation that the items seized were in fact the property of Dr. Evans," Walsh said, trying to gain some advantage in making the concession.

Duffy spoke. "We certainly will stipulate that the items were removed from the residence occupied by Dr. Evans, but no more."

"Sounds like we have a stipulation?" Judge looked at Walsh.

He hesitated briefly, resisted the urge to sigh, and said, "We do, Your Honor."

"Good, let's get a court reporter in here, get the stip on record, and be prepared for hearings on these three motions in my chambers tomorrow at 9:30 AM, sharp."

CHAPTER 99

THE HEARING BEFORE Judge Green was itself quite short. The judge had ruled early on that testimony for the most part was unnecessary, and that her intention would be to look at the four corners of the affidavit and warrant, and determine if probable cause had been established for the search. The defense had been permitted to submit (via affidavit) sworn statements of three reputable witnesses (for each item) that the items that had been seized were gifts to Dr. Evans, and as such could not possibly be trophies taken from accident or crime scenes.

The oral arguments of the various attorneys present, however, were another matter. Each attorney in the room seemed to have something to argue, and then in turn the attorneys on the other side had yet another attorney speak to refute that counter argument. Judge Green remained patient throughout. She even permitted some latitude to the assembled attorneys, allowing them to repeat certain arguments until everyone seemed to have had their say at least once, or twice.

"Justice delayed is justice denied," she announced. "As such, I issue the following order which will be reduced to writing as soon as I have it transcribed by the court reporter.

"I hereby rule that the affidavit of probable cause does not meet the standards necessary for issuance of a search warrant in the instant matter, and I hereby quash the warrant, without prejudice.

"I hereby rule that the motion for return of evidence is granted and pursuant to the stipulation of the parties that evidence will be returned to my chambers no later than ten days from today's date, the official date of this order. Mr. District Attorney, is it possible that we can have these items returned before then?"

DA Welsh did not hesitate. "Oh yes, Your Honor, I believe we can have these items returned to your chambers by noon tomorrow. Our tests are essentially complete."

Tom Wilson quickly rose. "We would of course insist upon a copy of all of the test reports, Your Honor."

"Yes," Judge Green chuckled, "I'm sure you would, however, police investigations are protected in a number of ways from discovery efforts until someone is actually charged with a crime, arrested, and has been held over for trial by a district court judge. So I'm afraid that motion is denied."

"I am further ruling that nothing that has been seized under this warrant can be used in the future by the police or the prosecution as evidence, unless it can be established that it has somehow been discovered through some source unrelated to this unlawful search.

"I thank all of you. I remind all of you, including our court staff, that this entire proceeding is under court-stipulated and a court-ordered gag, which means not one word of these proceedings or my findings will find its way out of this courtroom. I am certain that our local newspapers will challenge this ruling under *Lantz v. Welcott,* and we'll just see how that plays out."

The judge rose, walked off the bench, and into her chambers.

The tall, thin, conservatively-dressed woman at the defense counsel's table gave a very slight nod of thank you toward the judge, and turned to leave. Dr. Evans's attorneys had won, but she showed no jubilation, nor defiance, as she walked out of the courtroom. In the victory, her personal testimony had been unnecessary.

CHAPTER 100

T HE FIVE MEN sat around the table and sipped at their coffees. A box of donuts and pastries from the local Wawa sat in the middle of them, virtually untouched. The room was the interrogation room of the Uwchlan Township Police Department. It also served as their "war" room. The chief had requested three separate rooms in his budget, the first for holding prisoners, the second for processing prisoners, and the third for interrogation and as a war room. Two out of three ain't bad, the chief had thought. The supervisors of the township recognized the importance of a well-staffed, well-funded police department, but they also recognized their obligation to their citizens which extended much farther than simply the police and fire departments. The chief knew that and he appreciated the fact that he had at least gotten the two rooms.

The chief was sitting in one of the rooms now with two county detectives, his first sergeant and SB. The speakerphone was on and Spags was at the other end of the line, in theory, convalescing. Spags had been specifically ordered by the physicians not to come to work. The department was required by law to follow the conditions set by the physicians charged with the care of an injured officer. Neither the chief nor Spags, nor anyone in the room, was happy about the situation, but there it was. Nothing was going to change until the doctors released him.

SB spoke first.

"I think it is pretty obvious that Dr. Evans holds the key here. If we don't get that key, we are going to have a long and difficult winter because we are stuck with a set of physical evidences that leads to no logical conclusion in the murder of Elaine Kauffman. If we can't even determine whether there was one shooter or two, one gun or two, or even theoretically the caliber of the bullet that was removed in the operating theater on the night of the Kauffman shooting, we have literally nothing to work with. Even if we had a suspect, this case is simply a defense jury verdict waiting to happen, provided we could even get that far. The operative question, gentlemen, is what in the name of hell are we going to do about it?"

Everyone looked at the phone expecting Spags to make the first comment. He didn't, the chief did.

"Look, we all know we suffered a setback when the judge threw out the search warrant, but let's face the facts, the search only proved one thing, that Dr. Evans is one strange piece of work. SB, I love you dearly, but it's not as clear to me as it is to you. Do you really think that rich bitch is a souvenir hunter, or do you think that she is complicit in some way in the murder?"

"Murder? We seem to have several and let's not forget the hospital. There is no question in my mind that she is complicit in the removal of the bullet from Bill Kauffman. There is no other good explanation for the bullet's disappearance, and I also think she set us up. We pushed her and she decided to push back. She's wealthy, connected, and probably does pretty much whatever she wants. Daddy's money and lawyers are there if she needs them.

"Think about this, what if she just left those things around her haunted house just to put us in a position where we could never really go back after her. She may have set us up so we could not ever go after her for her souvenir-hunting antics, because we bungled our first attempt."

In his home, Spags cringed.

SB paused for effect and then continued. "She would appear to be the wrong height, according to our anonymous tipster, the wrong weight, the wrong gender, and the wrong shoe size. She has absolutely no motive that we can fathom for having been involved in any of the homicides here in the township, or for that matter at the hospital. I can't even begin to speculate on the homicide that occurred on Bill Kauffman's ward in Coatesville Hospital. I can't imagine how we could link that one with the others, or even some of the others with each other, be that as it may . . . "

SB had made a point. The problem was that no one really knew what to do about it. County Detective Art Grimes, a veteran of twenty-two years, spoke first.

"I think the only way we find anything out about the mystery woman is to put a tail on her. I know we're not going to be able to get a warrant for a wiretap, and I don't think she's dumb enough to use her phone to incriminate herself anyway. She seems very sharp, perhaps even more so than she's shown so far. If she really did have something to do with the murder of Mrs. Kauffman, then she's very nasty and very dangerous too. I will tell you that anyone that has been in that house of hers where she apparently has no furniture, sleeps on the floor, and eats next to nothing, has got to be spooked by her. She must have a ton of dough, doesn't spend any, could be in any hospital in the US, chooses Chester County, has what looks like a medieval torture machine that turns out to be her exercise machine, the ROM. She is in several words a scary lady."

Spags broke in. "She shouldn't be very hard to follow. She does a regular and fairly long shift at the hospital. We know where she lives, the make, model, and license plate number of her car, and we have good photos of her from the hospital and the DMV. She seems to be a social recluse. I doubt she stands around at local cocktail parties. It is pretty obvious that she has close family ties, but we have no indication that she spends any time with them. She has no alarm system in her house, doesn't own a dog or any kind of pet, appears to live in three, maybe four sets of clothes and workout outfits, other than her hospital clothes, and spends very little time at the hairdresser."

They all chuckled at the barb. The very Irish-looking doctor had a shock of hair that seemed to go in every direction, unless she had it pulled back on her head. It was well known that Dr. Evans's shock of strawberry blonde hair tended to vary between recently washed and combed on the one hand, and a massive tangle on the other.

She looks good to me either way, Grimes thought to himself, but said nothing.

Detective Benedict interjected. "She must have a stash somewhere. There must be a place where she stores things. There just isn't enough in that house for her to live on. I don't care how Spartan she is, she is in fact a female and females need shoes. We found no shoes other than the ones she had on her and a pair of cross training sneakers that looked like they had been worn to hell. We also know that she is an athlete and works out. Where the hell is her workout outfit? We found a tiny pair of shorts on the workout machine, but unless she works out virtually naked, we found nothing else. By the way, it turns out that machine costs over fourteen grand and is supposed to keep you in shape with only five minutes of workout, four times a week.

"It's called an ROM machine and it sells out of California. Doc looks to be in good shape and she doesn't seem to belong to a gym so . . . .

"We need to know these things and we need to know them fast. I think a soft tail is what we need to do, and once we gather the information, maybe we go with hard tail and warrants. Maybe even look to wiretap or search her hospital locker. Somehow I don't think we are going to have much luck with the DA's office, so for now we are on our own. If we end up in front of the same judge again, I think we all get sent to the gallows."

"So what else is new?" asked the chief, in as sarcastic a tone as he could muster.

The chief rubbed his chin and then rubbed both of his temples with his hands. He reached over, grabbed a croissant, took a big bite, and then a swallow of his coffee.

"OK. Obviously the political angle is going to create a problem for us if we go for warrants, so we've got to be smarter than that. I know there is not much on the Internet, but there has got to be some better info out there on who this doctor is, where she goes, and what she does. Let's put that soft tail on her; let's make it only from the time she leaves her house until she goes into the hospital, and vice versa. I don't want to the tail her at the hospital or even shadow her there. Makes no sense to do so. The second thing, Spags, got your computer at home?" the chief asked.

"Yep."

"OK. Get your buddies in the various surrounding police departments. Get a hold of your buddy at the state police in Maryland and follow up on that as hard as you can. Check with the guy in York County again and see if there is anything more he can provide. Those guys seem to have extremely good computer capability and we need to tap into it. As the cowboys on TV say, 'Let's git her done.' No screw ups."

No one had anything to say. They knew the meeting was over and they all exited. Spags hung up the phone and flipped his computer back on.

"Game on," was all he said.

CHAPTER 101

S PAGS SPENT THE rest of his day on his computer. He researched the Evans family and the Fitzpatricks every way he could fathom. What he found was a rather strange history followed by very public announcements and very little private information.

Dr. Evan's great, great, great, great, grandfather, one Sean Fitzpatrick had emigrated to the United States during one of the Irish Potato famines in the late 1840's, known as the Great Hunger. He had been a physician in Ireland who spent the very last of his monies on some food, water, and a ticket on a rickety ship known as the *Portubus* sailing from Dublin to New York.

There was nothing in the history that spoke of how a man who was not allowed to vote, own property, or receive a formal education had become a doctor in Ireland in that period of time. In addition, there was the death of one of his patients by violent means on the evening that he left the Emerald Isle, but with death being the order of the day in Ireland, there was no investigation.

Dr. Fitzpatrick set up practice in the Irish ghetto of New York and tended to all who came to him, whether or not they were capable of paying. He gained a reputation as a kind man but who harbored great ill will toward the British and had such a temper that he was nicknamed Mad Man Fitzpatrick by the non Irish population. He raised six children, two of whom died in the Civil War and three of whom went on to become doctors. All in all, it appeared that the original Fitzpatrick had spawned over one hundred progeny who became doctors, most of some significant note.

Dr. Evan's grandfather was one of the most respected surgeons in the country and several of her siblings were well-known research scientists in the field of medicine. Her family all in all had hundreds of patents on various pharmaceutical items ranging from over the counter remedies to sophisticated cancer treatments and various surgical devices as well. When Spags started looking at a long string of computer patents and software patents owned by the family or companies run by the family, he finally gave up. There was nothing in the public but accolades and press releases; the Fitzpatrick clan was very good at presenting their own public image.

CHAPTER 102

D R. EVANS HAD called a cab. There was no reason to take her car; someone might be trying to follow and she thought, We wouldn't want to make it is easy, would we? The cab drove her to the train station, and Dr. Evans purchased a round trip ticket to Philadelphia at the counter. If someone were following (she was convinced that they were), they would have no trouble with that.

When the train reached Philadelphia's Thirtieth Street Station, Dr. Evans exited and purchased a ticket for Penn Station, New York. It was a one-way ticket. The ticket was paid for in cash and was good for thirty days. There was a no-refund policy stated in small print at the back of the ticket. Did anyone really ever try to get a refund on a train ticket? she thought.

The train was to leave from the lower platform on its inexorable ride to New York City. Dr. Evans waited in line with the others, a hundred or so bored-looking people heading down to the platform both by escalator and stairway. Once down to the platform, Dr. Evans walked past six cars toward the end of the train, not quite to the last car, and boarded the train.

Dr. Evans carefully watched those who boarded behind her by placing herself in a seat that allowed her to look out the window, and at the same time look down the entire length of the car. Anyone coming into the front of the car was facing her, anyone who came in the back of the car had to walk past her or go the last car of the train. Either way, she'd see them, and know if they had gotten on the last car by reason of having passed her by.

She looked at her watch every few seconds, sure she had the right time and sure as well that this train would leave on time. When she had one minute left to spare, she calmly rose from her seat and walked off the train. She stood looking left and right, as if she were confused or she had misplaced a package. There were eleven people on the platform and that number soon became eight as the three stragglers hopped aboard the train. The other eight were all in blue uniforms and caps, four of them already about to pull themselves up onto the steps for departure.

"Ma'am, we're about to leave the station, is anything wrong?" The voice came from a tall, handsome middle-aged man wearing the uniform of the trainmen, standing with one foot on the platform and the other on the train step.

"Well . . . I just thought . . . did you see anyone get off the train?" she stammered, creating the impression that she was lost in thought, or just plain lost.

"Not in the last few minutes, before that, some people departed when we came into the station, if that's what you mean."

"All aboard!" The sound echoed down the platform while one trainman after another signaled by hand that all was clear. It was now her car's turn.

"Gotta go, ma'am, are you coming aboard?" he asked, some impatience showing through his friendly smile.

"I can't," she said, and stepped away. After two hasty ready signals from her car and the last car, the hiss of the air break releasing on the train filled the air, and she stepped behind a concrete abutment so fast that the trainmen on her car, standing in the entranceway of the now moving train, did a double take, but she was gone.

When the train had cleared the station, the man who had been tailing her casually strolled from the rear car to the second to last car on the train. Having walked the entire train's length, the tail shook his head once and cursed. She was gone.

CHAPTER 103

As soon as the train had cleared the platform, Dr. Evans hurried up the stairs, across the terminal, and up another flight of stairs, barely in time to catch the 6:41 to Clinton, New Jersey. She was the second to the last person on the train, and no one came bounding up the stairs behind her. She felt comfortable that she was either not being followed or had lost her tail. However, there was no way she was going to relax her vigil. Predators never did.

Dr. Evans had two other tickets that she had purchased almost a month earlier with cash. She had purchased one ticket from a remote location, which allowed her to exit at the first stop and one ticket to take another train to her actual destination in New Jersey.

She quickly boarded the second train as it was about to pull out of the station. She tucked her flaming red wig hair under a floppy hat and donned sunglasses. She turned her reversible jacket inside out and now was wearing a brown jacket with pink trim rather than the opposite. She rubbed off her lipstick and stuck her noise in a newspaper. Those minor changes made a major change in her appearance and if you didn't know her well, you would not have recognized her. She had left little margin for error. She knew that it made little difference in the overall scheme of things, but she knew that if she could take care of some loose ends, she could leave Pennsylvania for New York without any concerns.

She had a mental checklist for her meeting with Eddie and briefly but carefully ran through it. Eddie could be a problem. Even though Eddie did not know her, did not know what she looked like and did not know how to reach her, he was the only link that could even find its way back to her. Eddie was a professional burglar with some true talent in that area, but he was not very bright. He had never been arrested, so it was hard to determine how he would hold up under interrogation by the police, however remote that possibility was.

CHAPTER 104

THE UNDERCOVER OFFICER who had been following Dr. Evans, Pete Barnes, was in panic. When he realized that the train he was on did not contain the doctor and that she had eluded him, Pete buzzed his team in the parking lot below and told them he'd lost her. The team, believing that she was still in the station, got out of their vehicles and spread out inside along the various platforms. They all knew what Dr. Evans looked like and carried pictures of her just in case.

Dennis "Rabbit" Ravdin from the county office saw someone who fit the description boarding a train, but was unable to catch the train before its doors closed and the air brakes released. He radioed his team of the new development, and they scrambled to get to their cars. Rabbit grabbed a schedule, glanced at the first stops for the six trains that had just departed, and raced down to join his fellow officers.

The investigation of the murder of Elaine Kauffman had now centered on the evidence that the police were sure was stolen by Dr. Evans, and even though there was nothing tangible to tie her to the crime, SB, Kevin Moan, and Spags all believed now more than ever that she was the key. She was smart, medically trained, athletic, single, and unattached. It was impossible to prove, but it now appeared that Bill Kauffman had been having an affair. It had also come to light that a woman fitting Dr. Evans's description had dined with Bill Kauffman at least once at the Mendenhall Inn in southwestern Chester County. Several months earlier, Bill

Kauffman had switched from paying his hotel and bar tabs with a credit card to cash, very unusual for a man like him.

None of it made a great deal of sense to the detective team now following her, but that wasn't really important to them. They had been given the job of conducting surveillance on Dr. Evans on their own time at the request of Spags, and she wasn't making that easy.

Earlier that day, Dr. Evans had almost slipped the tailing policemen when she exited a small café in the Exton Mall through the rear door, and drove past one of the teams who had been unaware of the rear entrance.

Unfortunately for the team, Rabbit had not actually seen which train she had jumped on so they had to make some assumptions. To make it worse, the weekday schedule was quite different from the weekend schedule, which was different from the Sunday schedule, and it was Sunday. As bad luck would have it, they originally misread the schedule which had them heading for the first stop on the weekend schedule, which was the third stop on Sundays. This problem would ultimately cost them their surveillance.

When they arrived at Verdon Avenue Station, they knew something was wrong given the station was virtually empty, even for a Sunday. When the train finally rolled in fifteen minutes later, they all boarded and watched carefully to be sure their tail did not exit.

When the train rolled to a stop at its final destination, they had effectively searched every car, every restroom, and eyeballed every passenger that had exited. Dr. Evans was nowhere to be found.

CHAPTER 105

A T VINEARC, DR. Evans hailed a cab. The cabbie headed east at her instruction. She pretended that she had forgotten something at the station and asked the driver to double back. The driver was forced to make three left hand turns and began heading back to the station. She watched carefully to see if anyone else made three turns, and, satisfied that no one was following her, had asked the driver to drop her at the corner of Delaney and Squires. She gave him a mediocre tip, thanked him, and went on her way. She didn't believe she had given him any reason to remember her except the turnabout, and she had shown very little of her face or hair, so he would not have much to go by if he were asked to recall her.

After getting out of the cab, Dr. Evans headed straight for the Colonial Arms Hotel, six blocks away. The Colonial Arms had once been the Grand Inn, Restaurant and Pub. It had not been so for twenty years. The restaurant was still good, the inn was in disrepair, and the bar completely sealed off from the other two establishments with an entrance around the block. The bar was now more or less a dirty old man's bar, where men arrived at ten o'clock in the morning to drink a glass of milk before their first scotch of the day, and left when they were good and blind. These men usually left a lot of their money to someone else while playing pool or darts, or just betting on the New York Giants.

Since the Colonial Arms's owner was a female, and was known to contribute significant sums of money to a local battered women's shelter, the hotel was listed in various guides as being an appropriate and safe place for women traveling alone to lodge. The corridors were well lit and there was a panic button installed at both ends of every floor. The same panic button was also installed in every room. All a resident had to do was hit the button and, bingo, the local police were dispatched, the manager was alerted, and a security guard, who was actually armed and well trained, arrived at the panic button location in seconds.

The Arms's interior doors had old-fashioned key entry, but they also had real double-deep dead bolts drilled into the ancient walls, not just the doors frames. The rooms were quiet and the walls were thick. Discreet titanium bars adorned the windows. Each room had its own bath, miniature refrigerator, telephone, and WIFI hookup.

There was nothing unusual about Dr. Evans checking into this establishment. The fact that she had checked in under a false name, wore a wig, and tinted glasses would insure her ability to remain anonymous.

Dr. Evans paid cash when she checked in and asked for a second floor room that overlooked the street. There was no problem accommodating her on a Sunday evening this early, although the inn usually filled up as the night went on. After checking in, she went to her room and threw open the curtains. Dr. Evans had informed the manager that her luggage would arrive later, it having been sent on to Boston by the airlines. The manager smiled a knowing smile and suggested that if she needed anything, two of the women shops on Main Street were open until nine.

Directly across the street from the inn was Terri's Sports Bar. It had a large picture window that faced the street and its outside was all fresh paint, glass, and chrome. It was an upscale sports bar and had none of those tacky signs in the windows advertising free ribs or two-for-one hot dogs for Monday night football. She opened her bag and pulled out a bottle of Chivas Regal. She inspected the bottle and replaced it in the bag with two tumbler glasses she'd brought for the occasion. She sat down calmly and waited, watching the sports bar all the time. She didn't have long to wait.

CHAPTER 106

E DDIE WAS A very punctual man. He arrived at 6:30 PM as agreed, looked unobtrusively left and right as he entered the door, and went to the bar. He ordered a drink, paid for it in cash, and stood by the window. Dr. Evans had told him to wait by the window because she didn't know what he looked like and didn't want to get third parties involved in their mutual introduction.

Dr. Evans picked up the phone and dialed the sports bar number from a matchbook she'd taken from that establishment four months earlier. She was a blonde that night, small mole on her cheek, sweater too tight, and contact lenses that made her eyes water. She had not made much of an impression on anyone, just as she had planned. She had appeared that evening as just another bimbo looking for a jock.

"Terri's," said the voice, a little less cheerful than it should be.

"Yes," she said, "I'm terribly sorry but I'm late for a blind date. His name is Eddie, and he's supposed to meet me at the window, can you check for me?"

"Yeah, sure," said the voice. "Yo, boss, is your name Eddie? Gotta call here from a lady looking for Eddie."

Eddie smiled. He was extremely unhappy, scared, leery. The hairs on the back of his head telling him to put down his glass, walk out the door, and never look back. He shook his head slowly trying to focus his thoughts on what to do next. Greed won the day. He took the phone. "This is Eddie."

"Hi! Finish your drink if you like. Walk down two blocks and check into the Holiday Inn. Pay in cash. Don't worry, I'll pay you

back. Private's better, you know? I'll just follow you to your room."
Click.

Eddie was cool. "Yeah, OK," he said into the dead receiver.
"Thanks for the call."

He drank the rest of his drink and tipped the bartender.
"Thanks, pal. Thanks for the phone call, too," he said.

"No problem," said the bartender. "Stood you up, eh?" he
chuckled.

"Nah, nothing like that, thanks." He was out the door. Nothing
in his voice or mannerism showed how angry he was. *Who the hell
did this broad think she was screwing with anyway?* he thought.
A voice in the back of his head told him to turn around and walk
away. *No can do*, he thought. *He was going to get paid for this one,
boy was he going to get paid.*

He checked into the Holiday Inn. The desk clerk was not
particularly happy about his lack of luggage, but he was dressed
middle class, didn't speak like a punk, and they certainly had never
seen him before. He showed them a driver's license and told them
he didn't believe in credit cards, so they made him pay for two
nights in advance. *Welcome to America*, he thought. *I don't need a
card and so I gotta pay in advance and pay twice.*

He began rehearsing the calm, but disruptive, language he was
going to use on the lady. He even thought about upping his price.
In his business, that was usually bad for business, so he decided he
would play that part by ear. The jewelry burned a hole in his jacket
where he soon hoped to replace it with large crisp new bills.

His room was around the back. He thought that worked just
fine. He was no more in the door when Dr. Evans showed up.

"Before you start getting all pissed and crazy on me, just let me
explain. I don't want any trouble. I'm real careful. I didn't want to be
overheard saying anything in the bar or even being seen together,
OK? Here's an extra five hundred dollars for the room and for your
patience."

Eddie cooled down quickly. He knew he'd just made three
hundred and fifty extra dollars. His face showed nothing, but he
felt better. He quickly forgot any renegotiation and even the verbal
abuse he planned for her. She took the two glasses out of her
pocketbook and sat down at the small coffee table.

Eddie said, "Excuse me for a minute, I gotta hit the men's room. I'll be right back." He heard her twist the top off of a bottle as he closed the door.

He hadn't had time to check out the room so he wanted a minute or two to think. In the meantime, he checked out the bathroom, in the sink, cabinets, everywhere, but he could not find a wire, bug, or camera. He flushed the toilet, sprinkled water on his face and hands, grabbed a towel, and headed back into the bedroom.

"Place isn't bad. You been here before?" he asked.

"No. You look jumpy what's that matter?" she returned.

"Me, I don't think so, lady. Do I have something to be jumpy about?"

"Not from me," she said. She walked straight over to him, put her arms around him, and patted his back. Mistaking her move for passion he moved toward her and was caught off guard by her pat down. She even checked his pant legs and did not stop short of his crotch as he expected.

"Hey, what the hell . . . "

"Listen, you're acting funny. Why don't we call the whole thing off? Keep the Scotch, I'm outta here." She began to put the tumblers back in her purse.

Eddie was dumbfounded. He could see his money walking out the door and, for all his tough talk, he was not a tough guy. He didn't honestly believe he was capable of real violence.

"Hey, hey, hey! Take it easy. Let's face it, we two, we're not exactly in a trusting mood. Let's have that drink and just cool down. I'm no cop. I thought maybe you were. Listen, I have to tell you that when I read about that murder in the house, I was worried. Eddie doesn't do murder. Eddie's smooth, stays out of trouble and out of sight. I thought maybe somebody was trying to make me out to be a killer. I don't need that shit comin' down on me, you understand that don't you?"

Dr. Evans just stared at him for several moments. Then she took the tumbler back out of the bag, put the Chivas bottle on the table, and began pouring. When she had half filled both tumblers, she picked her tumbler up held it in the air and said, "They say you never get a second chance to make a first impression, but here's to trying."

Eddie reached for the glass in her hand, pushed the glass in front of him toward her and said, "They say that in the old days, kings had people taste testing their food and wine so they wouldn't get poisoned. I figure swapping glasses is about the same thing."

He took a long belt of Scotch without taking his eyes off hers. She in turn took a smaller, but significant drink from her glass, swallowed, shook her head twice, and put her glass down.

"Eddie, what if I knew you real well, and decided I'd trick you by poisoning my glass, knowing you'd make the swap?" His eyes went wide and he switched glasses back, as if by quickly changing them back he could undo some wrong.

"Gotcha!" she laughed and took a swig out of her original glass. The tension was broken and Eddie started to giggle, then to outright belly laugh as he took another hard swallow on the Scotch.

"Lady, you got a crazy sense of humor, but I like your style, and your Scotch ain't bad either. So let's talk money. I figure this job was a lot tougher than advertised, what with the murder and all. I figure that's worth an extra G, don't you?"

CHAPTER 107

THE LOOK ON Dr. Evan's face did not change but her body language was another thing, and this was not lost on Eddie.

"Eddie, don't fuck with me," she said coolly, with no particular emphasis and in a tone that was soft but menacing.

"Hey, lady, watch your language. I mean this job's gotta be worth more." Eddie finished his drink and poured himself a second tumbler.

"Eddie, tell me, what's the worst thing that ever happened to you?" she asked.

Eddie looked around the room as if the answer was somewhere hidden.

"Well, I was doing a job in Chester. Woman woke up from a dead sleep and started yelling. I put my hand over her mouth and she goes real quiet. Then this six-foot-eight guy comes through the door, and I mean through the door, and thinks he caught his old lady with some skinny white guy fooling around. Guy literally throws me out the window. Lucky for me, I land on the hood of a car and roll off running with this big son of a bitch chasin' me clear out of Chester. Yeah, that's the worst thing. I coulda been killed or in this guy's case, worse." Eddie took another long pull on the Scotch and a small dribble went down his chin.

Dr. Evans opened her bag and removed a chrome-plated forty-five caliber pistol, casually unfastening the safety and pointing it between Eddie's eyes. Eddie froze and began to hiccup.

CHAPTER 108

D R. EVANS LOWERED the gun to his chest level and smiled. "You know the worst thing that ever happened to me, Eddie? Someone took something of mine without my permission. Ever since I was a little girl, somebody takes something of mine without my permission and I get the same feeling. It's a really bad feeling and I have a great deal of difficulty keeping control. Right now you have some jewelry that I feel is mine. But you're telling me I can't have what's mine by holding me up for one thousand dollars. One thousand fucking dollars, Eddie. Do you know how bad that makes me feel?"

Eddie just shook his head slowly, hardly breathing, his hiccups gone away.

"Now, do you want to take that feeling away, Eddie? Because you can, you can put the jewelry on the table and pass it to me. Then I'll have what's mine and the feeling will go away. OK, Eddie?"

Eddie reached slowly inside his coat pocket and produced the folded envelope containing the jewelry. "Yes, ma'am."

Dr. Evans reached inside the bag and produced a sizable wad of hundreds and fifties, fanning them out on the table. "Count it, Eddie. I'm not a cheat."

"That's OK, lady. I'll take your count. Could you put that gun down?"

"Count it," she said, a little more forcefully the second time. He did.

After he finished the count, Dr. Evans lowered the gun to her lap and pushed her chair slightly back from the table.

"Sorry," she sounded contrite, "I guess I got carried away. Let's toast to the next time. Cheers." She sipped at her glass and Eddie, hands trembling, poured himself another large tumbler.

Eddie took a long pull on the Scotch and absently began to recount the twenties. He was having trouble focusing on the count. It was his first hint that something was wrong. He took another drink of his Scotch and shook his head, but it didn't help his focus, not even a little.

"I don't feel so good, is it hot in here?" Eddie's words were slightly slurred and he noticed his tongue felt thick.

"Here, Eddie," she said, sliding a typed piece of paper across the table with a pen. "Sign here and you'll feel better, and I'll throw in some extra incentive," she said.

Without thinking, he scribbled his name on the paper as the thought of getting a little action overrode the awful feeling in his chest.

"You sure it's not hoooottt in here?" Eddie mumbled.

"Feels fine to me, you must be coming down with something," she said.

"Yeah, comin' down wif somethin'..." Eddie felt like someone was lifting him out of his chair in a bear hug. He couldn't make out the twenties anymore and he couldn't remember what he'd just said. He didn't feel dizzy, just short of breath like he was being squeezed, and thick tongued like he'd drunk too much, too fast on a hot day.

"Where " He couldn't finish the thought. He was becoming scared; this was not a pleasant feeling. This was not good. He suddenly remembered the woman seated across from him.

"Hey, did yooouuu do sumpin, what, what didja doooo..." He was trying really hard not to sway, without success. He knew he was going to fall off the chair, and there didn't seem to be anything he could do about it.

He saw the woman picking up piles of green stuff just before he hit the floor. He couldn't make out what it was, but he had a feeling the green stuff belonged to him. He couldn't focus and he couldn't get angry. He was descending into a well and he had just about given up caring. The voice seemed distant, but clear.

"Sorry, Eddie, I'm just no good at sharing. The axlominate is now throughout your system and, coupled with the alcohol, will stop your heart, your breathing, even your brain functions. It's just a question of which will kill you. Oh, by the way, the whole bottle was spiked with the stuff, so switching glasses wouldn't help. If you weren't such a pig, you would have noticed that I barely sipped mine. You just signed your confession to the killing of Mrs. Kauffman, the theft of her jewelry, and shooting her poor husband in a panic when he came in by surprise. It's also your suicide note, so it's time for you to die.

"I did, of course, have the advantage of taking a large dose of steroids before I came here, which will go a long way toward preventing the small amount of axlominate I ingested from doing any permanent harm. Oh, I might have a flu-like symptom or two in the morning, but nothing to bother you with. I also took the antidote."

The note itself apologized for the murder, giving just enough detail to keep the authorities guessing if the confession was real or not. It was short, filled with typos, poor grammar, and misspelled words, and now it was signed. The note had been typed on an old Underwood typing machine two months earlier in a YMCA in West Virginia. Dr. Evans had been careful to steal the pen from a Holiday Inn in Kansas six months before, and to have never touched it. She left it behind so that Eddie's fingerprints would be found on the pen. She also left half the jewelry on the table.

Dr. Evans made a point of wiping down any surface that she had been near. She had tried very hard not to touch anything that she had not herself brought in, but it was extremely difficult to avoid touching certain things. She spent several minutes cleaning the door and the door handle with bleach. She used a dust buster to clean around the table in case she had left hair or other traces.

She took a gun out of a plastic bag wrapped in another plastic bag, and put the gun in Eddie's right hand. She then put his fingers on the outside of the gun and removed the magazine. After carefully taking the bullets out of the magazine, she took his left hand and ran the bullets one at a time over his finger before carefully replacing them in the gun.

She positioned the open Scotch bottle on the side of the table, close to the edge. Lifting Eddie's left hand, she knocked the bottle to the floor, spilling poisoned Scotch on the carpet, Eddie's pant leg, and the table itself.

She looked around and smiled. It was a good job indeed.

"Good-bye, Eddie," she said.

Eddie didn't hear anymore after that. Eddie just continued to slip down the well of unconsciousness until it all became black, and Eddie was gone.

CHAPTER 109

DETECTIVE SPAGNOLA HAD put the file back in the filing cabinet which unofficially meant he was no longer urgently interested in it. In the six weeks since his accident, he had healed well, but did not feel good about the Kauffman case. What they thought had been a serial killer had stopped killing or moved on, and they had no good evidence regarding who that person could be.

He looked over a photocopy of Ed Bearpark's confession. Forensics had verified his signature, but no one had been able to locate the typewriter upon which his confession had been typed. His DNA matched that of hairs found at the scene. Eddie had been found in a Holiday Inn in New Jersey by a maid. She had not wrecked the scene. Located on scene was the gun used to shoot Elaine Kauffman, the poison Eddie had apparently used to commit suicide, two pieces of Elaine Kauffman's jewelry, and the note itself. They had DNA from Bearpark that matched DNA from the door handle of the outside door of the Kauffman's home. It was far too tidy for Spagnola's taste, but what else was there?

He re-read the lines that stood out: "I did a lot of stealin' in my time, but I never hurt nobody. I never should hav brawt the gun. Sorry."

Spags had no witnesses, bupkus for forensics, no hard evidence, no motive, a dead husband who may or may not have had it in for his deceased wife, a brother who was the only one to profit from her death with an alibi Houdini couldn't dent, a boyfriend who couldn't hurt a fly . . . it went on and on. But, in the end, he had nothing.

Eddie's confession and the recovery of some of the jewelry just gave the entire Kauffman matter a worse smell. Spags did not believe for a moment that, based on his prior record, Eddie would have been carrying a gun, would have killed Mrs. Kauffman or Mr. Kauffman, unless . . . That was the problem, if Eddie, who was way out of his neighborhood on this particular adventure, had hooked up with someone else, then maybe it worked. But Eddie alone? It just didn't fit his style. Even the Scotch didn't fit from what they were able to find out. Eddie drank gin, gin and tonic to be exact, and never a lot.

For his trouble, he was in hot water with the DA, a female judge, and the district justice who had given him the search warrant. He had recovered from the three cracked ribs, a broken arm, a mild concussion, a bruised sternum, a strained knee, and various cuts and bruises. He had not recovered from the fact that someone had apparently lain in wait for him, crashed into his car, and walked away without a trace.

The investigations into the death of the nurse Rodriquez, Injun Joe and Kiefer Barney had gone nowhere.

As he waded though some paperwork, his phone rang.

"Detective Spagnola, Chester County, how can I help you?"

"Detective, my name is Special Agent Thomas Ambrose, and we have something in common."

Spags chuckled to himself. Yeah, right, he thought.

"And what might that be, Special Agent Ambrose?"

There was a short pause.

"I believe we share a common problem, one Carol Evans, MD."

CHAPTER 110

D<small>R. EVANS BOARDED</small> the Metro for Manhattan at Philadelphia 30th Street Station. She made no effort to conceal her destination. She made no effort to avoid being followed. There was no need, she thought. Her time in Southeastern Pennsylvania had come to an end.

She picked a seat in the middle of the second to the last car of the train. She faced forward and placed her overnight case directly across from her in hope of dissuading anyone from attempting to sit there. She lay her pocketbook and newspaper on the seat to her left, sitting next to the window which would face west on her short journey. The view would be pretty much the New Jersey Turnpike as soon as she passed Trenton. She enjoyed passing all the cars and trucks at eighty-five miles per hour.

The 3:00 PM Metro would sit in the station at Philly for just over five minutes before heading for Trenton, Newark, and finally at 34th Street Station in Manhattan. Dr. Evans had sold her car to a nice young graduate student at Villanova University. She knew that a car in a major metropolitan area was nothing but a nuisance, and an expensive one at that. It was not that she did not have the money, she made a very good living, was the beneficiary of a number of trusts, and stood to inherit even more, but she was frugal to a fault. Her personal items were being shipped from her apartment in Malvern and the house she rented in Exton. There was very little to ship: 4 pairs of shoes, two pairs of cross trainers, 3 changes of clothes, a running outfit and here exercise equipment the ROM. A girl shouldn't be without her gym, she thought.

She gazed out the grimy window at the even grimier station around the train. The station was three stories underground and was always damp. It had a smell that defied description. She closed her eyes upon hearing the "all aboard" signal followed by the distinct sound of the air brakes being disengaged. She knew they would not ask for tickets before Trenton but she put hers in the clip on the seat next to her in any event. She began to slowly eliminate the smell of the station and the sounds around her.

Once Dr. Evans had attained the proper state, she began to reflect on her time in Pennsylvania. Between her "locum tenans" appointment in York Medical Center and her job at the Brandywine Hospital Trauma Center, she had been in Pennsylvania for just under twenty three months. During that time she had killed four degenerates in York County; two would-be rapist truck drivers in Maryland, two worthless bums in Exton, and a cheating husband. Unfortunately in order to confuse the police and avoid prosecution she had also been required to kill Elaine Kauffman and Nurse Carmen Rodriquez, but that was the price one had to pay. She had also killed the professional burglar Eddie, poor soul, but he was not exactly the type of person who belonged with the herd of humanity, adding nothing to the gene pool, so it was just as well that he was gone.

All but one of the dead (in York) had been found and identified as homicides. She was quite proud of the work she had done with Bill Kaufman, but would not be sharing that pride anytime soon. With the exception of the trophy fiasco, no one would be able to link her to anything. The police had fallen for the bait with regard to the trophies and would now be unable to come after her again without looking vindictive and more importantly, without rubbing judges and the like the wrong way.

Dr. Evan's had "thinned the herd" a longstanding family tradition, she smiled at the irony. Since her twenty-first birthday she had killed thirty-seven persons and most of them shared the same trait, they were worthless human beings.

The death of Nurse Rodriquez was the nurse's own fault, she thought. The nurse was just too damn good and too damn conscientious at her job, making it very near impossible to murder Bill Kauffman in plain sight, so she had to go. Elaine had simply been a necessary casualty in order to kill the egocentric, philandering, scumbag Bill.

She had met Bill quite by accident in a restaurant in Delaware just over the Pennsylvania line. He had apparently been stood up, was into his cups, and feeling full of himself despite his circumstance. He had been quick to tell her about his marriage, his affairs, and even some pilfering he was doing at his employment. He also told her he was hoping his wife met with an accident so he could be free of her ala *Strangers on a Train* through a distorted mirror.

She had pre-arranged Eddie's burglary to help cover Elaine Kauffman's murder and reluctantly allowed Bill to talk her into being an accomplice. Bill's ego was such that in the end, he actually believed that it had been his idea to arrange for his phony shooting incident.

Spagnola and the medical examiner had presented a greater challenge than originally anticipated, but she had learned some valuable lessons about her opponents, lessons that could only be learned in the hunt.

The predator opened her eyes, glanced around and seeing no one looking, licked herself under her arm and purred.

EPILOGUE

THE PREDATOR HAD awakened just before two o'clock in the morning. She had taken a temporary leave of absence from the Brandywine Hospital Trauma team in order to tend to a "sick relative" on Long Island. She had paid three months of her lease in the Grapevine Apartments in Malvern in advance to the landlord. She had relayed the idea of the trip to Manhattan to her landlord, who was sympathetic and delighted with the advanced rent payment.

She now lumbered down a New York City street near the Hudson River, dressed as a bag lady, pulling a small cart packed with various items of clothing and food; just another bum in a city full of bums.

No need to be a Dr. Evans here to have a good hunt, she thought. No need to do that at all.

Another type of predator, very different from her, was standing in the shadows two blocks away. He answered to the name Tito, and claimed his last name was Morales. Both were false, but here in bum's alley New York, it made little difference.

Tito found his fun in and made his living by beating and robbing derelicts. This particular neighborhood was full of them. Most of his prey were instinctively afraid of him because he smelled good, dressed decent, and had none of the look of a bum about him, except his teeth which were as bad as any teeth in the neighborhood. Tito had thick black hair pulled back in a ponytail and a baggy shirt worn outside his pants, so as to conceal not one, but the two knives and the sap that he employed. Sometimes things got tough, and he had killed more than his share of bums over the past several years.

Even Tito was surprised how much cash and jewelry could be had from the bums of New York's worst neighborhoods. The bums made lousy witnesses and the police didn't care, so his hunting was smooth and relatively free of danger, until tonight.

He barely noticed the bag lady headed up the street. He knew bag ladies were bad news. His experiences with them had not been pleasant. Generally, they were loud, foul smelling, and more often than not, willing to fight to the death for their meager possessions. They were known to carry mace, knives, and even the occasional small pistol. Bad news, he thought. There was a bum about to nod off no more than thirty feet away from him, and he was looking at an easy score. He was a little tired so he might spare this one a beating, and surely wasn't in the mood to kill, although that had never stopped him in the past had the need arisen. Tito just wasn't in the mood to kill for the fun of it, tonight.

Tito casually stood up and walked down the steps, pausing at the sidewalk to take one last look around. He saw no one on the street except the bag lady, who now was only a block away. Tito decided to wait until she had passed before getting down to business. The bum was now asleep and was not going anywhere anytime soon.

Dr. Evans glanced at Tito from about forty feet away and started to steer to the other side of the street, as if to avoid him. Among other things, Tito fancied himself as having a good sense of humor. He couldn't resist.

"Hey, pretty lady. You don't like to be on the same side of the street as this handsome man?"

Dr. Evans hunched down, pulled herself further to the opposite side of the street, and muttered, "Fuck you."

This caught Tito off guard. He was not expecting a reply, but the "fuck you" should not have surprised him from a bag lady in New York. However, it did, and Tito's bad mood turned foul. He could feel the heat creeping up through his jacket despite the November chill. Just then, the bum groaned in his alcoholic-induced slumber, no doubt amidst a nightmare. Tito turned his attention to the bum and the bag lady quickened her pace, causing the cart to clatter on the uneven pavement.

"That's it, keep movin', you skanky bitch," called Tito, still full of rage, but deciding to take it out on the sleeping bum rather than getting involved with the bag lady. He took ten quick strides over toward the sleeping bum and kicked the bum hard in the ribs. The lightweight bum actually came part way off the ground from the force of the blow and immediately went into a fetal crouch, with an audible cough and groan. He followed that with a retching noise and vomited.

"You like that, you smelly bastard?" Tito was really worked up now and did not hear the approaching footfalls. At the last moment, he sensed someone behind him, but it was too late.

Dr. Evans swung the cut-off, forty-two ounce Louisville Slugger at Tito's right shoulder, so as not to kill him outright. The impact of the bat broke three ribs, pulled his shoulder muscle away from the tendons that attached them to his back, and knocked Tito to his knees. He barely had time to scream when the second blow, just a half-cocked one for minimal damage, struck him in the neck and laid him out on the ground.

Dr. Evans grabbed Tito by the collar and pulled him away from the bum who laid rocking and moaning on the ground. She turned Tito over so he could see her. All the bravado had left him.

"No, please, you take him. He's yours, no more, no more, please," Tito sputtered. He only wanted to get out of there and get something to ease his pain. His head had impacted with the sidewalk, and he could feel a warm trickle of his own blood run down the side of his face.

"You have been a bad person, Tito. You have hunted on my ground," she said, just before she jammed the short end of the bat into his mouth, breaking what little was left of his teeth. She methodically kicked him, first left foot then right, then finally she reached into her bag and took out several differently sized shoes, put them on her hands, and hit him with the shoes as if he had been kicked. When the police later found his body, it would appear that he had been savagely beaten and kicked by a group of assailants, just as she planned.

When she tired of beating him with her array of shoes, Dr. Evans dragged Tito by his feet up the staircase next to them, fourteen steps in all, and tumbled him down so that he left a trail of broken teeth and blood on each and every step. She chased Tito down to the bottom step with the grace of a cat. With the heel of the boot on her left foot, she crushed his larynx and, moments later, Tito was dead.

She pulled a vial of cat urine from under her coat and liberally sprinkled it all over him. The police would not want to get too near him.

On the ground, not ten feet from Tito, lay Gary Geigerich, former insurance salesman, now a seriously ill and injured, alcoholic, homeless bum, who had fallen back to sleep or passed out. He had survived Tito with only stomach bruises and a cracked rib. He had survived Dr. Evans, the predator, because it was not his time.